THE MARRIAGE
DALLAS SCHULZE

MIRA

MIRA

ISBN 1-55166-464-X

THE MARRIAGE

Copyright © 1999 by Dallas Schulze.

Printed in U.S.A.

To Bob Steingraber: guitarist extraordinaire, sometime Barbecue King and my favorite consultant on most things musical. Thanks for the Linus and Lucy. I couldn't have done it without them.

Prologue

"I don't see how anyone can stand to live out here, surrounded by so much nothing." Sylvie Lassiter shifted uneasily against the Jaguar's cream-colored leather seat and frowned at the endless expanse of sagebrush-covered prairie, visible through the tinted glass of the windshield. "Everything's so brown. Doesn't anything green grow in this state?"

"Wyoming doesn't get enough rain to be green." Duncan glanced away from the empty black ribbon of road long enough to smile at his wife. "This isn't New England, you know."

"*That's* perfectly obvious." Restless, she leaned forward and turned on the radio. The crackling hiss of empty airwaves filled the car as she twisted the dial back and forth. An occasional, half-heard voice made her hesitate, but the signals were weak and fuzzy, and after a moment she snapped the radio off and flounced back against her seat. "There aren't even any radio stations, for God's sake! You don't need rain to grow music, do you?"

"No, but you need people to listen to it, and Wyoming doesn't have a whole lot of those."

"I can see why," she muttered, scowling out the window. "Everything's so drab and ugly and just so...empty." She shivered a little, as if the emptiness of the land gave her a physical chill.

"Actually, it's a great place to grow up," Duncan said, raising his voice a little and throwing her a warning glance. "Horseback riding and fishing and all this open space. I loved it when I was a boy."

"Oh." Sylvie started guiltily and twisted to look over her shoulder at the car's other occupant. "Don't pay any attention to what I said, Ryan. Your father's right. This really is a wonderful place for a ten-year-old boy. I know you're going to love it here."

"Yeah. Sure." Her son lifted one shoulder in a half shrug and kept his gaze out the window.

"You're going to have so much fun, spending the summer with your grandfather on his ranch," Sylvie told him brightly, ignoring his obvious indifference. "Why, I expect you'll be a full-fledged cowboy by the time we see you again."

Her tinkling laugh drew a smile from her husband but not even a glance from her son, and she frowned. She wasn't accustomed to being ignored. An only child, born late in life to doting parents, she'd grown up in the spotlight of their adoration. She'd been blessed with striking beauty and an iron will wrapped in a spun sugar coating. What Sylvie wanted, she inevitably got, but she generally managed it with a pretty smile and a coaxing word. And if that didn't work, a suggestion of a pout and a few tears were sure to melt the hardest of hearts. Only rarely did anyone get a glimpse of the steely determination beneath the charming smile. Everyone adored Sylvie Marie Winthrup Lassiter. She made it her business to see to it that they did.

Until recently, her son's devotion had been complete and unquestioning. His uncomplicated adoration was, as far as she was concerned, the best thing about being a mother. But something had changed in the last year or so. When he looked at her now, there was an odd kind of cynicism in his eyes that disturbed her. No matter how she coaxed, she couldn't seem to break through the chilly barriers he'd raised between them. It was most annoying. She didn't like the feeling that he was judging her and finding her wanting in some way.

"Your father was a cowboy when I met him, you know," she said, addressing Ryan's profile. "He was so tall and handsome in his cowboy boots and hat." She sighed and cast a coquettish look at Duncan. "He just swept me right off my feet."

"Literally." Duncan laughed. "I wasn't watching where I was going, and I practically ran you down."

"I made it a point to get in your way." The story of their first meeting had been told so many times that they had the dialogue perfected. "I knew a good thing when I saw it."

"Lucky for me." Duncan's smile was warm as he reached out and patted his wife's leg.

"Me, too." Sylvie caught his hand in hers and brought it to her cheek, cradling it there for a moment. But her smile wilted around the edges a bit as she turned her attention back to the silent boy in the back seat. "I just know you're going to have a wonderful time this summer, Ryan."

Still looking out the window, his only response was a shrug. Sylvie's mouth tightened. Honestly, she didn't understand the boy. He'd been such a charming baby and a sweet, good-natured toddler. It was only recently that he'd started to get difficult. Sometimes he acted almost as if he didn't like her, which was ridiculous. Annoyance put an edge in her voice. "Aren't you excited about spending the summer on your grandfather's ranch?"

He turned his head to look at her, his eyes cool and much older than his years. "Does it matter?"

"Of course it matters." Surprise made her voice shrill, and she stopped and drew a deep breath before continuing. "Of course it matters. You know your father and I only want what's best for you."

He shrugged again and turned back to the window. Sylvie opened her mouth to demand a response, then shut it without speaking. Something told her that she might not like what she heard if she pushed him. Her expression set with annoyance, she jerked around to face forward.

Really, he was becoming absolutely impossible! If he wanted to sulk, she would just leave him to it. After all the trouble she'd gone to to arrange this visit with his grandfather, the least he could do was try to show a little enthusiasm. Maybe even some gratitude. It had taken her weeks to talk Duncan into contacting his father. The two of them had quarreled soon after her marriage to Duncan and hadn't spoken since, and it hadn't been easy to convince her husband to break a decade-long silence.

Sylvie's lower lip thrust out in an unconscious pout as she considered all the effort she'd put into arranging this visit. She could have just put him in a boarding school, the way so many of her friends did with their children. But she hadn't, she thought, conveniently forgetting that she would have done just that if Duncan hadn't reminded her of how much a good school would cost. Now, here she was, enduring an endless drive across this miserable state, all on her son's behalf, and he was acting as if *he* were suffering. Well, *she* certainly wasn't going to spend any more time trying to coax him out of his sulks!

"We've been on the road for hours," she said petulantly. "Where *is* this damned ranch, for God's sake?"

"Not far now." Duncan reached out to pat her arm, but she pulled away irritably, in no mood to be soothed.

"I hate this place," she muttered. "I don't know why we had to drive all this way. We could have arranged to have someone else pick him up in Denver."

"Dad asked us to bring him out ourselves, remember?"

Remember? Of course she remembered. Her father-in-law hadn't *asked* them to bring Ryan out, he'd *demanded* that they deliver the boy personally. Sylvie's pout became a scowl as she considered the unreasonableness of that. What right did he have to make demands on their time?

"We could be sunning on Dick and Jilly's yacht by now," she said irritably.

"We'll be able to meet up with them in Aruba in a couple of days," Duncan said soothingly.

"Well, I don't see why we had to waste all this time. I can't wait until we're on our way back to civilization. I don't want to spend a minute longer in this godforsaken place than I have to. As soon as we've dropped Ryan off, I want to get on the road again."

"Dad invited us to spend the night," Duncan reminded her. "You don't want to turn right around and drive back to Denver."

"Yes, I do." She shot him an impatient look. "It's not like there's any love lost between you and your father. I mean, you're not going to want to sit around and swap memories with him. You practically told me you hated him."

"I never said that," Duncan protested. He glanced uneasily in the rearview mirror, conscious of the fact that Ryan could hear the conversation. "We didn't exactly get along, but I don't hate him."

"Whatever." Sylvie rummaged in her purse for her compact. Snapping it open, she examined her reflection in the tiny mirror. Satisfied that she looked flawless, despite the difficulties she'd experienced, she shut the compact with a tiny sigh of satisfaction and turned a coaxing smile in her husband's direction. "It doesn't really matter one way or another. I just want to get back to the real world as quickly as possible. It's so annoying that Dick and Jilly had to start this trip without us."

"Honey, we're hours away from..."

Ryan tuned out the conversation in the front seat. He knew how it would end. His mother would get her way. She always did. His father would argue a little, then give in and do whatever she wanted. It always worked out that way.

He stared out at the rolling prairie, his expression bleak. She could talk all she wanted about how great it was going to be to spend the summer on a real ranch, but the only thing they really cared about was getting rid of him so they could spend the summer in Aruba with their friends. They were dumping him on his grandfather, just the way they'd been dumping him on friends and relatives for as long as he could remember. Six months with Sylvie's cousin in Milwaukee, three weeks with another cousin who lived in Florida, two months spent watching television with an elderly aunt and uncle in Phoenix, nearly four months with an old college roommate who had finally threatened to turn him over to Child Services if his parents didn't come back from Europe to get him. He could barely remember all the names and faces stretching back through the years.

Cynically, he wondered if his unknown grandfather knew what he was getting into. Did he know that Sylvie and Duncan were just as likely to go to Paris in the fall as they were to come back to Wyoming to get their son? In a few weeks, there would probably be a tearful phone call from his mother, saying how much they missed him but the *most fabulous* opportunity had just come up. They'd been invited to stay on a friend's yacht, seeing the Greek islands. Or they had a chance to go skiing in Saint Moritz. Or maybe it was a trip to the south of France. The excuse changed but the end result was always the same—they weren't coming back when they'd said they would, and whoever they'd dumped him on was stuck with him for a few more days or weeks.

He realized that his hand was clenched against his knee and made a conscious effort to relax it. He'd promised himself a long time ago that he wasn't going to let what they did matter ever again. They didn't want him—he'd figured *that* out years ago. He didn't know why, didn't know why they didn't love him the way other parents loved their kids. And it didn't matter. Not really. He wouldn't *let* it matter.

"Here's the road to the ranch," Duncan said.

The Jaguar swayed through the tight turn, tires rumbling across the cattle guard, dust rising up behind them.

Across the barbed wire fence that lined the road, there was a scattering of white-faced cattle. Some were grazing, others were lying down. A few turned to look at the sleek car without much interest. In the distance, there was a man on horseback riding among them. It was a scene right out of the old Western movies he'd seen on TV, and, despite himself, Ryan felt a stirring of interest. The land that looked barren and empty to his mother seemed beautiful and oddly familiar to him. There was power in the endless expanse of sky and land, freedom in the openness of it.

His father had grown up here and then left. Ryan couldn't imagine how anyone could live in a city apartment after this. He wanted to open the window to find out what the air smelled like, what it tasted like, but his mother was sure to have a fit about the wind messing up her carefully tousled hair, so he contented himself with looking, trying to absorb as much as he could through the tinted glass.

Somewhere inside him, there was a tentative unfurling of emotion, a faint, barely recognizable hope that maybe this was a place where he could belong. That maybe this could become home.

* * *

"Been a long time." The screen door thudded shut behind Sara McIntyre as she came to stand beside her employer near the porch railing.

"Ten years," Nathan Lassiter said without taking his eyes off the plume of dust making its way up the long dirt road from the highway. He was a tall man, with the narrow hips and broad shoulders of a rider. At fifty-two, his dark hair was threaded through with traces of silver, but his blue eyes were sharp and clear. He was the fourth generation of Lassiters to ranch on the Double L, and Sara knew just what it had meant to him when it became obvious that his son had no interest in following in his father's footsteps. She hoped he wasn't pinning too many hopes on the grandson he'd yet to meet.

"Mary Beth's funeral." Her dark eyes followed his.

Nathan's chest tightened at the sound of his wife's name. After all these years, there were times when the pain of her loss was still fresh inside him. His hand curled into a fist where it lay on the wooden railing. She'd been on his mind often in the days since Duncan had called.

The two of them had quarreled within hours of her funeral. It wasn't the first time—they'd been butting heads since Duncan was old enough to talk—but this time, without Mary Beth to step between them, they'd both said things that couldn't be forgotten. Duncan had left that night, and they hadn't spoken until his call a week ago. Now he was coming home, bringing his son.

My grandson, Nathan thought. *Our grandson. A second chance. A piece of the future.*

"The two of you never did get along worth a damn," Sara commented, her thoughts moving along a similar path.

"He was a pigheaded fool."

"And you're so easy to get along with." The look she slanted him was full of dry humor. The wife of Nathan's foreman, she'd known him too long to hesitate to say what she thought. She'd taken over the housekeeping chores after his wife's death, at first as a favor and then as a job, but she'd known the family for more than ten years before Mary Beth died, and she knew the fault had not all been on Duncan's side.

"Maybe not, but at least I'm not a damned fool, traipsing all over the world like a gypsy. That's no way to raise a child."

"Lots of folks travel," Sara said mildly

"I don't give a hoot in hell about how much they travel. I do care about the way my grandson is being raised. A boy needs roots. A place to belong. A home. How much of a home is he likely to find when they're never in one place more than a few months at a time?" He'd made it a point to keep track of Duncan over the years, especially after Ryan was born.

"There's those that say home is a state of mind."

"Maybe, but I'd be willing to bet it's easier to get in the right frame of mind if you settle in one spot."

The car slowed as it neared the ranch yard. Nathan snorted with disgust as the low-slung Jaguar bumped and shuddered its way over ruts left by spring rains. "Useless vehicle."

"I don't think it's supposed to be useful. I think it's supposed to look nice." Sara narrowed her eyes as the dusty car came to a halt a few yards from the house. "Wouldn't be much good for hauling hay or transporting a sick calf, but it's pretty enough."

"Useless," Nathan commented again, leaving her to wonder whether he meant the car or the woman who'd just gotten out of it.

At first glance, Sylvie Lassiter gave the impression of being a small woman. Fine boned and slender, she looked as fragile as a porcelain figurine, an impression that belied her five feet, ten inches. She was slim as a willow, with a tiny waist, small, high breasts and long, long legs.

She and Duncan had been married in Vegas, barely a week before his mother's death. Sara remembered her clearly from the funeral. With silvery blond hair, delicate features, and wearing an exquisite black silk suit with a skirt that ended somewhere above midthigh, Sylvie had been a little hard to forget. Particularly when she complained bitterly during the graveside service that she was getting mud on her brand-new Ferragamos. There had been some discussion afterward among the other mourners about what a Ferragamo might be, and the final conclusion was that it had to be the three-inch spike heels she'd been wearing.

This time, she was wearing a pair of black jeans tucked into tall black boots and a turquoise silk shirt with shiny silver buttons. Sara wondered if this was her idea of Western wear and felt a moment's curiosity about what might happen if she actually tried to straddle a horse in those skintight jeans.

"Hello!" Sylvie smiled and waved when she saw them. Nathan's only response was a barely perceptible sneer that curled one corner of his mouth. Sara waved with more enthusiasm than she felt to make up for it.

"You could at least try to be civil," she muttered.

But Nathan wasn't listening. His attention was all for the boy who was climbing out of the car behind his mother. He was tall for his age, and lanky, but his shoulders were broad, suggesting he would be a big man in a few years. His hair was as dark as Sylvie's was fair, a deep, dark brown with just a hint of red where the sun hit it—mahogany Mary Beth would have said.

As if sensing Nathan's gaze, Ryan looked toward the ranch house, his chin tilted at an angle that was both defensive and challenging. His features were even, holding the softness of childhood yet hinting at the adult he would soon be. It was a familiar face, one Nathan had known a long time ago.

His breath hissed out from between his teeth as the years rolled back. For just a moment, it was another boy standing there, chin tilted, eyes wary.

The heavy thud of a car door slamming shut shattered the image and snapped him back to the present. With an effort, Nathan dragged his gaze from his grandson and looked at his son. His eyes met Duncan's across the roof of the car, reading some of the same defensiveness and challenge there. He felt a twinge of regret and a kind of weariness. *Didn't things ever change?*

But the past was past, and it was too late for regrets. The old conflicts with Duncan no longer mattered. What he was interested in now was the future. It was hope for that future that brought him down off the porch to greet his son.

* * *

Ryan used the tip of his finger to push a cookie crumb around the edge of his plate. He glanced at the woman chopping vegetables at the counter but shifted his gaze away before her eyes could catch his. Sara McIntyre, she'd said her name was—chief cook and bottle washer. He thought that probably meant that she was his grandfather's housekeeper. Some of his parents' friends had housekeepers but none of them looked like this woman. She was nearly as tall as his mother, but built on more generous lines. Her hair was inky black and worn in a single long braid that hung down the middle of her back nearly to her waist. Her skin was a warm, coppery color that owed nothing to hours spent lying in a deck chair. She was wearing softly faded jeans and a blue-checkered shirt.

"You want another cookie?" she asked, catching his glance and smiling at him.

"No, thank you." The truth was, the two cookies he'd already eaten weren't sitting too well on his stomach as it was.

"If you'd like something besides chocolate chip, there's oatmeal cookies in that jar on the counter."

"I like chocolate chip fine, thank you. I'm just not very hungry."

Sara had a ten-year-old boy of her own, and, as far as she knew, Tucker had never seen any connection between chocolate chip cookies and actual hunger, but she didn't say as much. She was willing to bet that Ryan's lack of interest had more to do with nerves than anything else.

"They're talking about what to do with me, aren't they?" Ryan jerked his head in the direction of the study, where Nathan had taken his parents shortly after their arrival.

"They're talking about your stay here," Sara agreed. There was tension in the set of his shoulders, though he was doing his best to conceal it. "Your grandfather is looking forward to having you here."

"Is he?" The words were innocuous, but his obvious disbelief gave them a cynical twist.

Sara wondered what he was thinking, but it was too soon to push for answers. Her own son, Tucker, was an open book, easygoing and uncomplicated. Ryan had walls around him a mile thick.

Ryan got up abruptly and went to the open back door, leaning one shoulder against the doorjamb as he stared through the screen. The horizon was filled with the jagged blue bulk of the Rocky Mountains, and he felt a sudden, fierce longing to push open the door and run toward them. If he just ran fast enough and far enough, he could leave behind the uncertainty churning in his stomach. He wouldn't have to think about why his parents didn't want

him or worry about what was going to happen
when the time came that they couldn't find anyone
willing to be saddled with him.

His chest ached, and his eyes stung suddenly.
He was just so tired of being alone.

"I'm going to miss you so much, baby." Sylvie
knelt down to put her arms around her son, ignoring his stiffness as she pulled him against her in a
tight hug.

They were standing in the yard in front of the
ranch house—Duncan, Sylvie and Ryan. Nathan
stood a little ways away from the three of them,
distancing himself from his son and daughter-in-
law, even before they were gone. They'd been on
the ranch barely an hour, and he was not sorry to
see them go. If he'd held out any hope that time
might have closed the gap between him and his
son, it had soon faded. Whatever small closeness
he and Duncan might have had years ago was gone
now. He didn't know the man his son had become—didn't think he'd like him much if he did
get to know him.

His invitation to spend the night had been made
out of courtesy. When they'd refused, he hadn't
pressed them to stay. It was too late—years too
late—to rebuild the bridges he and Duncan had
burned between them, but he'd gotten what he

wanted out of the visit. He had Duncan's agreement that Ryan could stay on the Lazy L permanently, providing the boy took to the life. He'd been the one to stipulate that. He wasn't going to force the boy to stay. That was one lesson he'd learned—you couldn't make someone love the land.

Sylvie had protested at first, saying she couldn't possibly give up her only child. Nathan had wondered if perhaps he'd judged her too harshly, but the doubt had vanished when the real source of her concern became clear. *What would people say?* she'd asked, her forehead creasing with worry. Duncan at least had the grace to flush and look away from the contempt in his father's eyes. He'd been the one to persuade his wife to agree to the arrangement, and Nathan wanted to believe that it was because he knew it was the best thing for Ryan.

Watching them now, he wondered at the woman his son had chosen to marry. She was pretty enough. He couldn't deny that. But there was no staying power in her, no heart. She was all show, with nothing underneath to make her real. His upper lip curled in a faint sneer as he watched Sylvie press her cheek to her son's. The boy was stiff as a poker, but she didn't seem to notice. Or she just didn't care.

"I can hardly stand to leave you," she said as she drew back, her pretty blue eyes filling with easy tears.

Ryan squirmed out of her hold, taking a step back and out of her reach. He hated it when she acted like she cared about him; like she wanted to be with him but just couldn't. He wanted to shout that if she missed him so much, she didn't have to go on another stupid trip. But he didn't say anything. When he was little, he could remember begging them not to leave him, but it had never made any difference. And there'd come a point when he'd promised himself that he would never ask them to stay again. He didn't know why they didn't want him, but he'd made up his mind that he didn't want them, either.

"Are you going to miss me?" Sylvie coaxed. When Ryan didn't answer immediately, she allowed her lower lip to tremble slightly in a look that never failed to get her what she wanted. "Won't you miss me?"

Staring at the ground between them, Ryan shrugged. "Yeah. Sure."

"Tell Mama you'll miss her," she pressed, a queen demanding tribute from her subjects.

Ryan's mouth tightened, holding back an answer. He shoved his hands in the pockets of his jeans and looked past his mother's kneeling figure, focusing his attention on the big gray horse that had thrust its head over the top of a corral fence near the barn and seemed to be watching them. His chest tightened with a sudden wild yearning to be on that horse, riding somewhere far away from here.

"Ryan..." Annoyance edged Sylvie's voice.

"He won't have time to miss us." Duncan put his hand on his wife's shoulder and drew her to her feet. His glance veered from his son to his father and then back again. His smile was a little too broad, his voice a little too hearty. "There's so much to do here that you'll hardly know we're gone."

At that, Ryan lifted his eyes and looked directly at his father. "You're usually gone anyway, so what's the difference?" he asked coolly.

There was a moment of uncomfortable silence. A deep flush ran up under Duncan's skin, and something that might have been shame flickered in his eyes. At the same time, anger twisted Sylvie's pretty features into something not nearly so pretty. She started to speak, but Duncan's fingers tightened on her arm, cutting off whatever she might have said.

Nathan wondered if he was trying to protect her or the boy. Either way, it was time to put an end to this scene. He stepped forward and set his hand on Ryan's shoulder, feeling the tension humming through muscle and bone. "You'd better get on the road if you hope to make it to Cheyenne tonight. It's a long drive."

"Yes. Yes, it is." Duncan looked grateful for the intervention, but there was nothing of gratitude in his wife's expression.

"Let's go," she snapped. "I can't wait to get out of this godforsaken place." She stalked off without another glance at the son she could "hardly stand" to leave behind.

Duncan hesitated a moment, his expression uncertain as he looked at the boy. Ryan met his eyes, his own face still and hard, older than his years— impenetrable as a wall of ice. Sylvie's car door shut with a slam, the sound seeming to echo off the mountains that loomed behind the ranch house. Duncan started. Whatever momentary doubts he might have had were pushed aside, and he smiled at Ryan without really seeing him, his thoughts already focused elsewhere.

"Take care and have fun." He lifted one hand in a vague half wave, then turned and walked to the car.

Ryan didn't say a word as his father backed the Jaguar into a tight turn and drove out the gate. He stood there, his slim body rigid with tension, his expression empty of all emotion. It was only when the dust grew thick enough to obscure the vehicle that he moved. He stepped out from under his grandfather's hand and turned to face him, his chin tilted in a subtle challenge.

"They won't come back when they said they would." His tone dared Nathan to disagree. "They never do."

"No?" Nathan shrugged. "Then I guess you'll be here longer."

"They won't give you any money, either." Ryan threw the words out like a duelist throwing down a gauntlet. "Not even if they said they would. They never pay people for looking after me."

"I don't want money," Nathan said calmly. Seeing the confusion in his grandson's eyes, he decided to lay his cards on the table. He hadn't planned on saying anything so soon. He'd thought to wait, let the boy settle in, start getting a feel for ranch life. But maybe it was better this way. Let him know he was wanted, and then he could mull the idea over in his own time. He met Ryan's gaze directly. "I want you to stay with me as long as you want. Permanently, if you like it here."

"Permanently?" Ryan was shocked out of his pose of indifference. "You mean, like, live here forever?"

"As long as you want to stay." Disbelief and suspicion warred in the boy's eyes, but Nathan knew better than to try to convince him that he

meant what he said. He suspected the boy had little
reason to value promises.

"Why?"

It seemed to Nathan that there was a lifetime of
hurt in the stark question, and he had to clear his
throat of a sudden tightness before he could speak.
"You're my grandson. This is your home, if you
want it to be."

Ryan stared at him in confusion. Something in
him wanted to believe this lean old man, but he
pushed the idea aside. Experience had taught him
that adults were better at making promises than
keeping them. It was easy enough for his grandfather to say he wanted him to stay forever, but
that wouldn't last. Before too long, he'd be looking
for a way to get rid of him, counting the days until
Duncan and Sylvie came to get him. That was the
way it always worked.

He looked away, shrugging to show how little it
meant to him one way or the other. "Whatever."

Nathan saw the walls come up in the boy's eyes
in the instant before he looked away, but he wasn't
discouraged. They'd come down for a minute.
Given time, he hoped they would come down permanently. Trust wasn't earned in an instant. He
would give the boy some room and let time prove
the truth of what he was saying. The land—and the
life—could argue its own case to those who had
ears to listen.

Chapter One

Twenty years later

"And so I says to Davis that if'n he didn't want me to fetch him up alongside the head with my fist, then he'd better figure on doing some pretty fast talking, 'cause I wasn't going to sit there and let him bad-mouth a lady like Belinda. And Davis, he says to me..."

Ryan shifted, trying to find a comfortable position—a vain hope at the best of times, considering the battered condition of the truck's bench seat. With a sling on one arm and taped ribs, all he could manage was to find a position that minimized the aches. Tugging a dusty gray Stetson lower on his forehead, he closed his eyes and tried to visualize

himself alone on a desert island, with only the
whisper of waves against the sand to break the silence. A bottle of cold beer in one hand, a good
book in the other, nothing but sun and sand and...

"...and when they let us out of jail, Davis, he
bought me the best damned breakfast I'd had in a
month of Sundays, and we..."

Maybe the old cabin tucked back in a canyon in
the mountains that marked the western edge of his
grandfather's ranch. It was the middle of winter,
just after a blizzard. A stillness so profound that he
could almost hear the air rushing through the wings
of the hawk wheeling overhead. A cup of hot black
coffee and...

"...course, Davis, he ain't the brightest fellow
you're ever going to meet. Fact is, the light in his
eyes is most likely the sun shinin' through the back
of his head. But he..."

Or maybe a hidden oasis in the middle of miles
of burning sand. No sound but the murmur of the
wind through the palms. An icy cold glass of...

"...brains ain't everything, but Davis, he don't
know enough to tamp sand down a rat hole, and
I—"

"I swear to God, Doug, your tongue must be
hinged in the middle so it can flap at both ends."
Ignoring the warning twinges from his cracked
ribs, Ryan sat up and glared across the cab of the

truck. "You haven't shut up for the last two hundred miles. Don't you ever draw a breath?"

"I try to time it so's I can breathe between sentences." Grinning, Doug glanced at Ryan. "It's sort of like one of those high-class opry singers, learning to breathe in amongst the caterwauling. Not everybody has the knack for it," he added with a simple pride that drew a reluctant laugh from Ryan.

"I should have hitched a ride home," he muttered without heat. Giving up the idea of dozing, he sat up straight, shifting automatically to avoid a broken spring and settling his aching arm into a more comfortable position against his stomach.

"How many folks you figure are going to give a ride to a busted-up cowboy and that flea bait horse of yours?" Doug jerked his head in the direction of the horse trailer they were towing. "You'd have ended up walking all the way to Wyoming."

"Maybe, but at least I wouldn't have had to listen to you flap your lips for two solid days," Ryan grumbled.

"You've been in a bad mood ever since you took that little spill."

"Little spill?" Ryan arched his brows. He owed his current battered condition to a bronc named Lucky Streak, who had expressed his annoyance at the whole rodeo experience by throwing his rider in six seconds flat and then doing his best to grind Ryan into the dirt. "That damned horse did the polka up and down my body. It wasn't exactly a little spill."

"Looked more like a tango to me," Doug said consideringly. "Had him a real nice rhythm going, come to think of it."

"Guess I was too busy getting stomped to appreciate the subtleties of his performance," Ryan said dryly.

"I ever tell you 'bout the time I won me a set of dancing lessons from Fred MacMurray?"

"Fred MacMurray?" Ryan's eyebrows shot up. "You mean Arthur Murray?"

"Coulda been." Doug shrugged. "Don't matter one way or the other. It was a Murray of some sort, and they was dancing lessons. I wasn't going to go, but I was dating a little gal that set store by fancy footwork, so I figured I'd..."

Ryan had heard the story before, so he knew the ending. Doug had learned to do a passable waltz just in time for the "little gal" to run off to Tulsa with an oil rig monkey who had two left feet. Keeping half an ear on his friend's monologue, he let his attention wander.

The landscape outside the truck's windows was familiar. An hour or less and he'd be home. Four years, he thought. Four years since he'd spent more than a few days at a stretch on the Double L. A long time to be away from home.

He rubbed his left thumb against the base of his ring finger, absently searching for a ring that was no longer there. Catching himself, he splayed his fingers out flat for an instant and then, with a conscious effort, relaxed his hand. No more looking back. He'd promised himself that while he was lying in the hospital waiting for the doctor to set his wrist. It had hit him suddenly that he was tired— bone deep tired of life on the road.

He wasn't sure what had triggered the sudden decision to go home. He'd been stomped by broncs before and had the scars to show for it—two broken collarbones, one broken leg and more stitches than he could remember. Injuries were a part of the rodeo game—a bad spill from a horse, an angry bull. Hell, he knew a rider once who slipped on a puddle of spilled soft drink, fell out of the viewing stands and broke both arms. He'd been back in the saddle as soon as the casts came off. Unless an injury was life threatening, it was hardly worth noticing.

No, it hadn't been getting hurt that had made him decide to hang up his spurs. And it hadn't been the fact that, since the start of the season in January, he'd been pulling nothing but bad broncs and worse luck. That was a part of the game, too. Some years you were in the money, some years you couldn't win for losing. He'd made enough to pay expenses, which was better than a lot of cowboys could say.

He didn't know what had triggered it, but the decision had been made in the space between one breath and the next. He'd been lying in the emergency room, staring at a poster stressing the importance of regular breast exams, listening to the subdued bustle going on beyond the curtain they'd pulled between his bed and the next, and he'd suddenly wondered what the hell he was doing here— not here in the hospital, but *here*—a thousand miles from the quiet spaces of the Double L. A thousand miles from home.

He'd always known he would go back one day. No matter how far he went or how long he stayed away, the ranch had always been there, pulling at him, calling to him as softly as a lover whispering in his ear. Sitting in a smoky bar in Abilene, he had only to close his eyes to smell the sagebrush and hear the endless sigh of the wind. Caught in a snarl of traffic on the outskirts of Denver, he could look up at the mountains and remember the crisp smell of pines, the crunch of snow under his horse's hooves.

Lying in the hospital bed, with his wrist aching

in rhythm to the moans coming from some unseen sufferer beyond the curtain and his nose full of the warring scents of antiseptic, fear and a wholly incongruous whiff of White Shoulders, he'd decided to go home. Not just to wait out the weeks it would take for his wrist to heal, but to stay. It was time. He'd been running from the past for too long. It had taken him four years, but he'd finally figured out that you couldn't outrun a memory.

Now, only a few miles from the ranch, Ryan wondered what the old man would say when he saw him. Nathan hadn't made any secret of how he felt about his grandson's chosen profession. They'd quarreled bitterly when he came home at Christmas.

"Stupid way for a grown man to make a living," Nathan had snarled, glaring at the silver-and-gold trophy buckle Ryan had won at the National Finals in Vegas less than two weeks before. If he felt a twinge of pride at seeing his grandson place at the top of the competition, he'd be damned if he'd let it show. "Goddamn waste of time and money."

"It's my time and my money," Ryan answered, his smile tight and hard.

"You can't run forever," Nathan said and saw Ryan stiffen, his expression closing up. Fear made him ignore the warning in his grandson's eyes— fear that the boy was going to kill himself trying to hide from his grief. He plowed on. "Breaking your fool neck by falling off a horse in front of five thousand people isn't going to bring Sally back."

"This isn't about Sally," Ryan had said, not sure if it was a lie or not. "I'm a good bronc rider. Damn near the best in the country. I made good money this year."

"And spent most of it staying in the game," Nathan barked. He knew what it cost cowboys to compete. Between travel expenses and the cost of entering the competition, most of them were lucky to break even.

"It's my time and money," Ryan said again, shrugging. Hoping his grandfather would let the subject drop, he lifted his glass of eggnog and sipped it. Sara's special mix: cream, eggs, a dash of nutmeg—and enough brandy to knock a mule to its knees. He'd been twelve the first time he snuck a taste of it; seventeen the first time his grandfather served him a glass of his own. All these years later, it still tasted like sin.

Less than a week earlier, he'd been standing in the dust and noise of an arena in Las Vegas, listening to the crowd roar and thinking about getting home for the holidays. This wasn't exactly what he'd had in mind. He tried a change of topic. "How does the herd look this year?"

Nathan's jaw knotted with frustration. This wasn't the first time they'd argued about the way Ryan was living. Or rather, *Nathan* had argued. Ryan refused, turning it into a joke or changing the subject.

"What the hell do you care how the herd looks?" he snapped. "You don't get fancy gold buckles nursing a herd of cows. I didn't raise you to be a goddamn rhinestone cowboy! It's time you came home."

Ryan's glass rang sharply against the polished wood of the coffee table. He rose to his feet in a single, quick motion that spoke of checked temper, and looked down at his grandfather. "I'm not a child anymore—"

"Couldn't prove it by the way you're acting," Nathan cut in. He stood, and the two of them faced each other across the living room—blue eyes clashing, expressions set and hard. In that moment, though there was no one there to appreciate it, the resemblance between them was striking. There was no give in Ryan's face, and frustration had Nathan speaking too quickly. "I'm not leaving the Double L to some urban cowboy with a collection of fancy buckles. If you want this place, you're by God going to have to prove you can run it."

Angry color ran up under Ryan's skin and then receded, leaving him unnaturally pale beneath his tan, his eyes glittering like blue fire in contrast. When he spoke, his voice was barely above a whisper.

"Don't try to blackmail me, old man."

He'd gone too far, and he knew it, but Nathan wasn't going to back down an inch. "I'm just stating facts. I've put my whole life into this place. I'm going to make damned sure I leave it in good hands."

"I don't give a rat's ass what you do with this place," Ryan lied. "Just don't try to use it to whip me into line."

The arrival of the McIntyres had put an end to the conversation, which was just as well. The argument could only have gone from bad to worse. When he'd left just before New Year's, the atmosphere between him and his grandfather had still been cool. Thinking about it now, months later, Ryan shifted uneasily on the truck's seat. This wasn't the way he'd envisioned his homecoming— injured and more or less flat broke. Time was, he wouldn't have given it any thought. He'd never felt as if he had to prove anything to his grandfather. But things had changed over the past few years. He rubbed his thumb absently against the base of his empty ring finger. A lot of things had changed.

"Looks like we got us a damsel in distress," Doug said, snapping Ryan out of his thoughts.

A pale blue compact was pulled off to the side of the road, hood up and emergency lights blinking. Doug was already pulling the truck off onto the shoulder. There was no question of not stopping. In country like this, where cars were few and far between, you just didn't leave a fellow motorist stranded.

Ryan swallowed a groan as he dropped to the ground. It had been nearly three weeks since his close—and painful—encounter with the dirt floor of the arena but his body still felt every bump as if it had been yesterday. Another sign it was time to get out of the game—he was just getting too damned old for it.

"Now that's what I call a proper damsel," Doug murmured as he and Ryan met near the front of the truck.

Ryan followed his gaze to the woman standing next to the stalled car. She wasn't very big, probably not more than an inch or two over five feet, but they were certainly nicely packed inches, he thought, admiring the full curves of breasts and hips beneath her jeans and T-shirt. Very nicely packed. Her hair was a little past shoulder length, honey blond, sun streaked with pure gold and casually tousled. Pillow rumpled. She probably used half a can of hair spray to get it to look like that, he thought cynically. As if in response to his thought, she reached up and shoved the weight of it back from her face, and the carelessness of the gesture made it obvious that the tousled look came quite naturally. He found that sexier than any amount of planning could have been.

His mood took a swing upward. If you were going to rescue a damsel in distress, it didn't hurt if the damsel was easy on the eyes.

Maggie Drummond had mixed feelings as she watched the truck coast to a stop. The battered red pickup towing a faded blue horse trailer was the first sign of life she'd seen in the thirty minutes since her car had broken down, unless you counted the two jackrabbits that had hopped across the road and the half dozen pronghorns she'd seen off in the distance. Neither the jackrabbits nor the antelope had shown any interest in her or her dead car, and she'd begun to contemplate the possibility of a fifteen-mile walk into town, most of it done after dark on a road that had never so much as heard of a streetlight. The alternative—spending the night in the car—didn't hold much more appeal.

When she saw the truck, she felt a surge of relief, but, as she watched the two men walk toward her, she was suddenly vividly aware that they were in the middle of nowhere, with nothing but the sky and the wind to hear a scream. Not that there was any reason for anyone to scream, she told herself. And she certainly hoped she didn't need to run, either, she thought uneasily, eyeing the long legs on the taller of the two. Still, she found herself edging back toward the car and mentally calculating how much time she would need to open the door and get inside.

"Howdy, ma'am." It was the shorter one who spoke. He reached up and pushed his cowboy hat back with the edge of his thumb, revealing a shock of sandy hair, an appealingly homely face and a pair of smiling brown eyes. "Looks like you got yourself some trouble."

Maggie felt herself relax. It might not be logical, but she simply couldn't be afraid of a man who reminded her of a basset hound. "I was starting to think I was going to have to walk into town," she said, returning his smile.

"Bit of a hike." It was the other one who spoke this time, his voice as soft and dark as midnight. Maggie felt an odd little shock of awareness when she looked at him. The words *tall, dark and handsome* popped into her head, but the old cliché didn't really do him justice. He *was* tall, an inch or two over six feet, and his hair was dark—a deep, rich brown. But *handsome* wasn't the right word to describe him. His features were a little too sharply defined, his chin too stubborn, his nose too

definite, for such a simple word. He was...
arresting, she decided. The sort of man you'd look
at twice if you passed him on the street. Broad
shouldered and narrow through the hips, he looked
like the epitome of a cowboy—the Marlboro man
come to life. The sling on his left arm didn't detract
from the image.

"I'm Doug Tennent and this stove-up cowboy
is Ryan Lassiter." It was the sandy-haired one who
spoke, and Maggie was relieved to have an excuse
to look away from his friend.

"Maggie Drummond," she said, but didn't offer
her hand. In her experience, Western men didn't
expect to shake hands with a woman. She hadn't
figured out yet if it was chauvinism or some sort
of courtesy or a little of both.

"Pleased to meet you." Doug's smile emphasized the friendly puppy look of him, and Maggie
felt the last trace of uneasiness disappear. If this
guy was dangerous, she was Cindy Crawford. Too
many years of living in the city, she thought. It
made a woman paranoid.

"I could take a look at your car," Doug offered.
"See if I can figure out what's wrong. Maybe the
fan belt went."

"It's not a fan belt," Maggie said, shaking her
head. "I carry a spare. Actually, I'm pretty sure

it's the transmission. I just left the hood up so the car would be more visible.''

"I reckon I could give it a look-see." Doug sounded willing but not eager.

"But only if you tell him where the transmission is first," Ryan drawled.

"I know where the transmission is," Doug said defensively. "I even know what it looks like. Had one practically fall out of my truck near about five years ago. Different truck, of course. I was in the middle of bald ass desert—begging your pardon, ma'am—on my way to a rodeo in Sante Fe. There was this awful clanging sound, and the blasted truck just stopped dead. Nothin' for miles but cactus and rattlesnakes, and me with a truck that's deader than damn it—beggin' your pardon again, ma'am. It's a good thing I had me a case of Lone Star in the cooler, else I'd probably have died of dehydration before somebody else come along. I—"

"I don't want to hear a blow-by-blow account of your survival in the New Mexican desert," Ryan interrupted ruthlessly. From long experience, he knew it was better to stop Doug before he got started. "And I'm sure the lady doesn't, either."

"How do you know? Maybe she'd find it real interestin'."

"I know because I've heard that story before,

and it's duller than ditch water. Your own mother wouldn't find it interesting.''

''What about the snake?'' Doug asked indignantly. ''Big around as my arm, and the meanest eyes I ever did see, fangs as big as knives.''

''All it did was crawl across the road. Now, if it had actually stopped long enough to bite you, *that* would be interesting.''

Maggie felt like a spectator at a tennis match, her eyes moving from one to the other as she followed the exchange. It had taken her only a moment to realize that there was no heat in their bickering. From the sounds of it, this wasn't the first time they'd had this conversation or one similar to it.

''You'd like to hear about the snake, wouldn't you, ma'am?'' Doug asked, unexpectedly drawing her into the conversation.

''Well, I...''

''She wants her car fixed, and neither you nor I can help her with that.'' Ryan reached up and tilted his hat back, revealing a pair of smiling blue eyes that made Maggie's pulse flutter. ''The fact is, unless you've got a flat tire or a busted fan belt, we aren't much for car repairs.''

''We're cowboys,'' Doug said, as if that was all the explanation necessary. ''We can do a fair amount with spit and baling wire, but I'd guess a transmission needs a bit more than that.''

''Cowboys can't be mechanics, too?'' Maggie asked, slightly bemused at having this easy, light-hearted conversation with two strangers.

''There's nothing in the handbook against it,'' Ryan said. ''But it does seem to work out that way more often than not.''

''There's a cowboy handbook?'' Maggie's brows shot up.

''Yes, ma'am.'' Doug pulled his craggy features into a solemn expression. ''That's where we get the cowboy oath and the secret handshake.''

''Yeah, and if you send in three box tops and a dollar bill, you'll get a secret decoder ring that glows in the dark,'' Ryan added dryly.

Her grin revealed a slightly crooked front tooth. It was an oddly charming little flaw, Ryan thought. He was relieved to see that the fear had disappeared from her eyes. They were very nice eyes—a kind of smoky gray, warm and changeable, reflecting her emotions as easily as a mirror.

When he and Doug had first approached, she'd watched them warily. Not that he could blame her. Despite the legends, even in the Old West a woman hadn't always been safe, and these days, crime didn't stop at the Wyoming border. But as soon as Doug smiled, she'd started to relax. Ryan had seen

the reaction before. There was something about
Doug's broken nose and gap-toothed smile that put
women instantly at ease. He could have told Maggie that Doug Tennent wasn't nearly as harmless
as his homely puppy exterior led women to believe.
Over the years, he'd cut a considerable swath
through the buckle bunnies who hung out around
the chutes wearing painted-on jeans and batting
mascaraed lashes at the cowboys who swaggered
by. There was no explaining it, but there was something about his slightly goofy smile that just
mowed them down.

Whatever it was, it also appeared to work won-
ders on stranded damsels in distress, Ryan noted
with amused exasperation.

"We could give you a lift into town, if you'd
like," Doug offered, and Ms. Maggie Drummond,
who moments ago had watched their approach with
wide, wary eyes, accepted the offer without a second's hesitation.

The world was just not designed for people who
were a scant inch over five feet tall, Maggie
thought, as Ryan pulled open the door of the truck
and stepped back to allow her to get in first. Pants
were too long, kitchen counters were too tall, cupboard shelves were out of reach, and there was no
graceful way to step up into a truck. Ordinarily,

she would simply have climbed up into the seat without giving much thought to whether or not she looked graceful, but she was ridiculously aware of those brilliant blue eyes watching her. Stupid, she thought. As if a man like that would notice whether or not she looked graceful while getting into a truck. As if he'd notice her at all, she thought wistfully.

"Here." Ryan set his hand under her elbow as she reached for the armrest to balance herself. The unexpected warmth of his touch surprised her into looking at him. "It's a bit of a step up," he said, smiling.

"Thanks." She was startled by the breathless sound of her own voice. She didn't normally go all breathy just because an attractive man offered her a little polite assistance. It must be relief that she wasn't going to end up a permanent part of the local landscape. That was why she was overreacting. Hadn't she read somewhere that when a person was rescued from terrible danger, they sometimes developed a tremendous attachment to the person who rescued them? Of course, she hadn't been in terrible danger, exactly. The worst that was likely to have happened to her was a bit of acute discomfort. But still, she *was* very relieved to have a ride into town. That must be causing her to overreact. Wasn't there a name for that kind of thing? Stockholm Syndrome? No, that was for hostage situations. And why did they call it *Stockholm* Syndrome, anyway? Did they have a lot of kidnappings in Stockholm? The Swiss seemed too orderly to allow kidnappers to run rampant. Stockholm *was* in Switzerland, wasn't it? Geography had never been her strong suit.

"Is something wrong?"

Ryan's question made her realize that she was still standing in the open doorway like a statue. Startled, she said the first thing that popped into her head.

"I was just trying to remember where Stockholm is."

His dark brows climbed ever so slightly, his eyes widening in surprise. "It's in Sweden, last time I looked."

"Not Switzerland?"

"Not unless they've moved it." He gave her a cautious look. "Is it important?"

"No. I was just wondering." *Good going, Maggie. You've just convinced him that you're a lunatic.* With a sigh for her own foolishness, she climbed into the truck and scooted into the middle of the bench seat.

The interior of the truck showed as much wear as the exterior. The dashboard was cracked from the sun. A tattered old army blanket had been thrown over the seat, but Maggie could still feel something jabbing the back of her thigh, even through the thick layers of wool. The knob to wind down the passenger window was either broken or someone really hated fresh air, because the handle was secured against the door with an X-shaped bandage of duct tape. The floor was nearly covered with empty Twinkie wrappers and crumpled fast-food bags. She tried to subtly nudge aside the Jack-in-the-Box bag that was leaning against her ankle.

Unconcerned with subtlety, Ryan used the toe of his boot to shove the sack toward the firewall. "Doug single-handedly supports half the fast-food franchises in the country."

"Wasn't me that ate two Big Macs for breakfast," Doug said as he turned the key in the ignition.

"Hunger can drive a man to do things he wouldn't ordinarily do," Ryan said darkly.

"Yeah, like order an extra side of fries." Doug automatically glanced in the rearview mirror before pulling back out on to the highway. Ryan caught Maggie's concerned look as they drove past her car.

"It will be okay there. Nobody's likely to disturb it."

"I know. This isn't like Detroit, where I might come back in a few hours and find it stripped. I was just wondering if it's going to need a new transmission.''

''If you need a good mechanic, Frank Luddy has a place on the north side of town,'' Ryan said.

''Thanks, but I'll let Luke take a look at it first. He's pretty good with cars.''

Luke. A boyfriend? Husband? Ryan glanced at her hands. She wasn't wearing a ring, but that didn't necessarily mean anything. He found the thought that she might be attached less than appealing, and the reaction caught him off guard. It had been a long time since he'd given more than a passing thought to whether or not a woman was attached. And longer still since he'd cared one way or the other. He would prefer it if things stayed that way a while longer. The last thing he needed— or wanted—was any kind of involvement with the opposite sex. He had other things on his plate right now, he thought, rubbing his thumb absently against the base of his ring finger.

''Detroit?'' Doug asked. ''That where you're from?''

''Born and raised there, though I have a hard time believing it sometimes. After three years out here, Michigan seems like a foreign country.''

''Never spent much time in Michigan that I can recall. Guess they don't do a whole lot of rodeos in Detroit.''

"Not that I recall," Maggie said. "Are you a rodeo cowboy?"

"I sure enough am. I been cowboying since I was a pup. My daddy has him a place in North Dakota, and me and my brothers grew up ropin' and ridin'. Wasn't room for all of us on the ranch, though, so I figured I'd best take to the road and earn me enough to buy a little place of my own."

Ryan listened to the conversation with half an ear. He already knew Doug's background. Ninety percent of the cowboys riding the circuit were looking to earn enough to "buy a little place" of their own. Doug was one of the few who had a shot at actually doing it. There was a lot more to Doug Tennent than he generally let show. He had grown up on a ranch, and he was a damned fine bull rider, but he also had a degree in economics from the University of Washington, and he knew the stock market inside and out. His reading material was as likely to be the *Wall Street Journal* as it was *American Horseman*. He cultivated the folksy image the way some people cultivated a finely toned body.

Maggie laughed at something he said, and Ryan found himself smiling in response. Her laugh was like her smile—warm and friendly, making you want to laugh with her. Doug was telling one of his stories, this one involving a particularly ill-tempered Brahma bull with whom he'd had a running battle a couple of years ago. He'd drawn the animal several times, and it had left him eating arena dirt every time.

"Do you both ride bulls for a living?" Maggie asked, glancing up at Ryan.

"No, ma'am," Doug answered for both of them. "Ryan, here, he likes to take it easy. He's a bronc rider. That's a little like riding a rocking horse. He got that busted arm when he went to sleep in the saddle and fell right off."

Ryan caught Maggie's uncertain glance and smiled. "He can't help lying, ma'am. He's landed on his head one too many times. It's sort of addled his thinking a bit."

"I'm not the one wearin' a cast," Doug noted. "One thing you got to learn, boy, is not to play carpet for eight hundred pounds of horse."

"You've got a point there," Ryan conceded with a grin. "I'll try to remember that."

"Speaking of carpets, I ever tell you about the bearskin rug in my daddy's den? Tom, my oldest brother, and me was out fishing one day when we heard something crashing through the underbrush. We figured..."

Maggie had only known Doug a few minutes, but that was long enough to recognize that he was launching into a lengthy—and probably highly exaggerated—story. She instinctively glanced at Ryan, and their eyes met, bright with humor and a certain wry resignation on his part. It was an instant of perfect communication, and Maggie couldn't help but feel a momentary pang of regret that she wasn't a tall, svelte platinum blonde, the sort of woman a man couldn't help but look at twice.

She looked away and focused her gaze determinedly out the windshield and her attention firmly on Doug's story, which seemed to involve him and his brother, armed only with fishing poles and a rock, battling a twelve-foot tall grizzly bear. It seemed improbable, but no more improbable than a man like Ryan Lassiter suddenly finding himself wildly attracted to a short, plump woman with no particular claim to beauty. Not that she cared one way or the other, she reminded herself. She wasn't looking for involvement with the opposite sex right now. She had more than enough to deal with already.

One of the things Maggie liked most about the town of Willow Flat was that it had no pretensions. There was no cute Welcome sign hung out at the edge of town, no building codes requiring a clever Western motif to unify the commercial buildings and give the two-block-long downtown an "authentic" Western look. Even the name was simple.

The land was flat. Thanks to a rare, dependable source of water, there were willows. Hence, it was called Willow Flat, a name as practical and unadorned as the town itself.

It had started out as a frontier town whose main function had been to provide services for the surrounding ranches, and, a hundred and twenty years later, nothing much had changed. The streets had been paved, and cattlemen no longer drove herds of cattle through the middle of town. The general store now had a corner where you could rent video tapes, right next to the display of Bag Balm and the neatly stacked shelves of blue jeans. Lucille Devlin, owner of Lucille's Grille, had put in a cappuccino machine a year or so ago, and, while the town wasn't exactly overrun with double mocha decaf latte drinkers, curiosity had brought in enough extra business to pay for her investment.

All in all, Maggie liked to think that one of the original settlers would still feel pretty well at home if he happened to fall through a time warp and land in the middle of town. Coming from a big city, where whole neighborhoods seemed to rise and fall overnight, the stability of Willow Flat was a welcome change. Her sister, Noreen, called it stagnation and despised the town for all the same reasons Maggie liked it. She frequently talked about shaking the Wyoming dust from her shoes and moving to a place where there was real life, like Los Angeles or San Francisco, or maybe even New York. But, since she spent money faster than she made it, it didn't seem likely that she would be leaving anytime soon.

"Place never changes much," Ryan said as they reached the edge of town. His tone was neutral, but Maggie responded as if the comment had been full of enthusiasm.

"That's what I like about it," she said, looking at the architecturally uninspired buildings around them. "There's something kind of nice about knowing that it looks just the same way it must have ten years ago, isn't there?"

"Actually, it looks pretty much the same way it did twenty years ago," he said, smiling a little at her pleasure. Willow Flat wasn't the sort of place to inspire excitement. It was just a small, dusty Western town, more functional than beautiful. Within his memory, it had always looked pretty much the same. He'd never considered it a reason for either celebration or complaint. It was just the way things were.

"Turn here," Maggie said, and Doug obediently turned right.

The businesses in Willow Flat were all strung out along a single stretch of the road that ran through town. Behind them, the residential areas sprawled with careless abandon. There were no neat developments with tidy rows of houses and neatly watered lawns. Homes had been built as the need arose, with practicality the first consideration. There was no cohesive style—no recognizable style at all, actually. These weren't bungalows or ranch houses or the pseudo-Spanish style homes so ubiquitous in states farther west or south. They were just houses. The lots were large and mostly unfenced, though here and there a chain-link fence had been thrown up to keep dogs and small children out of the street. Behind the houses, you could catch glimpses of outbuildings, a small stable here, or there a chicken house or toolshed. The neighborhood straddled the line between town and country, too haphazard for one, too organized for the other.

The pavement disappeared within a few yards of the main road, and the truck's tires crunched over a mixture of gravel and dirt. A dog barked in a desultory fashion as they drove past, then settled back down to nap. Maggie directed Doug to a house near the end of the road. It was a bit scruffier than most of its neighbors, in desperate need of paint, and the roof had a tired look about it that said it might not survive another winter's worth of snow. The yard was mostly dirt, though a few patchy areas of grass suggested there might once have been a lawn there. In contrast to the generally unkempt appearance, there were two neat flower beds lined up on either side of the sagging porch. This early in the year, they held only the tantalizing promise of color to come, but the soil was rich and black, and the crisp green leaves were full of life. Ryan was willing to bet that, in a few weeks, the beds would be a riot of color. He was also willing to bet that Maggie was responsible for that bright promise, though he couldn't have said why he was so sure of that. For all he knew, "Luke" was a master gardener.

"Thank you so much for the ride," Maggie said to Doug. "I would probably still be sitting out there in the middle of nowhere if you hadn't come along."

"My pleasure, ma'am." Doug tilted his hat back and gave her a toothy grin. "Rescuing pretty ladies is something of a hobby of mine."

"Well, you're very good at it," she said, smiling. "Good luck at the next rodeo."

"Ain't a matter of luck," he assured her solemnly. He slanted a pointed look in Ryan's direction. "It's pure skill. Some of us just have a bit more of it than others."

"Yeah, and some of us hold a lot more hot air than others," Ryan said as he pushed open the passenger door and stepped out of the truck, his battered ribs protesting the movement.

"Here." He offered Maggie his hand as she slid to the end of the seat. She seemed to hesitate the merest fraction of a second before setting her hand in his. Her hand was small, but her grip was firm. Despite her size, there was nothing delicate or fragile about Maggie Drummond. There was something appealingly...sturdy about her. And he doubted if there was a woman alive who'd appreciate hearing herself described that way, he thought with a twinge of amusement.

"Thanks so much," she said, pulling her hand away as soon as she was on the ground. "I really do appreciate the help."

"Don't thank me. I'm not much good at rescuing damsels in distress with this thing." He lifted the cast a little for emphasis, his mouth curving in a self-deprecating smile. He was going to tell her to have a nice day or some other banality, tip his hat and climb back in Doug's truck. No one was more surprised than he was when he said, "I'll be staying on my grandfather's place, the Double L. Maybe I'll see you around town?"

It wasn't exactly a proposal of marriage. It wasn't even a request for a date, but it was a lot more than he'd planned on saying, and, from the way her gray eyes widened in surprise, it was more than Maggie had expected to hear.

"That would be nice," she said, after a barely perceptible pause. She hesitated a moment longer, then gave him a quick, uncertain smile and turned and walked toward the house.

Ryan ignored the impulse to stand and watch her walk away. He'd already done more than he intended. It was just that he'd made a lot of changes in his life recently—giving up the circuit, coming home. All that change had thrown him off balance. He wasn't really thinking about looking Maggie Drummond up and asking her out. He stepped into the truck and shut the door with a solid thud. Out of sight, out of mind, he told himself.

"She's real pretty," Doug said, leaning one arm on the steering wheel and watching her walk up the cracked concrete walkway.

"Yup."

"Seems like a real nice little gal."

"Yup." Almost without his volition, his eyes followed Doug's. She was small, but she was very nicely packaged, he thought, admiring the soft, womanly curves of her body.

"Gal like that makes a man think about home-cooked dinners," Doug said soulfully. "Picket fences, some of them flowery curtains at the windows, maybe a fire in the—"

"You paint a deeply moving picture of domestic bliss." Ryan's voice was dry as dust. "Maybe you should see about getting yourself a nice, steady job in town and then call on her. Last I heard, we didn't have a village idiot. You just might qualify. Pay's lousy, and the benefits aren't much, but you can always live on love."

"Wasn't me she was making eyes at," Doug said, unmoved by his friend's sarcasm. Maggie turned to wave when she reached the porch, and Doug lifted his hand in return before dropping it to the gear shift. He grinned knowingly at Ryan. "Come to think of it, wasn't *me* making eyes at *her*."

"No one was making eyes at anyone," Ryan said grumpily. He just wished he was as sure as he sounded. Not that it mattered, because there was no reason for his path and Maggie Drummond's to cross again.

Chapter Two

Maggie stood just inside the screen door and watched the rusty pickup pull out. Doug would turn around at the end of the road. If she stood here, she could see the truck drive by again, but they wouldn't be able to see her. Of course, she was well past the age of doing something so sophomoric. Besides, Ryan would be on the opposite side of the truck anyway—not that she'd necessarily be watching to get another glimpse of him in particular. And if this wasn't the stupidest conversation she'd ever had with herself, she didn't know what was. But she stayed where she was, hidden behind the grainy protection of the screen.

"Who was that?" Maggie jumped guiltily and spun away from the door. Her sister, Noreen, stood just behind her, looking over her shoulder.

"My car died a few miles outside of town. A couple of guys gave me a ride home."

"Somebody you know?"

Maggie knew better than to think the question was asked out of concern for her safety. Among Noreen's many complaints about living in a small town was the fact that the pool of available men was severely limited. *Of course, most women didn't require quite such a large pool.* The sheer bitchiness of the thought startled Maggie. She'd come to terms with the way her sister chose to live her life a long time ago. At least, she thought she had.

"I haven't seen them around town," she said, answering Noreen's question.

"Haven't seen who around town?" Her mother stuck her head through the living room door.

"A couple of strange men picked Maggie up and gave her a ride into town," Noreen said, her eyes sparkling with malice.

"You needn't make it sound like we had an orgy in the back of the pickup," Maggie snapped. Behind her, she heard Doug's truck heading back up the street, but she didn't turn to look. Moving away from the door, she headed for the kitchen. It was almost six o'clock, but she knew better than to think that anyone would have started dinner.

"I'd never accuse *you* of having an orgy," Noreen said, following her. "The way you're headed, you're probably going to end up as the world's oldest living virgin.''

Maggie hung her purse over the back of a chair and closed her eyes for an instant, gathering the mental threads of self-control. It took more of an effort than it usually did to swallow the several nasty—and quite true—responses that came to mind. Quarreling with Noreen was a waste of time. She'd learned that early in life.

"Everybody has to have a goal in life," she said lightly and had the satisfaction of knowing her calm response had annoyed her sister more than any catty remark could have.

"Of course, it's not as if you're turning down dates," Noreen said spitefully.

"Don't quarrel, girls," Lydia Drummond ordered as she entered the kitchen behind her oldest daughter. "I don't know why the two of you can't get along." She tugged fretfully at the moth-eaten pink sweater she wore over a pair of faded gray stretch pants and an old flannel shirt. Bright pink patches of blusher angled across her cheekbones, and thick, black liner circled her eyes, making her look like a startled raccoon. Looking at her, Maggie found it hard to remember that she'd once thought her mother the most beautiful woman in the world. Age had set a heavy hand on Lydia Drummond.

"So who was it that dropped you off, Maggie?" she asked.

"My car died," Maggie explained again. "I was lucky enough to get a ride into town with a couple of cowboys."

"Cowboys." Noreen's tone made the word something less than a compliment. "Every man in the whole damned state is a cowboy or pretending to be one. I swear to God, if I never saw another pair of pointy-toed boots or one of those damned hats again, I could die a happy woman."

"This is ranching country," Maggie said as she opened the refrigerator and took out ingredients for a casserole. "Loafers and pink pullovers with little animals on them would look a bit out of place."

Noreen leaned one hip against the counter and watched as Maggie chopped onions with swift efficiency. It didn't occur to her to offer to help, and it didn't occur to Maggie to ask. "So, did these cowboys who came to your rescue have names?"

"Doug Tennent and Ryan Lassiter," Maggie said, a little surprised by her own reluctance to give out even that much information. It wasn't as if there were anything to hide. It was just that the little bit of time she'd spent with Doug and Ryan had been so pleasant. She didn't want it tainted by Noreen's peculiar view of the world.

"Lassiter." Lydia repeated the name thoughtfully. "Isn't that the name of that old man who owns the big place west of here?"

"The Double L?" Maggie could practically see Noreen's ears prick up.

"Was this Lassiter one of *the* Lassiters?"

"Probably. He said something about staying at his grandfather's place," Maggie said, keeping her tone indifferent.

"The Double L is a huge spread. Some of their hands come into the Dew Drop, and I've heard them talk." Noreen served drinks at the Dew Drop Inn, a bar on the outskirts of town. "This must be the Lassiter that's been riding rodeo for the past few years. I've heard him mentioned a couple of times. They've got tons of land, about a zillion cattle. They're loaded. As far as I know, he's the only grandson, so I imagine everything will go to him when his grandfather dies, and I think he's pretty old. He probably won't be around much longer."

The naked greed in Noreen's voice had Maggie's fingers clenching around the head of lettuce she'd just pulled from the vegetable crisper. There were moments—many of them—when she wondered how it was possible that she and Noreen were related.

"Anything I can do to help?" Lydia asked, one foot already out the door. The television was chattering in the living room and she hated to miss "Wheel of Fortune." She liked to see what Vanna was wearing to turn the tiles.

"I've got it," Maggie said, aware that she was talking to the back of her mother's head. Not that it mattered. Lydia was singularly useless in the kitchen. Maggie was caught off guard by the sudden, sharp twinge of resentment that the task of cooking dinner always fell to her, just like most of the cleaning and paying the bills and making sure there was food in the house to start with. It had been the same for so long that she rarely thought about it, but there were moments when she questioned her own sanity in letting things stay the way they were. It just seemed easier than trying to persuade her mother or sister to take on some of the chores. *And if you're not careful, you're going to turn into a complete doormat, Maggie.*

"Is he good-looking?" Noreen asked, settling herself more comfortably against the counter.

"Who?" Maggie asked, deliberately dense.

"This Ryan Lassiter," Noreen prodded impatiently. "Is he good-looking?"

Good-looking? Maggie thought of Ryan's sky blue eyes and the dimple that appeared in his cheek when he smiled and the thick fall of dark hair. Two things struck her—*good-looking* was a hopelessly inadequate description, and she wasn't at all sure she liked the fact that his image was so sharp and clear in her mind.

"He's attractive," she said finally.

"Attractive and loaded." Noreen's mouth curved in a feline smile. "My favorite kind of man."

"I didn't know you had a preference," Maggie muttered under her breath as she turned on the water in the sink.

"What rotten luck that it was *your* car that died," Noreen said irritably, missing the comment. "I could really have done something with a chance like that."

"I just bet you could." Maggie turned the faucet off with a sharp twist of her wrist.

"What did you say?" Noreen's blue eyes narrowed in suspicious question.

"I said, I'm sure you could have done something with a golden opportunity like that." She smiled at her sister. "Not every woman knows how to make the most out of a dead transmission, several hundred square miles of empty countryside and two strange men, but I'm sure you would have."

Noreen frowned, and Maggie could see the wheels turning in her mind. There was an insult in there. She knew there was. But Maggie's expression was guileless, nothing but sincerity in her tone. And she hadn't actually *said* anything unpleasant. After a moment, Noreen shrugged, apparently deciding to take the comment at face value.

"I'm sure if I put my mind to it, I can figure a way to meet this guy." She smoothed one hand absently over the slim curve of her hip.

Maggie was sure she could, too, and she didn't like the idea at all. Men had a tendency to look at Noreen's willowy figure, mile-long legs and the lush invitation of her mouth and lose sight of the cold calculation in her eyes. There was no reason to think Ryan Lassiter would be any different. Not that it was any of her concern, she told herself. It wasn't as if she had any claim on him. Or even wanted to have any.

She resisted the urge to cross her eyes and look down at her own nose to see if it had grown a couple of inches. Did just *thinking* a lie make your nose grow?

"He didn't say how long he'd be in town," she said.

"Well, I imagine we'll run into each other." Noreen straightened away from the counter. She smiled, a feline curve of her lips that made Maggie want to heave a salad bowl at her head. "I'll make sure we do." She sauntered from the kitchen.

Maggie didn't know what annoyed her most—Noreen's blatant gold digging or the fact that she let it bother her. Heaven knew, her sister's attitude was hardly a surprise. It wasn't as if she didn't know what Noreen was. Or what her mother was, for that matter. She just didn't usually let it bother her.

There was a nasty headache building in her temples, and Maggie let her hands drop to the counter as she closed her eyes and willed the pain to fade. *Your choice,* she reminded herself. She didn't have to stay. She was not a child anymore, forced to abide by the decisions of the adults who controlled her fate. She could leave. But even as she thought it, she knew she wouldn't go. Duty or stupidity, she wasn't sure anymore which it was, but she wasn't going anywhere. At least, not immediately.

Sighing, she opened her eyes. There was nothing she hated more than whining. God knew, she listened to more than enough of it from her mother. And if there was guilt in the thought, that didn't change the truth of it. She'd made her choices, and, if life wasn't working out quite the way she'd dreamed it would when she was a little girl, she had no one to blame but herself.

There was a window over the sink, and, if she stood on her toes and leaned slightly to the left, she could see past the trailer parked in the backyard of the house next door and get a glimpse of the mountains. She fantasized sometimes about losing herself in the cool green canyons and never coming back.

With a sigh, Maggie settled back down on her heels, giving up the view of the mountains for the chipped yellow paint on the cupboard. Unbidden, a sudden image of Ryan Lassiter's smile popped into her head. She wondered what he'd meant when he said he would see her around town. Was it just wishful thinking that made it sound like he *hoped* he'd see her around? On the other hand, in a town the size of Willow Flat, you saw everybody around town, sooner or later. Maybe he'd simply been stating the obvious.

Maggie sighed as she got out a skillet. If there was one thing she'd learned in her not quite twenty-four years, it was that expectations led to disappointment more often than not. A practical woman would put Ryan Lassiter and his blue eyes and dimples right out of her mind. She dropped a chunk of butter into the pan and watched it start to melt.

Practicality sucked.

In 1865, wearied by the fighting in the East, Quintin Lassiter had journeyed west, looking for a place to build a new home, a place not tainted by the stench of old hatreds. He'd settled on a stretch of land at the foot of the Wind River range, in the untamed Wyoming Territory. It was a lonely, isolated place, far from anything that might be called civilization, but, where most people saw nothing but an empty land inhabited by antelope, jackrabbits and hostile Indians, he saw a cattle range, a place to build a home and raise a family.

By the end of his first year, he had a small but sturdy cabin built of logs he'd snaked out of the nearby mountains on horseback. His herd was still small, but the cattle were thriving on the rich grass. He sent to Virginia and asked his wife to join him. Marilee Lassiter was a small woman with masses of pale blond hair and a delicate beauty that seemed out of place in the vast emptiness of the new land, but her fragile looks disguised a will and determination to match her husband's. They'd left nothing behind but smoke and rubble. This was where they would build a new life.

Less than a year after she arrived, while Quintin was away from the ranch, a party of Kiowa, raiding north of their usual range, stumbled across the small ranch. They struck without warning, severely wounding the Lassiters' only hired hand. Marilee, seven months pregnant with her first child, took his rifle and, firing through the rifle slits built into the walls of the cabin, killed one brave and two of their horses before the Indians decided they'd had enough. Quintin came home to find their hired hand delirious with fever and his wife, a former belle of Virginia society, dividing her time between nursing him and clearing the rubble from the burned outbuildings so they could be rebuilt.

When the hired hand recovered, he told Quintin that he should count himself as one lucky son of a bitch that Marilee was on his side, because he'd seen what she could do when she got riled up. Laughing, Quintin had decided to name the ranch Lassiter's Luck and the Double L brand had been born.

Nathan Lassiter stared absently at the formal portrait of Quintin and Marilee Lassiter that hung over the mantel in his study. They'd fought Indians, squatters and the land itself to lay a foundation for future generations. And each generation since had built on that foundation. At a time when family-owned ranches were sinking under the combined pressures of taxes, developers and the growing American obsession with low-fat everything, the Double L was on solid financial footing. He'd spent most of his life working to keep it that way, though for a while there, it had seemed as if he might be the last generation of Lassiters on the Double L.

But that was before Duncan and Sylvie had brought Ryan to him. The boy had taken to ranch life like a duck to water. He'd wanted to know everything, wanted to learn everything. After Duncan's indifference, Nathan had been startled by his grandson's avid interest in everything to do with ranching. Duncan had found the ranch confining; Ryan reveled in the freedom it offered. Duncan was never more than a competent horseman; Ryan rode as if he'd been born in the saddle. The constant sigh of the wind grated on Duncan's nerves; Ryan loved the mixed scents of pine and sagebrush that rode on it.

Nathan's worries about the future of the ranch had faded. His grandson's love of the ranch was as deep and strong as his own. When Ryan married Sally McIntyre, it had been yet another tie to the future. John McIntyre had been foreman on the Double L for close to a quarter century. He'd taken over the job from his father. The McIntyres were as much a part of the Double L as the Lassiters. Their son, Tucker, was Ryan's best friend and, when Ryan fell in love with their youngest daughter, everything seemed perfect.

Maybe too perfect, Nathan thought now, remembering the long months of Sally's illness and the cold, still look in Ryan's eyes as he'd watched them bury his wife.

He turned away from the portrait and walked to the window. Ryan and his friend were on their way up to the house. He'd heard the truck pull in, had seen Seth Balkins come out of the bunkhouse and help them unload the mare before unhitching the horse trailer. Another one of Ryan's rescue projects, no doubt. The boy had a weakness for injured birds, three-legged dogs and horses no one else wanted. Damned stupid attitude in a rancher, Nathan thought, shaking his head in exasperation. On a ranch, everyone had to carry their own weight, including the animals. His mouth curved in a half smile as he thought of some of the useless creatures that had lived out their days on the Double L over the last twenty years.

Ryan laughed at something Doug said and Nathan's smile widened a little. He hadn't heard Ryan laugh much these past few years. He'd taken Sally's death hard. They all had. She'd been so young and so full of life. No one had said Ryan shouldn't grieve. But it had been four years now, and the boy was still living like there was no tomorrow, spending his time chasing after fancy buckles and trying to break his neck on the back of a bucking horse. If he kept at it, he was bound to succeed sooner or later.

Now, here he was home again. And he was hurt again. It wasn't the first time he'd come home to wait out an injury. Each time, Nathan had thought the boy might finally realize it was time to come home for good, time to put the past behind him. And each time he'd gone back out on the road as soon as the broken bones had knitted. One of these days, he wasn't going to come back at all.

Nathan's hand clenched where it rested on the back of the worn leather sofa, and his jaw set with determination. Thirty years ago he'd lost his son, for all intents and purposes. He wasn't going to lose his grandson. Not if he could do something to prevent it.

"What have you done to yourself this time?" Sara McIntyre shook her head in exasperation as she looked at the cast on Ryan's arm.

"The horse's name was Lucky Streak," he said, then grinned at her quick bark of laughter.

"I'd think you'd have more sense than to get on a horse with a name like that. You should have known you were asking for trouble."

"I'll try to remember that." He put his good arm around her shoulders and drew her close for a hug. "I came home so you could nurse me back to health."

"If you think I'm going to wait on you hand and foot after you were stupid enough to get yourself thrown off a horse, you'd better think again," she told him firmly. "I'm more likely to put you to work."

Sara concealed a worried frown when she felt the stiffness of the bandage around his ribs. She wondered if there were any other injuries but knew better than to ask. And, if his movements were a little careful, she wouldn't mention that, either. She'd never known anyone more allergic to fussing than he was.

"You remember Doug," Ryan's tone made it half question, half statement.

"Of course." Sara's smile was quick and welcoming. "You spent Thanksgiving with us two years ago. How are you?"

"Can't complain." Doug grinned at Ryan. "'Specially now that I'm getting shut of this broken-down cowboy. He just about talked my ear off the last couple of days."

"He always was a chatterbox." Sara's smile widened. She remembered Doug quite well and was willing to bet that, if anyone had done a lot of talking, it hadn't been Ryan. "There's no point in standing in the hall," she said, suddenly aware that they hadn't made it out of the entryway. "Come on in and we'll get you fixed up with a room."

"I appreciate the invite, but I've got to be gettin' back on the road," Doug told her. "I've got me an appointment with a bull in Montana day after tomorrow, and I can make another two or three hundred miles tonight."

"I don't suppose the bull could wait?" Sara asked, already knowing the answer.

"No, ma'am. Bulls, they don't have much patience." Doug shook his head and looked solemn. "Waitin' tends to sort of ruffle their feathers a mite, makes them hard to get along with, so I'd best be on my way."

"Not before I fix you up some sandwiches to take with you," she said firmly. "And maybe you could take time for a bowl of soup? There's some vegetable beef soup left over from last night's supper, and I'm likely to have to throw it out unless I can coax someone into finishing it up."

"Well, I reckon a few more minutes wouldn't do any harm," Doug said, weakening in the face of severe temptation.

"Of course it wouldn't. How about you, Ryan?"

He shook his head. "I can wait 'til supper. I'll just take my stuff up to my room."

"I don't suppose it would do any good to point out that you probably shouldn't be carrying that duffel bag upstairs." Sara allowed a trace of exasperation to enter her voice.

"No good at all," he told her with a smile.

"He's not near as bad off as he looks," Doug told her. He dropped his hat on the hall table and ran his fingers through his sandy hair, combing it into a vague sort of order. "I know he looks kind of puny, but you got to be careful not to encourage him to malinger. You know how it is with bronc riders, they're prone to make a fuss over the littlest thing.''

''Why don't you go eat before I decide to deprive you of the use of a few of your teeth?'' Ryan threatened lightly.

Doug grinned at him and threw his arm around Sara's shoulders. ''Truth is, you'd just be casting pearls before swine, Miz McIntyre, feeding your good cooking to him. He ain't got no taste at all. Now, I haven't had a home-cooked meal in a month of Sundays. Not since last time I was home and Mama fried up a mess of Rocky Mountain oysters. You know, it puts me in mind of the time my uncle Leonard paid us a visit. He's got him a little place down New Mexico way, and he don't eat nothin' unless it's chock full of hot peppers. He brought a batch of them with him, and Mama just about had a conniption fit when he asked her to add some to a batch of...''

Ryan shook his head as Doug's voice faded into the distance. If there was an occasion for which he didn't have a story, he'd yet to see it. He turned and leaned down to pick up his duffel bag, allowing himself a muttered curse as his ribs grumbled about the weight. He didn't remember it hurting this much the last time he'd busted a couple of ribs. Had to be age creeping up on him.

"How bad is it this time?"

The question startled Ryan into straightening too quickly. He barely noticed the pain that shot across his chest as he turned toward the sound of his grandfather's voice. Nathan stood just outside the door that led to his den, his expression unreadable.

Something about the way he stood there, half in shadow, half in light, stripped away the familiarity, made him look like a stranger. For an instant Ryan was swept back twenty years. He was ten years old again, meeting his grandfather for the first time, unsure of his welcome, wondering if there was a place for him here. The feeling was gone as quickly as it had come, but the uncertainty lingered. They hadn't parted on good terms.

"Broken arm, three broken ribs," he said, answering Nathan's question. His smile was lopsided. "According to Doug, the horse did a nice little tango right over the top of me."

Nathan nodded without smiling. "Good thing it wasn't your head."

"I appreciated that."

"Saw you unloading a mare." Nathan moved farther into the entryway as he spoke. "Another one of your charity cases?"

"She's got a few problems, but she comes from

good lines. It may take a little work, but I think she'll make a good cutting horse." Ryan tightened his grip on the duffel bag. He was tired, and he hurt. The mare had spooked when they were unloading her. She'd lunged, knocking him into the side of the trailer and reawakening every ache and pain he'd been trying to forget.

Nathan snorted. "In other words, she was on her way to the canners when you bought her."

Ryan shrugged. He couldn't deny it. Nor could he explain what had made him buy a mare that everyone else thought was untrainable. There had just been something in her eyes that had made it impossible for him to stand by and see her sold to the canners.

"I can work with her," was all he said.

"For how long?" Nathan gestured sharply to the cast. "Until you get that thing off and head back to the circuit? Goddamn it, Ryan, this isn't a rest home for broken-down rodeo bums and glue factory rejects."

Ryan stiffened, his eyes taking on an icy chill. "I can go elsewhere, if you'd prefer."

Temper nearly had Nathan telling him to do just that, but a small voice of sanity stopped him. Looking into his grandson's eyes, he knew that if Ryan left now, he might not come back. Since that was exactly what he wanted to prevent, he struggled to tamp down the worry-driven anger.

"This is your home," he said stiffly. "Even if you don't seem to remember that very often."

Ryan swallowed a sharp response. He was tired of the anger between them. He could probably end it once and for all by telling his grandfather that he'd come home for good, but pride wouldn't let him say the words. He wasn't going to let the old man think he could dictate his life.

"Thanks," he said, struggling to keep his voice even.

"This is your home," Nathan said again.

The silence that fell between them swirled with undercurrents—anger and frustration, words unspoken, stubborn pride. In the barn, a horse whinnied, the sound carrying easily through the stillness. It served to break the tense silence that filled the entryway.

"I'm going to go unpack," Ryan said.

"You'll be down to supper?"

"Sure." He hesitated a moment, wanting to say something more, wanting to bridge the gap that had grown between them, but he didn't have the words. Maybe there were no words, he thought tiredly. Without speaking again, he walked past his grandfather and started up the stairs. He wondered if he'd made a mistake in coming home.

* * *

Nathan stood in the entryway and watched until his grandson was out of sight. Though Ryan tried to hide it, his movements were slow and stiff. He'd lost weight since Christmas. A few weeks of Sara's cooking would put some meat back on his bones but it would take more than good food to drive the shadows from his eyes. It was time he came home. Past time. And Nathan was going to do whatever it took to make his grandson see that.

"If you're trying to make him leave, you're off to a fine start."

Sara's voice came from behind, startling him. He turned to look at her, his dark brows hooking together in a frown.

"I know how to handle him."

She snorted, unimpressed by his scowl. She'd left Doug finishing up his soup in the kitchen and had come out in time to hear the end of the conversation between Nathan and Ryan. "If you handled cattle as poorly as you handle your grandson, this place would have gone under years ago. You push him too hard. He's not a child anymore."

"It's time he came home. I didn't raise him for the past twenty years just so he could waste his time entertaining a bunch of urban cowboys by getting himself stomped by a damned horse," he said, his frustration spilling over.

"You didn't raise him to take orders, either," she reminded him.

"The boy's stubborn as a damned mule," he said huffily, bypassing the truth of her words for an easier accusation.

"He's not a boy. And he's too much like you for his own good." Sara met his glare without flinching. "Give him some rope, Nathan, or you're going to push him away for good."

"I've given him plenty of rope. Seems to me he's trying to hang himself with it!" Nathan ended the conversation by going back into his den and shutting the door.

Sara stared at the closed door for a moment, her dark eyes bright with annoyance. She would have given a great deal to be able to knock some sense into the two of them.

Chapter Three

In the week since her car had broken down, Maggie had thought about a lot of things. She'd thought about how much it was going to cost to get her car fixed, and had debated whether or not to sell it and buy a vehicle with fewer miles on it. She'd thought about getting a place of her own, which would mean giving up on the idea that she and her mother would ever grow closer. She'd wondered if the fact that, for the past three years, she'd been reasonably content with her job as a waitress at Bill's Place said something terrible about her lack of ambition. She'd even given serious consideration to whether the next president was going to be a Democrat or a Republican. Since the election was still several years away, this hadn't held her interest for long.

The one thing she hadn't let herself think about was Ryan Lassiter.

She had, in the course of her almost twenty-four years, had her share of dreams. When she was a little girl, she'd fantasized that the father who'd left when she was a few months old had actually been kidnapped by a mysterious cult and had spent all the years of her childhood longing to return to the family he'd seemingly abandoned. By the time she reached her teens, the fantasy had taken on a more worldly tone—he returned for her high school graduation, bearing gifts and begging her forgiveness for the mistakes he'd made. Naturally, she was the epitome of graciousness, accepting both his gifts and his apologies.

There had been other dreams—being a prima ballerina, becoming a world famous photographer, being hired to be White House chef, waking up one morning to find that she was eight inches taller and ten pounds lighter.

She'd eventually given up on her father; accepted that short, plump ballerinas were regrettably out of fashion and decided that Washington, D.C. was too humid, especially if you had to spend all day in the kitchen. But she still dabbled with photography, and, while she hadn't won a Pulitzer yet, she'd had some very nice rejections from wildlife magazines. She also refused to abandon the fantasy about growing eight inches and losing ten pounds overnight, but she was philosophical about the unlikelihood of having it actually happen.

As far as she was concerned, dreams made life worth living. Whether or not they came true wasn't nearly as important as the dreams themselves. But you had to be careful. If you counted on your dreams too much, you could end up with a broken heart. It was safest to build fantasies around the unlikely or the downright impossible. The trouble came when you risked dreaming about things that were almost within reach.

Ryan Lassiter definitely fell into the high-risk category. *Maybe I'll see you around town.* Maggie shook her head as she swiped a damp cloth across a table, wiping up a scattering of spilled salt and a smear of ketchup. It was obvious her social life was in sad shape when she actually spent time thinking about a meaningless remark like that. Maybe if she actually *had* a social life, she wouldn't have so much time to spend not thinking about a pair of clear blue eyes and a wickedly attractive smile.

"Hey, Maggie, how about another round?"

"How about you go home, Virgil?" Grateful for the distraction, Maggie dropped the rag into a pocket in her apron and turned toward the speaker. Virgil Mortenson was a regular at Bill's Place. He came in during the afternoon two or three times a week. He sat in the same booth and didn't socialize with the other clientele. He never got loud or obnoxious, his hands never wandered, and he was unfailingly polite, no matter how much Jack Daniel's he'd poured down.

In the three years she'd worked here, she'd seen a lot of different styles of drinkers. Some were social drinkers—they were in a bar, so they had a drink or three. A few drank because they loved the taste of it, and they savored the smooth fire of their chosen drink—whether it was whiskey or Scotch— the same way a wine connoisseur might savor a fine pinot noir. But it seemed to her that the majority of people who drank to excess did it because it gave them an excuse to make an ass of themselves. No matter what they did, the next morning, they could blame it on the booze.

Virgil was a unique case in her experience. He simply sat, all alone at his table, and drank steadily. He seemed to know exactly how much he could drink without passing out. At some point, he reached his limit, paid his tab and made his unsteady way out of the bar and walked two blocks down the street to the room he rented above the general store. Maggie knew that because she'd followed him a couple of times, worried that he might not make it home.

Bill's wasn't really the kind of place that catered

to serious drinkers, but Virgil wasn't the first one she'd seen. Now and again, someone overestimated his own capacity and passed out at the bar. She'd never felt the same concern for any of them that she did for Virgil.

According to what Bill had told her, he used to have his own place and had built quite a reputation as the man to see if you had a horse you couldn't tame. Nearly six years ago, his wife and two children had been on their way home from a trip to Cheyenne when a late spring blizzard caught them miles from the nearest town. It had been several days before the bodies were found.

A couple of years later, he lost the ranch, the victim of bad luck or bad management, depending on who was telling the story. Bill said his heart just hadn't been in it anymore. With the ranch gone, he moved into town and rented a room above the general store. He did odd jobs and part-time work to keep body and soul together, and he was reliable enough when he was working, but he spent most of his earnings on liquor. He'd only been coming into Bill's for the past few months, but, from what she'd been told, he'd been doing his best to drink himself to death for a couple of years.

"Go home, Virgil," she said again, compassion softening her voice.

"Ain't nothing there," he said in response.

There was no self-pity in the words. They were just a statement of fact. He gave her a crooked half smile that broke her heart. For a moment, a spark of humor edged out the emptiness in his dark eyes, giving her a glimpse of the man he might once have been. "Besides, I hear tell, it ain't healthy to drink alone."

"Well, at least have something to eat, then. I'll bring you a burger." She'd been watching him drink himself into a stupor for too long, and she'd suddenly had enough.

"I'm not hungry," he said, looking surprised. "Just need another drink."

"Well, you're not getting another drink until you put something solid in your stomach. And don't tell me you can't afford a meal," she told him, anticipating his argument. "We've got a special on cheeseburgers today. A buck fifty, and it comes with an order of fries and a glass of milk. How do you like your burgers—rare, medium or well-done?"

"Rare," he answered automatically.

"Fine. I'll be right back with your milk."

"But, I—"

Maggie walked away, ignoring his feeble attempt at protest. When she returned with the glass of milk, he was still looking confused. She set the glass down and left without giving him a chance to argue.

"A special on cheeseburgers?" Bill Martin raised one bushy brow in question as she returned to the bar. It was the middle of the afternoon on a weekday, and the bar was nearly empty, so there had been nothing to distract him from watching the exchange between her and Virgil.

"He looks like he hasn't had a decent meal in weeks. I'll pay the difference in price."

"Don't worry about it." He waved his hand dismissively. "Virgil used to be a good man. It's worth the price of a few ounces of beef to see somebody shake him up a little." He grinned as he looked past her to where Virgil sat staring at the glass of milk as if trying to figure out how it had come to be there. "I just hope the shock doesn't do him in."

"He needs help," she said, frowning.

"That he does," Bill agreed. "But no one can force him to get it."

"I suppose not." Maggie sighed. She knew he was right. No one could help Virgil unless he was willing to help himself. "Well, at least I'll know he's eaten a decent meal today."

"Your heart's too soft, Maggie," Bill told her. "It's going to end up broken one of these days."

"My heart's tougher than you think." She was

smiling as she turned away, but the smile faded when, for no reason that she could imagine, a vision of Ryan Lassiter's face popped into her mind. Talk about your potential heartbreak, she thought with a sigh. Not for her. She wasn't the sort likely to get her heart broken by a man like that, but some woman, somewhere, was going to either get her heart broken or all her dreams fulfilled.

Ryan's first visit to Bill's Place had been just a few weeks after he came to stay with his grandfather. He'd only just begun to believe that Nathan really wanted him to stay, and he was trying to absorb everything about his new home all in one great gulp. He'd come into town with one of the hands to get some supplies. By his own account, Lou Kleinman had been on the Double L longer than God, having worked for Nathan's father since before Nathan was born. The elderly cowboy had been willing to answer Ryan's endless stream of questions, never losing patience and never getting tired of talking about the life of a working cowboy, and Ryan had been his shadow most of that first summer.

On the way home, Lou had stopped in at Bill's for a beer, *Just to wet my whistle*. The big room had seemed the epitome of a Western bar to Ryan's inexperienced eye. Twenty years later, it still did, he thought as he pushed open the door. Low-ceilinged, and dimly lit except for the square lights that hung over the pool tables, everything was dark wood and worn burgundy vinyl seating. As a boy, he'd loved to sit at the long bar, his toes just touching the railing. Bill would serve him a Coke with three maraschino cherries or a Roy Rogers, a sticky sweet concoction of sugar and food coloring designed to rot a child's teeth in record time. He would sip his drink and listen to the men around him talk about the price of beef and the latest football scores, good horses and balky cows, complain about wives who didn't understand them and complain even more about the ones who did.

Those afternoon visits had established his image of the true Westerner. A certain pride that came of living close to the land and a long way from civilization; an independence born of both temperament and necessity; the belief that a man's word was his bond; the idea that a woman deserved a man's respect and protection. As he got older, he'd realized that living in the West didn't make a person any more likely to live up to those standards than those living in other parts of the country, but the ideals had stayed with him all these years, and he liked to think he lived up to them more often than not.

"Heard you were home," Bill said as Ryan

walked up to the bar and dropped his hat on an empty stool. "Heard you were among the walking wounded, too." He nodded to the cast. "Couldn't get a clear idea of what was wrong, though. Depending on who was telling the tale, you'd broken both legs, both arms, your collarbone or you were in a full body cast—injury unknown. And somebody said it was a broken finger."

"Nice to know the grapevine's as dependable as ever." Ryan was grinning as he slid onto a stool. "For the record, I broke my wrist and a couple of ribs."

"Hell, no wonder they embellished it. Body cast is a lot more interesting. The usual?"

"Why don't you throw in an extra cherry? I feel like living dangerously."

Bill chuckled as he filled a glass with ice and then spun his wheelchair with a quick flick of his wrist and got a bottle of Coke out of the cooler. Four maraschino cherries later, he pushed the glass across the bar to Ryan.

"Too many customers like you and I'd go out of business."

"Can I help it if I think most liquor tastes like lighter fluid?"

"It's downright un-American," Bill grumbled as he turned and wheeled down the bar to pour a beer for another customer.

Ryan took a deep swallow of icy Coke and let the atmosphere soak into his bones. On the jukebox, Alan Jackson mourned the fact that everything he loved was killing him. Two old men played a slow game of pool at one of the tables in the back of the room. The smell of cigarette smoke, whiskey and French fries blended into an odor that swept him back through the years.

Like the rest of the town, Bill's hadn't changed since he was a kid. As far as he could tell, neither had Bill. There was a little more gray in his hair and maybe a few more lines in his face, but those were small changes, hardly worth noticing.

He'd been a champion bull rider in his youth, but a bad spill had left him paralyzed from the waist down. Never one to waste time on mourning what couldn't be changed, he'd bought a run-down bar and restaurant with the money he'd been saving to buy a ranch and installed a ramp so he could tend bar from his wheelchair. That had been close to thirty years ago, and most of the locals found it hard to remember a time when Bill's Place hadn't been there.

"How's it going?" Ryan asked as Bill returned to his end of the bar.

"Can't complain. Business is pretty good. Too good, in some cases."

Ryan's stool squeaked a complaint as he turned

to look in the direction of Bill's nod. "Virgil still trying to drink himself to death?" he asked as he turned back.

"Giving it a fair shot." Bill wiped a damp rag over an invisible spot on the gleaming surface of the bar. "Damn shame."

"Anybody try to talk to him lately?" Ryan rubbed his thumb absently over the base of his empty ring finger.

"Bobby Rayczek gave it a shot a couple of months back. Offered him a job on the Rocking D."

"And?"

Bill shook his head. "Virgil turned him down. Didn't give a reason. Just said he wasn't interested."

"Can't help him if he won't let you."

"That's what I told Maggie a little bit ago."

"Maggie?" Ryan glanced across the bar at him, his interest sharpened. "Maggie Drummond?"

"You know her?" Bill looked only slightly surprised. In a town the size of Willow Flat, most people crossed paths sooner or later.

"Doug Tennent and I gave her a lift into town when her car broke down last week." And he'd thought about her more than he'd expected—or liked—in the days since then.

"Great little gal. Heart as big as Texas." Bill

nodded in Virgil's direction again, his mouth quirk-
ing in remembered amusement. "She just told Virgil he wasn't getting another drink until he ate
some lunch. Bullied him into it."

Ryan tried to picture the pretty little blonde with
the friendly smile bullying anyone into anything,
but the image wouldn't come clear. The image of
Maggie Drummond herself was crystal clear,
though. He frowned down into his glass. He'd certainly forgotten prettier women in his time. But
something about Maggie had stuck with him—the
warmth of her smile, the way her gray eyes reflected her emotions. Or maybe it was the odd little
flash of awareness he'd felt when he took her hand
to help her step out of the truck. He didn't particularly like it, but he couldn't deny that she'd lingered in his thoughts.

He glanced up as the swinging door that led to
the kitchen opened and Maggie came through, carrying a red plastic basket with a cheeseburger and
a mound of fries in it. She was wearing jeans and
a short-sleeved cotton shirt in a soft, dusty shade
of blue. Her streaky blond hair was caught up in a
ponytail, and there was a simple white apron tied
around her waist, not the frilly kind, but one that
looked a little like a carpenter's utility belt.

She didn't see him. From the look of determination on her face, he doubted if she saw anyone

but Virgil Mortenson. Looking at the firm set of her jaw, he revised his opinion about her ability to bully.

"Watch," Bill said quietly, his voice laced with anticipation. Ryan didn't need any urging. He was already turning on his stool, his eyes following Maggie's relentless progress across the room.

Virgil looked up apprehensively as she neared the booth. "Now, Maggie, I appreciate this, but I don't want—"

"Eat it. And drink the milk, too." She smacked the basket down in front of him like a gunfighter throwing down a gauntlet.

"I don't see why it's any of your business," Virgil protested in a tone that hovered somewhere between a complaint and a whine.

"Because I've made it my business," she told him flatly.

"I don't have to come in here," he told her, half bravado, half threat. "There's other places I can go."

"Yes, there are." Maggie didn't look disturbed by the possibility that he might take his business elsewhere. She simply stood there, hands on her hips, and waited.

Virgil looked down at the food and then looked back up at her. "You'll bring me another drink?"

"When you've eaten all of it," she promised, not softening her stance.

"I ain't had a glass of milk since I was a kid," he muttered, reaching reluctantly for a French fry.

"Then this will be a treat, won't it?" Her tone was ruthlessly cheerful, and Ryan bit back a grin. Poor Virgil looked as if he didn't know what had hit him.

"I can go somewhere else," Virgil muttered as he picked up the burger. This time, he sounded as if he was reassuring himself more than threatening her.

"It's a free country," Maggie agreed as she turned away from the booth.

"I want my drink when this here's gone," he called after her.

"I'll bring it."

"You planning on driving all my customers away?" Bill asked as she approached the bar.

Since he was smiling when he said it, Maggie knew he was kidding, but she was just a little shaken by her own actions. When it came right down to it, maybe Virgil was right—maybe it wasn't any of her business if he chose to drink himself into a stupor three days out of five.

"Maybe I shouldn't have said anything to him," she began guiltily.

"Sure you should. It will do Virgil a world of good to have someone push him around a bit."

It wasn't until he spoke that she really looked at the man sitting across the bar from Bill. Wearing a pair of faded jeans and a blue chambray shirt that reflected the color of his eyes, his dark hair slightly rumpled as if he'd combed his fingers through it, Ryan Lassiter looked even better than she'd remembered, and her heart bumped against her breastbone when their eyes met. She felt her cheeks warm and hoped the light was dim enough that he wouldn't be able to see the sudden surge of color.

Despite all her best efforts, she'd thought of him a lot this past week, wondered if she would see him again. She'd imagined bumping into him in the general store, or maybe he would be driving past and see her walking along the sidewalk. Briefly, she'd entertained the thought that his "maybe I'll see you around town" might actually mean that he would show up at her home. The thought had brought with it a mixture of anticipation—if he came looking for her, it had to mean she hadn't been the only one to feel that spark of attraction—and dread—what if Noreen was there? The one scenario that hadn't crossed her mind was that he would walk into Bill's, which was the most likely one of all. Practically everyone in town came through Bill's at one time or another.

"Maggie?" Bill's questioning tone made Maggie realize that she'd been standing there staring at Ryan without speaking.

"I didn't expect to see you here," she said, rushing to cover her lengthy silence. Ryan's surprised look had her hurrying on. "I mean, I didn't expect to see you anywhere. In particular, I mean. Anywhere in particular. Or at all, for that matter. Not specifically, I mean."

She trailed off, aware that what should have been a casual exchange of greetings had somehow become a tangled mess. Bill's bushy eyebrows had risen halfway up his forehead, and he was looking at her as if wondering about her sanity. Not that she blamed him. She was afraid to look at Ryan again. Her cheeks felt hot enough for spontaneous combustion to be a real possibility, and she cursed the fairness of her skin. Her face must look like a Stop sign, she thought despairingly. Where was a bolt of lightning when you needed one?

"I've known Bill since I was a kid," Ryan said, apparently deciding that a noncommittal response was his best bet. "I haven't been in much the past few years, though."

"Oh." Maggie cleared her throat and forced herself to *look* at him. He didn't look as if he thought she was dangerously deranged. Maybe they could just start over. She tried a tentative smile. "I didn't see you come in."

"You were in the kitchen getting food to shove down poor old Virgil's throat."

"I didn't exactly shove it down his throat," she protested, her embarrassment forgotten as she shot a guilty look across the room to where Virgil was gloomily making his way through the cheeseburger.

"You looked like you might if he didn't eat it voluntarily. Sure put the fear of God in me." His grin was irresistible, and Maggie let her own smile widen.

"I just couldn't take one more afternoon of watching him sit there and drink himself into a stupor without *doing* something."

"Other folks have tried to get through to him," Bill commented. "I don't think anyone's tried force-feeding him, though."

Maggie flushed again, but her chin came up at the same time. "I know he needs a lot more than just a decent meal, but it's better than nothing."

"Much better," Ryan said, firmly enough to reassure her.

"Losing his family like that is a terrible thing, but there's no sense in him throwing his own life away. You can't just jump into the grave when you lose someone you love."

There was a pause, hardly enough to be noticed, so Maggie might have thought she'd imagined it if she hadn't seen the quick, sharp glance Bill sent in Ryan's direction. Ryan didn't return the look, didn't seem to notice it, but she'd seen it, and she wondered what it meant.

"I've never thought jumping into the grave was the smart choice," he said with an odd little half smile that didn't quite fit with the shadows in his eyes. He picked up his drink and took a long swallow before setting the glass back down. When he looked at her, the shadows were gone, but she knew they'd been there, if only for an instant. "Did you get your car fixed?"

She accepted his lead, but she filed the incident in the back of her mind to examine later. "It needs a new transmission, so I took your suggestion and took it to Frank Luddy."

"Your friend, Luke, couldn't do the work?" Ryan asked casually. But maybe not casually enough, he thought, catching Bill's questioning look.

"It was a bigger job than he wanted to tackle," Maggie said. "He agreed with you that Luddy's was a good place to take it."

"Glad to have my opinion confirmed." Ryan was careful to keep the edge out of his voice, but the gleam in Bill's eyes told him that he hadn't been entirely successful.

"I didn't know Luke Brakman was doing any work at all these days," Bill said, putting a subtle emphasis on the name. "You remember old Luke, don't you, Ryan? He lives just down the street from Maggie. Used to own Luddy's place, didn't he?"

"That's what he said." Maggie smiled, apparently unaware of the undercurrents in the conversation. "I've been trading homemade cinnamon rolls for tune-ups for the last couple of years, but he said there weren't enough cinnamon rolls in the world for him to tackle a transmission job. Said he was too old for it."

"He's getting up there, all right. Luke must be...what? Seventy-five or so by now, wouldn't you say, Ryan?" Bill asked blandly.

"Something like that." People who knew you too well were a curse, Ryan decided. Especially when they knew you well enough to read things in your voice that you weren't even ready to admit to yourself.

The muted buzz of a phone provided a welcome distraction, at least as far as Ryan was concerned, particularly since the phone was at the other end of the bar. With a muttered apology, Bill turned his wheelchair and moved down the bar to answer it, leaving Ryan more or less alone with Maggie.

Looking at her, he still couldn't see any obvious reason why he hadn't been able to get her out of his mind. She was pretty, but in a quiet way—not the sort of woman who would turn heads on the street but, once you'd really looked at her, there was something about her. He couldn't put his finger on what it was, but he'd remembered every detail of her. There was that oddly appealing little overlap on her front teeth and the slightly crooked tilt to her mouth. Her nose was short and straight but otherwise unremarkable. Her eyes were probably her best feature, he thought—wide set, thickly lashed and bright with life, as if she found the world vastly interesting. Today, they were more blue than gray, picking up the color of her shirt. She wore the shirt tucked into her jeans, and he couldn't help but notice the nicely rounded lines of her body. He'd always thought jeans looked best on flat-hipped, long-legged women, but he could see his thinking had been too narrow. The snug denim did very nice things for Maggie's fuller curves.

"Would you like another drink?" she asked, going behind the bar as she spoke. Ryan swallowed a sigh of regret as his view was cut off.

"Are you going to make me eat something if I do?"

Color rose in her cheeks. "I think the maraschino cherries will provide sufficient nutrition."

The contrast between the prim set of her mouth and the smile in her eyes was enticing, and Ryan was surprised by how much he wanted to lean across the bar and see if he could taste the smile she was trying so hard to hide.

"I didn't realize there was any nutrition in maraschino cherries," he said, pushing his glass toward her. "Plain Coke."

"Cherries are a fruit," she said as she picked up the glass.

"Yeah, but after they've added all that sugar, red dye and assorted chemicals, these are cherries in name only."

"In name only?" She slid the newly filled glass back across the bar. "Sounds like something out of a soap opera."

"'As the Stone Turns'?" Ryan suggested and was absurdly pleased with himself when she giggled. He hadn't felt much like smiling lately.

It had been a long, difficult week. Whoever had said that you couldn't go home again should have added that you would have a damned, difficult time of it if you ever dared to try. The cast on his arm kept him sidelined from a lot of the day-to-day work of the ranch, making him feel like a guest rather than a part of ranch life. And, judging from his grandfather's attitude, he wasn't sure he was a particularly welcome guest. The fact that he could end the tension by telling the old man that he was home for good didn't help matters any. Maybe it was pigheaded of him, but he would be damned if he was going to let Nathan think he'd won the battle of wills between them. If he stayed on the Double L, he wanted it understood that he was doing it because it was what *he* chose to do, not because he was caving in to his grandfather.

"How's Doug?" Maggie asked, and Ryan welcomed the interruption to his thoughts. He'd spent too much time brooding about the situation already.

"He was headed for Montana when he left here. Then Oregon and California."

"That's a lot of miles on the road."

"When you follow the circuit, you spend a lot more time behind the wheel than you do on the back of a horse—or a bull, in Doug's case. Some of the cowboys put in better than a hundred thousand miles a year."

"Bull riding." Maggie shook her head. "I can't imagine why anyone would want to do that."

"Neither can I," Ryan said with an exaggerated shudder.

She grinned and nodded at his cast. "I can't see that getting on a bucking horse is much safer."

"Horses don't have horns," he explained solemnly. "That's what I don't like about bulls. If they didn't have horns, I'd like them just fine."

"Wouldn't they look kind of funny?" she asked, wrinkling her nose.

"I'd never thought about it quite that way, but I guess they would." He grinned, envisioning a cartoon image of a bull without horns. "Kind of like Daffy Duck when Elmer Fudd shoots his bill off."

Maggie's giggle was irresistible. "Guess you're just going to have to stick to those nice, gentle horses," she said teasingly.

"Not gentle enough." He lifted his cast for emphasis. He shook his head, his smile fading. "Actually, this is about it for me. I'm quitting the circuit." It felt strange to hear himself actually say the words out loud. And strange that she should be the first person he said them to.

"How long have you been working in rodeo?"

"Off and on since high school. Full-time for the past four years. And don't let my grandfather hear you call it working," he said dryly. "He thinks it's a damn fool way for a grown man to spend his time."

"Maybe he's worried about you getting hurt," she suggested.

"Maybe." Thinking about the conflicts with his grandfather made him restless. He finished off his drink, and the glass pinged sharply against the bar when he set it down. "I should get going."

Ryan slid off his stool and pulled money out of his pocket, but, after he'd set it on the bar, he hesitated. He wasn't particularly anxious to go home. There was nothing waiting for him at home except a testy old man and a horse who viewed him with the same warmth she would have given to a hungry mountain lion. But he would look like a damned fool if he changed his mind and asked for another drink. Not that he wanted another Coke, he thought. What he really wanted to do was ask Maggie-of-the-big-gray-eyes if he could see her again.

"It was nice seeing you again," Maggie said, her smile a little shy.

"You, too." He hesitated, caution warring with the urge to see more of her.

"I'm ready for that drink, Maggie." Virgil's voice seemed unnaturally loud. Ryan started and turned to look at the other man. He'd known Virgil Mortenson a long time. He'd known him when his eyes were clear, his hair was neatly combed and his skin had a healthy tan. He'd known him before his wife died and he'd started falling apart from the inside out until he was hardly even a shell of what he'd once been. He'd seen the changes come over Virgil after he lost his family, seen what loss had done to him. It scared the hell out of him, because he knew that it wouldn't have taken much to nudge him down the same path.

Feeling oddly chilled inside, Ryan turned back to Maggie. He smiled without really looking at her. "Tell Bill I'll drop in and whip him in a game of poker one of these days."

"I will."

He picked up his hat and nodded farewell, his eyes distant. "I'll see you around."

"Sure."

Halfway to the door, Ryan abruptly changed direction. "Hey, Virgil."

"Hey, Ryan." Virgil looked up as he approached the booth. "Heard you was hurt bad."

"Just a busted wing." Ryan lifted the cast for emphasis. "How you been?"

"I'm makin' out." Virgil's eyes shifted away. He moved the empty burger basket a little closer to the middle of the table, then slid the salt shaker into better alignment with the pepper.

Ryan was already regretting the impulse that had made him stop. He knew Virgil the same way he knew most of the local folks—to say hello to, to shoot the breeze with over a beer. They were friendly acquaintances rather than friends. The fact that they'd each lost a wife hadn't really changed that, but it *had* created a sort of bond between them. Shared misery, Ryan thought ruefully. He hadn't made the same choices Virgil had, but he understood—more than he liked—the pain that drove the other man.

"I bought a horse while I was in Texas," he said.

"I hear tell they have a lot of them down there," Virgil said, glancing up at him for a moment before looking past him to see if Maggie was bringing his drink.

"She's not real fond of people right about now," Ryan said. "From the scars, I'd say she doesn't have much reason to trust."

Virgil's head was down, his attention apparently all for the napkin he was folding into ever smaller squares. If it hadn't been for the tense set of the other man's shoulders, Ryan might have thought he was talking to himself.

"I was thinking maybe you could take a look at her, maybe work with her a little. I've never seen anyone better with a balky horse."

Virgil jerked as if from a physical blow. His eyes flickered up to Ryan's and then away again. "That was a long time ago," he muttered. "I don't do that kind of thing anymore."

Ryan hesitated, torn between the urge to push harder and the need to put distance between himself and everything Virgil represented. He saw Virgil look past him and guessed that Maggie must be bringing the promised drink, and the decision was made for him. He didn't want to see her again. She made him think about things he didn't want to think about; feel things he didn't want to feel. He straightened away from the corner of the booth.

"Well, if you change your mind, I'd appreciate you taking a look at the mare," he told Virgil, knowing the offer would never be accepted. Barely waiting for the other man to nod, he turned and walked away.

Maggie told herself that she didn't feel disappointed that Ryan hadn't waited to speak to her again. And she certainly hadn't thought he would say something about seeing her again. You could only be disappointed if you had expectations, and she certainly didn't have any where he was concerned. A little wishful thinking, maybe, but no expectations.

She refused to let her eyes follow Ryan's tall figure. But even without looking, she knew the exact moment when the door shut behind him. Not a good sign, she thought, with a sigh for her own foolishness.

Virgil gave her a self-conscious smile when she brought his drink. "Tasted pretty good," he said.

"Best burgers in the state." She picked up the basket, pleased to see that he'd eaten it all. Maybe food wouldn't solve all his problems—or even help them much—but a decent meal couldn't hurt.

"I guess maybe I was a mite hungry after all."

"Man does not live by Jack Daniel's alone, you know."

"I guess not." Virgil cupped his fingers around the glass and slid it toward himself but didn't immediately pick it up. "A man gets into habits, I guess."

"I guess a man can get out of them, too. If he really wants to." Maggie felt hopelessly inadequate to be trying to offer him advice. She was not a therapist, and what she knew about alcoholism could be written on the head of a pin. He needed professional help, not an amateur do-gooder.

"Ain't always that easy," he muttered, seeming to withdraw back into his shell.

"Sometimes the best thing for you is the hardest thing to do."

He lifted one shoulder in a half shrug and picked up the glass, and she didn't need to be told that the brief moment of communication was over. She turned away before he took the first drink. Like Bill had said, no one could force Virgil to get help. He had to want it for himself.

"Can't expect one cheeseburger to change a man's life," Bill said as she walked back to the bar. His phone call at an end, he was checking the bar stock, making note of what needed to be re-ordered.

"I didn't expect it to. Not really, anyway," she added, smiling a little when she caught his doubtful look.

"You care too much," he said, repeating his earlier warning. "People make bad choices in their lives. You can't fix them all."

"I know. It would be nice to fix one or two of them, though," Maggie said, sounding slightly wistful. She glanced around the bar to make sure that no one needed her at the moment, then slid onto a stool and leaned her elbows on the bar. One of the first things she'd learned about being a waitress was to sit down every chance she got. A few minutes of rest here and there during the day made life easier for her feet.

"Your heart's just too big, Maggie." Bill checked the contents of a bottle of J. & B. and set it back in place with a little more force than was strictly necessary.

"Sounds like a medical condition," she said lightly.

"Could be, if it gets bruised often enough."

"I'm not going to let my heart get bruised over Virgil. I just wish he'd get some real help." She curled her toes inside her sneakers in a sort of reverse stretch that helped ease the ache in her instep.

"Wasn't Virgil I was thinking about." Bill glanced up at her, his dark eyes sharp and probing. "I had Ryan Lassiter more in mind."

"Ryan?" She managed to sound surprised, but she could feel the color coming up in her cheeks, mocking her incredulous tone. She shrugged for emphasis. "I barely know him."

"Just because my legs don't work, doesn't make me deaf, dumb and blind," he said dryly. "And that's what I'd have to be to miss seeing the sparks between the two of you."

"You're imagining things." *Sparks between the two of them?* So maybe she hadn't imagined that Ryan felt that little tug of attraction, too? The possibility helped make up for his abrupt departure.

"I don't think so." Bill shook his head as he looked at the little smile that curved her mouth. He set down a bottle of whiskey and rested his heavily muscled forearms along the arms of his wheelchair. "Look, I suppose it isn't any of my business, but I've known Ryan since he came to live with his grandfather when he was a boy. Knew his father, too. Duncan wasn't a bad sort, but he didn't have sense enough to pour piss out of a boot. Still, he might have done okay if he hadn't up and married a woman with a brain the size of a thimble. They dumped Ryan on the Double L when he was ten or so and went off to be part of the jet set or whatever they call themselves these days.

"Useless as tits on a boar hog," he muttered, shaking his head in disgust. "Both of them. Leaving Ryan here was probably the only smart thing they ever did."

It occurred to Maggie that Ryan might not appreciate Bill telling her his past history, but her interest outweighed her nobler instincts.

"John McIntyre is foreman on the Double L. You've probably seen him in here a time or two."

Maggie nodded, picturing a stocky man with sandy hair, streaked with gray, and dark eyes. He didn't come in often, and he didn't say much when he did come in, but he had a nice smile, and he always left a generous tip.

"Well, Ryan pretty well grew up with the McIntyre kids," Bill continued. "Three girls and a boy—Tucker. He's the eldest, and he and Ryan are about the same age. The two of them are like brothers, and I guess the girls pretty much thought of Ryan as another brother. Leastways, the older two did, and maybe Sally did, too, until she grew up."

Bill's eyes were distant, as if he was seeing into the past. "I knew all the McIntyre kids. They'd come in with their folks now and again, have lunch on a Saturday afternoon sometimes. Tucker fancied himself a dangerous man with a pool cue, but the oldest girl, Annie, could beat him six ways from Sunday. Used to drive him and Ryan crazy. She's married to a rancher up in Idaho. Lorraine was the middle girl. She was real quiet. Ended up going to college in Denver and becoming a teacher.

"Sally was the baby of the family, and she was always up to her neck in some sort of mischief—getting thrown off horses she wasn't supposed to ride, shinnying up windmills and then needing someone to climb up and rescue her—there wasn't much she wouldn't tackle.

"She was always tall for her age, and skinny as a rail. She was all arms and legs, long black hair and big eyes. When she was a kid, you'd never have expected her to grow up to be much to look at, but nature has a way of playing tricks on you. I never did figure it out how it happened, but one day she was just a skinny kid, then she turned sixteen and she was suddenly so damned beautiful she just about took your breath away."

He paused, apparently lost in memory. Maggie shifted uncomfortably on the stool. She had the feeling she wasn't going to like the rest of this story, particularly the parts about the breathtakingly beautiful Sally McIntyre, but she was too caught up in it to stop him.

Bill seemed to shake himself a little, as if physically coming out of the past. When he continued, his voice was brisk. "Ryan had been away at college and hadn't seen her in almost a year, but when he came home that summer, he took one look at her and it was all over but the shouting. Sally was all for getting married right away, but her parents said she had to wait until she graduated high school. I think Sally would have eloped if Ryan would have gone along with it. She led him quite a dance for the next couple of years, but there was never any doubt that they were going to end up together. Lord, she was a handful." He laughed a little, his rugged features soft with remembrance. "They got married two weeks after she graduated from high school. Seemed like everybody in the state was at the wedding, and you never saw two people more in love."

Funny, how, now that her feet weren't hurting, there seemed to be an odd little ache starting up in her chest. And wasn't it about time somebody signaled for a drink or a new customer strolled through the front door? Maggie glanced around hopefully, but no one seemed to want anything, and the door remained stubbornly closed.

"They had everything going for them. She'd grown up on the Double L and loved it as much as he did. And she loved rodeo. For a couple of years, she and Ryan did the rodeo circuit together.

Sally was a barrel racer, won some buckles, had a shot at being a champion, but they both wanted to stay on the ranch. They were so happy together that it made you feel good just to be around them.''

"What happened?" Maggie asked, not at all sure she wanted to know the answer. She told herself that she didn't mind hearing that Ryan and his breathtakingly beautiful, born-in-the-saddle bride had been blissfully happy, but there was a pinched feeling in her chest that suggested otherwise.

"She died."

His answer was so unexpected that it took her a moment to absorb the sense of the words. She'd expected to hear that the ever so perfect Sally had run away with an insurance salesman from Des Moines, or had traded in her horse for a surfboard and was living on the beach in Hawaii, waiting for the perfect curl, or even that she had fallen in love with a rodeo clown and gone off to live amid the smells of greasepaint and wear baggy pants. She hadn't been prepared to hear that she was dead. For some reason, that upset her more than anything else he'd told her.

"What happened?"

"Leukemia." Bill bit the word off. "When she was diagnosed, Ryan moved her to Denver to be closer to her doctors. They tried every treatment available, but nothing worked. After a few months, it was pretty obvious there was nothing they could do for her, and she decided to come home. The doctors pitched a fit about her being so far from medical care, but she said she wanted to die where she could see blue sky and hear the wind, so Ryan brought her back to the ranch. She was gone a few weeks later, just after her twenty-fourth birthday.''

"How awful.'' It sounded hopelessly inadequate, but there were tragedies that went too deep for words.

"It was rough,'' Bill said, a laconic bit of Western understatement that might have been almost funny under other circumstances. He picked up a half-full bottle of bourbon, looked at it and then set it down again. His hands flexed on the arms of the wheelchair. "Ryan hasn't been back here for more than a week or two since he buried Sally.''

"Too many memories,'' Maggie murmured. She thought about what he'd said about leaving the circuit and wondered if he had decided it was time to face those memories.

"I suppose so.'' Bill nodded to the booth where Virgil sat nursing his drink. "Ryan didn't throw himself into the grave with Sally, and he didn't try to drown himself in a bottle, but he comes with a load of baggage. Any woman who gets involved with him ought to know what she's getting into.''

"I'm not involved with him.'' Maggie tried for

a dismissive laugh, but her throat was too tight. She settled for what she hoped was an unconcerned smile instead.

"Any woman *thinking* about getting involved with him," Bill amended.

"I'm not—" She caught his eye and couldn't finish the lie. She shrugged, her eyes dropping to the polished surface of the bar. "I barely even know him. I may not see him again." Her smile was self-deprecating. "Besides, it takes two people to get involved. Maybe he's not interested."

Bill had known Ryan long enough to be willing to take bets that he was interested. Whether or not he would do anything about it was something else altogether. As far as he knew, Ryan had been careful to avoid anything that smacked of involvement since Sally's death. Looking at Maggie, he thought it was a damned shame. A man would have a hard time finding a sweeter incentive to leave the past behind.

She cared about people—not just people like Virgil who were in trouble, but everyone she met. He'd watched her with the customers. She remembered whether they wanted their burgers well-done or extra ice with their drinks but she also remembered who had kids in 4H or wives expecting a new baby. People liked her—young and old, male and female. On a purely practical level, she'd been good for business. On a more personal level, he'd grown fond of her over the last three years.

"I just don't want to see you get hurt," he said gruffly.

"I'm a lot tougher than I look." She smiled as she said it, then slid off the bar stool in answer to a wave from one of the two old men playing pool.

Bill watched her walk away, her blond ponytail swinging with each step. She greeted the old men by name, asked how the game was going and listened with apparent interest as Ernie Lamott described the shot with which he'd sunk the eight ball in the last game. Maggie widened her eyes and looked impressed, which made Ernie's thin chest puff out and made Walter Sinclair remember a shot he'd made once that put Ernie's latest effort to shame. She listened without any sign of impatience or disbelief, which couldn't have been easy, considering the fact that Walter's miracle shot appeared to involve banking the ball off the bumpers at least thirteen times before sinking the eight ball for a win.

Smiling a little, Bill went back to checking his inventory. The day Walter Sinclair made a shot like that would be the same day the sun rose in the west. And about the same time the word *tough* would apply to Maggie Drummond.

Chapter Four

The first thing Maggie did when she got home
was take off her shoes and socks, sighing with
pleasure as her bare feet met the cool surface of
the aging linoleum of the entryway floor. Frank
Luddy had promised to have her car done the day
after tomorrow, which just happened to be payday.
Then, no more walking home from work. After
spending eight hours on her feet, that additional
fifteen minutes was sheer torture.

"Well, hello, Max." She smiled as a huge orange tomcat with three white socks trotted in from
the direction of the kitchen. He meowed a greeting
in a voice that was absurdly high and light for a
cat who weighed almost fifteen pounds. Maggie
bent to scoop him up. "Did you miss me?" she
asked, nuzzling her face against his fur.

When he began to purr and knead his paws against her arm, she took it as an affirmative. Max had belonged to a couple who lived across the street. When they moved to Cheyenne, they didn't bother to take Max with them. The day after they left, Max was waiting for Maggie when she got home from work. He followed her into the house as if he'd lived there all his life. Maggie was touched by his trust in her; Noreen said he knew a sucker when he saw one. Either way, Max had become a member of the household.

She could hear the sound of the television coming from the living room, as usual. Her mother turned it on when she got up in the morning and didn't turn it off until she went to bed. She watched the news, talk shows, soap operas, reruns of "Little House on the Prairie," game shows and sitcoms— she wasn't hard to please. And she wasn't one of those people who turned the TV on and let it run in the background while she did other things. Lydia stared at the flickering images on the screen as if the secret to life would be revealed to her if only she watched long enough. All day, every day, she sat drinking endless cups of coffee, smoking countless cigarettes and watching other people's lives on TV.

Maggie had tried suggesting that she get out more, but, in Lydia's opinion, there was nothing in

Willow Flat that rivaled the entertainment provided by television. The landscape and wildlife that Maggie found endlessly fascinating didn't hold any interest for her mother. When Lydia said there was nowhere to go, she meant there were no nightclubs, no restaurants, no piano bars where a woman wearing sequins and Chanel No. 5 might luck out and meet an interesting man. The Dew Drop Inn, with its jukebox full of country music, line dancing and occasional barroom brawl, didn't even warrant mention.

Listening to the artificial heartiness of canned laughter, Maggie briefly considered tiptoeing past the living room and going straight to her room, but she suppressed the urge. No doubt she was hopelessly naive, but there was still a part of her hoping that, if she just tried hard enough, said or did the right things, she and her mother would somehow find at least a piece of that closeness that mothers and daughters were supposed to share.

"Hi, Mom," she said cheerfully, raising her voice to be heard over the patter of the game show host. Still carrying Max, she stepped into the living room and felt her heart sink.

On the TV, Vanna's smile was dazzling as she turned letters on the big board, accompanied by squeals of delight from one of the contestants. Maggie didn't share her pleasure as her eyes swept over the opened boxes and packing material scattered on the floor.

"Maggie!" Lydia spun around, her eyes wide and startled, like a child who'd just been caught doing something forbidden. "I didn't expect you home so soon."

"I got off at the regular time." Maggie looked at the heavy bracelet clasped around her mother's thin wrist, all bright, colored stones and glaring imitation gold. A matching necklace was around her neck, a splash of sparkling color against the pilled gray fabric of her sweatshirt.

"I guess I lost track of the time." Lydia lifted her hand to brush her hair back from her face, setting the bracelet jangling.

"I guess so," Maggie said, her eyes moving slowly over the wreck of the living room. As near as she could tell, there were two boxes that had yet to be opened. An unidentifiable appliance sat on the coffee table, pink electric cord dangling over the edge. Some miracle beauty gadget, no doubt, guaranteed to add new shine to damaged hair, do away with wrinkles forever or restore youthful firmness to sagging breasts. A length of fuchsia-colored silk spilled over the arm of the sofa. It was a terrible color for her mother, she thought absently. The bright pink would leach the color from her already pale skin and make her hair look even more brassy.

"Mom..."

"Now, don't start on me, Maggie." Lydia lifted her chin and gave her daughter a look of mixed guilt and defiance. "It's just a few little things, and they were real bargains." She reached up to touch the gaudy necklace. "You wouldn't believe how little I paid for this set, and it even came with earrings."

Whatever it was, it was too much, Maggie thought. Max pushed against her hold, and she bent to set him on the floor. He sauntered over to a fuchsia sleeve that dangled close to the floor and sniffed curiously.

"Don't let him get his claws in it!"

At Lydia's shriek, Max glanced over his shoulder at her. If he'd had an upper lip, it would have curled. Ignoring her moans of fear, he sniffed the dangling sleeve again and then, with a contemptuous flick of his tail, sauntered out of the living room.

"He could have ruined it!" As soon as he'd disappeared, Lydia lunged forward and snatched up the garment, holding it out as if to check for hidden damage. Maggie blinked as the full glory of fuchsia background, purple and turquoise flowers and deep green foliage was revealed. She tried to imagine her mother in the jacket and, when that failed, tried to imagine *anyone* other than a circus performer wearing it. She was relieved when Lydia folded it carefully and draped it over her arm.

"That cat is a menace," she said angrily. "This is pure silk."

"He didn't touch it."

"He might have, if I hadn't been here."

Privately, Maggie doubted Max would have touched the jacket even if bribed with a can of tuna. He had his standards.

"Mom, I thought you decided that you weren't going to watch the home shopping channels." Looking at the boxes, she wondered how much Lydia had spent.

"*You* decided, you mean." Lydia thrust her lower lip out in a pout that had been sweetly sexy when she was a girl. "I like having pretty things around me. It doesn't matter so much when you're plain, like you, but pretty women should have pretty things," she said, repeating words once said to her by an admirer twenty years before.

"I don't want you to do without pretty things," Maggie said, absorbing the comment about her looks without a flinch. It wasn't the first time she'd heard it. Her mother's opinions of her attractiveness varied, depending on whether she was annoyed or trying to talk Maggie into doing something she wanted. Then Lydia would tell her that she was really quite pretty—if only she would lose a little weight and maybe do something with her hair. Maggie paid no more attention to the half-hearted flattery than she did to the insults.

"I thought we agreed that we were going to try to save money so we could put a new roof on this summer."

"A roof." Lydia wrinkled her nose. "That's so boring."

"But necessary," Maggie said, grabbing for her patience.

"Necessary." Lydia made it sound like an epithet. She jangled the bracelet on her arm. More squeals of delight spilled from the television, and Vanna clapped her hands, her smile glossy and unchanging. "You spend too much time worrying about necessities."

"Somebody has to," Maggie snapped.

"Somebody has to what?" Noreen asked as she wandered into the room. Wearing a thigh-length blue silk robe, her pale blond hair tumbled around her shoulders, she'd obviously just gotten out of bed. She worked nights at the Dew Drop and, as often as not, went home with one of the cowboys who went there to drink. Maggie had never understood it, but she'd stopped questioning her sister's choices a long time ago.

"Maggie's all upset with me because I bought a few things." Knowing she would have an ally in Noreen, Lydia's tone shifted to a plaintive whine. "She's harping on the stupid roof again."

"You know what Craig Chapman said when he came out and looked at the roof—" Maggie began.

"I know he was so busy ogling your sister's legs that he hardly looked at the roof. He probably just said we needed a new roof so he'd have an excuse to come here and gawk some more."

"Craig is happily married and has three kids." Maggie knew, even as she said it, that she was wasting her breath.

"He can't be all that happy if he's spending his time looking at another woman's legs." Noreen perched on the arm of the sofa and stretched her legs out in front of her, admiring their smooth length. The gesture made her loosely tied robe fall partially open, exposing one hip and a few pale curls of pubic hair. Well aware that the casual lack of modesty was meant to embarrass her, Maggie kept her eyes on her sister's face.

"Craig is an honest man. If he says this roof won't make it through the winter, I believe him."

"Your privilege." Noreen shrugged, and the robe fell open another couple of inches, revealing the inner curves of her breasts. "Personally, I think Mom should sell this piece of crap house and move somewhere with a little more life. Maybe L.A. or Vegas. This town is so boring that it's no wonder she ends up watching the shopping channels. It beats sitting and watching the grass grow for entertainment.''

''Property prices around here aren't exactly high.'' Maggie struggled for patience. ''Even if she could find someone to buy it, she couldn't get enough money for this house to buy anything somewhere else.''

''So?'' Noreen reached in the pocket of her robe for her cigarettes. ''Who says she has to buy again? She could take the money and rent a little apartment somewhere. She could get a decent wardrobe, have her hair done. She could maybe take a cruise. I hear those cruise ships are pretty much a supermarket for singles of a certain age looking for a significant other. Mom could probably find herself a studly dude with big bucks who'd like nothing better than to keep her in minks and diamonds.''

She grinned at her mother, and Lydia giggled and clasped her hands together in front of her like a child contemplating a promised treat. ''A cruise! Oh, that would be so much fun!''

''And what is she going to live on when the money's all spent and she hasn't found her 'studly dude'?'' Maggie asked.

"She's got her disability check," Noreen said, shrugging as she lit her cigarette.

"That's right, I've got my disability check," Lydia parroted, giving Maggie a defiant look.

"You know that's not enough to keep her going." Knowing her mother was already caught up in a fantasy image of herself aboard a luxury liner, being wined and dined by handsome men, Maggie directed her words to her sister. "That's the reason we moved out here when Aunt Margaret died and left Mom this house, because it was paid for and the money would stretch further."

"Aunt Margaret was supposed to be leaving Mom a big ranch," Noreen objected. Her full mouth tightened in remembered anger. "The Flying M!" She exhaled a sharp stream of smoke. "How the hell were we supposed to know anyone would name something like this piece of crap?"

Maggie actually thought it was rather sweet that her great-aunt had given her modest home such a grandiose name. She couldn't deny that she'd been as surprised as her mother and sister when they'd arrived in Willow Flat and found the ranch they'd been expecting was actually half an acre of overgrown shrubs and struggling trees, and that the only livestock was the neighbor's dog, who liked to sleep under the straggly elm that hung over the garage, and Max, the neighbor's cat.

But she liked it here. The house wasn't much, but it was better than the apartment her mother had had in Detroit, and she didn't have to pay rent. The disability check she received for a back injury she'd gotten in a fall at work was enough, with a little care, to pay her expenses. Except when she spent it all on mail-order junk, Maggie thought, giving the boxes an exasperated look.

"It may not be much, but it gives Mom a roof over her head and a little security."

"Some of us want more out of life than security," Noreen said contemptuously. "Some of us actually want to live, not just exist. Mom's still a relatively young woman. I hate to see her burying herself out here in the back of beyond when she could be actually having a life somewhere else. I'd like to see her happy."

"And you think I don't?"

"I don't know. Maybe you need to take a closer look at your motives." As Noreen stood up, the slippery silk belt dropped to the floor and her robe fell open. Without hurrying, she bent to pick it up but didn't bother to put it on again, leaving the robe hanging open, a silky frame for her magnificent body. Maggie knew it was deliberate, but she could feel her face heating. Noreen looked at her through a veil of smoke, her crystal blue eyes bright with malicious amusement, and Maggie looked away, cursing the fair skin that made it impossible for her to conceal her reactions. The fact that Lydia didn't seem to even notice her older daughter's semi-nudity only made Maggie feel more foolish for letting it embarrass her.

"I don't want to see her end up broke," she said, keeping her voice even with an effort.

"And I don't want to see her end up old and alone. It's fine if *you're* content waiting tables all day and coming home to a cat at night, but maybe Mom wants something more in her life."

"Of course I do!" Lydia glared at Maggie as if she'd been trying to force her to renounce all of life's pleasures for a life of deprivation and drudgery.

Maggie opened her mouth to deny the unspoken charge and then closed it without speaking. What was the point? she thought. She knew that Noreen's interest wasn't as selfless as she pretended. If Lydia sold the house, Noreen was sure to help herself to a good-size chunk of the proceeds. That was the only reason she'd come to Wyoming when she heard about her mother's inheritance. She'd been picturing a spectacular ranch, like something out of an old rerun of "The Big Valley." Money and plenty of good-looking cowboys to jump at her commands. The reality had been a bitter disappointment, and she'd been pushing Lydia to sell the house ever since. Only Maggie's determined practicality had so far kept it from happening.

Glancing at the boxes and scattering of foam packing peanuts that dotted the dull beige carpet, Maggie wondered why she bothered. God knew, it wasn't appreciated. This battle, at least, was lost. Lydia had spent the money, and it was, as Noreen had pointed out, her money to spend. And if the roof gave out, well, they probably both figured they could count on good old Maggie to come up with the money to fix it. Didn't she always think of something?

"Do what you want," she said, suddenly weary of the argument.

"I certainly will," Lydia said, her voice sharp with indignation. Maggie half expected her to toss in a defiant "you're not the boss of me."

Noreen began belting her robe as Maggie walked out of the room, and Maggie shook her head in disbelief. She'd never figured out why Noreen took such delight in making her uncomfortable, but it had been going on as long as she could remember. It might make sense if she were jealous, but the idea of Noreen being jealous of her was so far-fetched it was laughable.

She sighed as she shut her bedroom door behind her. Max was sitting in the middle of the bed, the tip of his tail curled neatly over his front paws, his green eyes watching her with what she chose to believe was sympathy. Maggie sank down on the side of the bed, and he immediately walked over and butted his head against her arm.

"Well, at least someone is glad to see me." She scratched behind his ear and was rewarded with a rumbling purr. Petting him, she felt the tension ease from her shoulders and the headache that had begun to nibble at the edges of her consciousness retreat a little.

"You're better than a therapeutic massage," she told him. He responded by purring louder and rolling over on his back so she could scratch his tummy. She obliged, smiling when he batted at her hand with his front paws, but, somewhere in the back of her mind, there was a niggling sense of unease. Noreen's comment about spending the rest of her life waiting tables and coming home to a cat hadn't been intended to do anything except sting, and it had. But not in quite the way Noreen might have wanted.

"Time's flying, Max, and I'm standing still. If I don't look out, I'm going to end up exactly the way she described, old and all alone except for a cat. Not that you're not perfectly delightful company," she assured him as she scratched under his chin. "But, if you don't mind my saying so, your conversational skills are a bit limited. I'm not criticizing, mind you, but you don't read anything more complicated than the label on a tuna can, and there's only so much depth and meaning there.''

Abruptly tiring of the attention, Max rolled out from under her hand and got to his feet. He sauntered to the top of the bed, settled in against the pillows and began bathing himself. Maggie watched him, but her thoughts were elsewhere. She was only twenty-three and the future stretched out for a long way ahead of her. But you didn't have to be middle-aged to know how quickly time passed. It hardly seemed possible that three years had gone by since she'd started working at Bill's. It was a little scary to think that three more could go by just as quickly.

She fell back across the bed and stared up at a crack in the ceiling and the yellowed splotch of an old water stain. *No one dreams of growing up to become a waitress,* she thought. It wasn't the sort of job that they talked about in school on Career Day. No parent visited her child's second-grade class to tell the children about her exciting job waiting tables at the local diner. There was no vocational training available to teach you how to serve a hamburger or keep smiling when an indecisive diner changed his order for the third time. No ads on late-night TV promising a rewarding career waiting tables if you called the number on the bottom of your screen.

It was okay to be a waitress as long as you were on your way to being something else—a movie star or an artist, or maybe you were penning the next Great American Novel. Then you had tradition on your side. It seemed as if every celebrity had spent time waiting tables before achieving success.

But what if you didn't have anything else in mind? What if you didn't have any driving ambitions pushing you toward greater things? What if all you had was a vague idea that you'd like someone special in your life, a home, children perhaps, maybe a little more time to spend with your camera, time to pursue the half-formed dream of putting together a book of photographs. Nothing grand, nothing that hadn't been done before; just a new view of nature's beauty.

What were you supposed to do if your dreams were small things and you had no idea how to go about making them come true?

"Tucker got home last night," Nathan said as he slathered butter on a stack of pancakes.

Ryan had been pouring himself a cup of coffee, and his grandfather's sudden announcement nearly made him drop the pot. One of the first things he'd learned when he came to live on the Double L twenty years ago was not to talk to the old man until he was on his third or fourth cup of coffee, at least. Add to that the fact that, since he'd come home two weeks ago, the atmosphere between them had been on the cool side and having Nathan, barely halfway through his second cup of coffee, speak to him in such a pleasant tone was quite a shock.

"I thought I heard some commotion last night." He set the coffeepot down and reached for the sugar, but Nathan was already pushing it toward him.

"Going to rot your teeth out," he said genially, and Ryan hesitated before spooning sugar into his coffee.

Maybe he was asleep and just dreaming that the two of them were sitting in the kitchen at half past daylight. But if this was a dream, would he be able to feel the place on his hand where bacon grease had spattered and left a stinging little burn? And if he was going to have a dream, wouldn't he dream his arm out of this damned cast?

"I thought Tucker was due back next week," Ryan said.

"He finished his business sooner than he expected. Sounds like he made a good deal on some breeding stock."

"Good." Ryan poured syrup on his pancakes

and wondered what had brought on this sudden surge of civility.

"Seems he ran into Shelly Taylor in Los Angeles," Nathan said as he poured his third cup of coffee. "Brought her back with him. You heard Leland Taylor died a couple of months ago?"

Ryan nodded. "I was sorry to hear it. He was a good man, and I know the two of you had been friends for a long time."

"Better than fifty years," Nathan murmured. He stared down at his plate, but he was seeing more than half a century of friendship. He'd been a couple of years shy of twenty when Leland's father bought the neighboring ranch. The two of them had met at a dance, and, before the evening was over, they'd gotten into a fight over the prettiest girl there. He'd blacked Leland's eye and gotten a bloody nose in return. Remembering, he smiled. He couldn't even remember the name of the girl now. Alice? Betty? Her family had moved away a couple of years later, and she'd soon been forgotten. But he and Leland had ended up friends.

Leland had married late in life, and his wife had died when their only child was still in leading strings. He'd never remarried, and Shelly had become the center of his universe. He'd built High Reaches Ranch as a legacy for her, the same way Nathan had done for Ryan.

They'd talked a time or two about joining their two spreads, about how nice it would be if Nathan's grandson and Leland's daughter just happened to fall in love. They hadn't made plans—this wasn't the Middle Ages, after all, where you could go around arranging marriages. They'd just talked about it a little. And there had been a time, when Ryan and Shelly were in high school, when it looked as if that half-formed dream might actually come true. And why shouldn't it? They were both healthy, attractive young animals, they could fall in love with each other as easily as with anyone else. Then Shelly had gotten it into her head that she wanted to be a movie star, and Ryan had gone off to college. Even then, Nathan had hoped that, once they'd both matured a bit...

But Ryan had fallen in love with Sally McIntyre, and it wasn't possible to regret that. Even if Nathan hadn't already loved Sally for her own sake, he would have accepted her for the happiness she brought his grandson. But she was gone now, and it was time Ryan moved on with his life, time he settled down and started looking to the future. Time he had children of his own, damn it.

He shook off the memories and looked across the table at his grandson. "Shelly inherited the ranch, of course."

"Can't imagine Leland leaving it to anyone

else," Ryan said as he used the side of his fork to cut off a bite of pancakes. He'd be glad when he got this cast off and could use a knife and fork again. Eating one-handed made him feel like a slightly backward six-year-old.

"Ray Wellman is running the place for her."

"He's been foreman there as long as I can remember," Ryan said. "He'll do right by her."

"Seems likely Shelly will be coming back to stay, now that her daddy's gone," Nathan said casually. "Far as I can tell, she hasn't set Hollywood on fire, and she's not a kid anymore. She'll probably be looking to settle down, maybe start a family. Ray isn't getting any younger. He's got a son up in Idaho, runs some cattle, a few head of horses. Boy's been after him to come help him take care of things up there. Wouldn't be surprised if Ray took him up on it one of these days. Shelly will need someone to help her run things."

So now he knew why the old man was suddenly feeling so chatty, Ryan thought. He set his coffee cup down very carefully and looked across the table at his grandfather.

"No."

"No, what?" Nathan's confused look might have been funny if Ryan had been in the mood to be amused.

"Don't start getting any ideas about founding a dynasty. It isn't going to happen."

"I don't know what you're talking about." Nathan freshened his coffee and shoved his empty plate away from him. "I'm making conversation."

"No, you're not." Better to cut this off here and now. He had enough problems in his life without dealing with his grandfather's heavy-handed matchmaking. "I'm not going to marry Shelly."

"Nobody said anything about marrying her," Nathan protested. Forgetting he'd just refilled the cup, he took a swallow of coffee and burned his mouth. "God damn it!" Coffee sloshed over the side of the cup as he set it down too quickly.

Ryan watched impassively as Nathan dabbed at the spill with his napkin. "I know you and Leland had some idea that Shelly and I were going to fall in love and unite the Double L and High Reaches in holy matrimony, but it isn't going to happen."

"How do you know? You haven't seen her in years," Nathan said, switching from denial to persuasion. "You dated in high school."

"We fought like cats and dogs, and we stopped dating. That ought to tell you something."

"People change."

"Not that much."

Nathan stood abruptly, the legs of his chair scraping across the floor. He picked up his empty plate and carried it to the sink. He rinsed it off and set it on the counter before turning to look at Ryan. "I'm asking her to come here for supper tomorrow night."

"Okay." Ryan kept a tight rein on his temper.

"I'll expect you to be here." He read refusal in his grandson's eyes and continued before Ryan could speak. "She's an old friend of the family, and she lost her father not long ago. It doesn't seem too much for you to say hello and offer your condolences."

Neatly done, Ryan thought, grinding his teeth together. How could he refuse now?

"I'll be here."

"Good." Nathan wasn't foolish enough to allow any hint of smugness to enter his expression. And he didn't kid himself that he'd done anything to change his grandson's mind. But you never knew what might happen if you threw a couple of attractive young people together. He hadn't really expected Ryan to be enthused about the idea right off, anyway, so, all in all, he wasn't unhappy with the way the conversation had gone, he thought as he lifted his hat off the rack next to the door on his way out.

Ryan watched him leave the kitchen and then looked down at his half-eaten breakfast. His appetite wasn't what it had been. As soon as the old man spoke to him in a civil tone, he should have run for his life, he thought, torn between irritation and amusement. But the amusement faded as he considered just how uncomfortable Nathan could make things. What his grandfather lacked in subtlety, he made up in tenacity. If he'd decided that he and Shelly were a match made in heaven, he would do everything he could to push them together.

Maybe he would luck out and Shelly would turn out to be already engaged to some blow-dried actor type. That would put an end to his grandfather's dynastic vision. Well, at least he could be reasonably confident that Shelly wouldn't be any more receptive to this idea than he was. If he remembered correctly, at the end of their last date she'd called him a scum-sucking slime worm and threatened to take out a contract on his life if he ever so much as looked in her direction again.

Ryan grinned at the memory. Of course, that had been fifteen years ago. As far as he knew, Shelly no longer wanted him dead. Their paths had crossed a few times, and she hadn't shown any signs of hostility. The last time he'd seen her had been at Sally's funeral, he remembered, his smile fading. He rubbed his thumb against the base of his empty ring finger, his eyes distant.

He shook his head as if to physically throw off

the memories. There was no point in worrying about his grandfather's matchmaking schemes. Sooner or later, he would have to give up on them. The cast clunked against the edge of the table as he pushed his chair back and stood up. If it hadn't been for a horse named Lucky Streak, he could have been a thousand miles from here, getting thrown on his head in the middle of a dusty arena. At the moment, it seemed a bit less risky than coming home might turn out to be.

The mare had gotten to the point where she no longer immediately ran for the opposite side of the corral when Ryan approached. That was progress of a sort. Of course, she didn't exactly look happy when she saw him, either, he admitted as he propped his cast on the top rail of the fence and set one booted foot on the bottom rail. The mare stood her ground in the middle of the corral but eyed him with deep suspicion. Not that he blamed her.

As near as he could tell, she hadn't exactly seen a whole lot of kindness from the humans in her life. Still, she had good blood. Her father was a champion cutting horse, and some of her half brothers and sisters had sold for thousands. But she'd resisted every effort to break her. Her owner had tried selling her as a bucking horse, but she wouldn't buck when the clock was ticking. A horse that couldn't be ridden and wouldn't buck in an arena wasn't worth more than a few cents a pound. If he hadn't bought her, she would have ended up at the slaughterhouse.

"I hear tell you're planning on breedin' a new kind of horse, one that nobody can ride."

Grinning, Ryan turned to face the speaker. Tucker McIntyre had been his best friend since the summer he'd come to live on the Double L. Tall and broad shouldered, with jet-black hair and dark eyes, he showed his mother's Native American heritage more clearly than any of her daughters except Sally. Seeing him now brought an odd little shock of recognition.

"You know me, I always did like to break new ground," he said, holding out his hand.

"Among other things." Tucker nodded to the cast on Ryan's arm.

"Among other things," he agreed. "How the hell have you been?"

"Fair to middlin'." Tucker grinned as they shook hands. "How about yourself?"

"Can't complain. Well, I could," he amended, lifting the cast. "But it wouldn't do me much good. Grandad said you were in L.A. I figured you'd come back with a surfboard and one of those flowered shirts."

"You're thinking of Hawaii. It's a little farther west. L.A.'s the place with all the movie stars."

"I hear you brought one of them back with you." Ryan grimaced, remembering his grandfather's heavy-handed matchmaking plans.

"Shelly was heading in this direction," Tucker said. He set his back to the corral fence, lifting one foot to brace his boot against the bottom rail as he reached in his shirt pocket for his cigarettes. "Seemed unneighborly to make her hitchhike."

"She planning on staying around?" Ryan set his arm along the top of the fence and let his eyes drift to the mare. She was watching them warily, but she still hadn't retreated to the far side of the corral. Progress, he thought again.

"I suspect so." Tucker struck a match on the bottom of his boot and cupped his hands around the flame as he brought it up to light his smoke. The sun was shining, and the sky was a pale, clear blue, but the wind was always present, whispering around the edges of a man's consciousness, soft as a lover's caress but holding the threat of leashed power.

Tucker lifted his head as he shook out the match. "I don't think Hollywood has lived up to Shelly's dreams. Couple of made-for-TV movies, one straight-to-video feature and some commercials. Better than most do, probably, but not exactly interviews on Oprah and a star on Hollywood Boulevard.''

"She always did dream big," Ryan commented, remembering some of the quarrels they'd had when they were dating. She'd been sure that she was going to take Hollywood by storm, and she hadn't much appreciated his suggestion that she ought to have a way to earn a living while she was waiting for stardom to find her.

"Not much point in dreaming small," Tucker commented.

"I guess not." He glanced at his friend. "You think Shelly's going to try to run High Reaches herself?"

"Maybe. She didn't talk about it much, but, from what little she did say, it sounded like she was planning on staying around. Seems likely, anyway." Tucker shrugged. "Her daddy hadn't been in the best of health the past couple of years. Ray Wellman has been pretty much running things. I imagine he'll stay on, but Ray's not the sort to want full responsibility. He'll want someone to at least give the go-ahead to any decisions."

Ryan nodded. That was pretty much his impression of the foreman at High Reaches—a good man, but not the sort who would be comfortable running things for an absentee owner. "Grandad says Ray's thinking about going to Idaho to help his son run his place up there.''

Tucker's dark brows rose as he considered that possibility. After a moment, he nodded slowly. ''Makes sense. I hear tell Andy's doing pretty well for himself. Has a couple of kids. He and Ray got on well together, and Ray might want to be closer to the grandkids.'' He drew deeply on the cigarette, narrowing his eyes against the smoke as he exhaled. ''If he goes, it will leave Shelly in a world of trouble. She's smarter than she likes to let on, but she's ten years or more away from ranching. She'd have a hard time handling things on her own.''

''Grandad figures if I marry her, I can run the place,'' Ryan said, keeping his tone casual but slanting a look in Tucker's direction to catch his reaction. He wasn't disappointed.

Tucker had just lifted the cigarette to his mouth, and surprise had him drawing a quick startled breath, sucking the smoke down the wrong way. Ryan waited out the subsequent coughing fit.

''You want to run that by me again?'' Tucker asked, when he could breathe again.

Ryan turned to look at him, leaning his hip against the railing, his mouth twisted in a half smile. ''He's decided that Shelly and I are a match made in heaven. He won't admit it, but I think he and Leland had some idea of combining the two spreads, and he figures Shelly coming home like this is a golden opportunity to fulfill that dream. I told him it isn't going to happen, but he's not listening. You know what he's like once he's got his mind made up. It's like talking to a mud fence. He's inviting her to dinner tomorrow night. I think he's got some idea that if he parades her in front of me, I'll be overcome with lust.''

Tucker studied the tip of his cigarette, his expression unreadable. ''She's still real easy on the eyes.''

''And real hard on everything else.'' Ryan shook his head. ''I've never come closer to murdering anyone in my life. And she felt the same. Hell, she blacked my eye the night of the senior prom.''

''I'd almost forgotten that.'' Tucker grinned at the memory. ''You told everybody a rabbit ran across the road and you hit your head on the steering wheel when you braked.''

''Well, I sure as hell wasn't going to tell them my girlfriend had decked me.''

''Maybe if you told your grandfather you're afraid of her, he'd back off,'' Tucker suggested, tongue in cheek.

''Don't tempt me,'' Ryan said gloomily. He grinned reluctantly when Tucker laughed. ''I get the feeling you're not taking this as seriously as you might.''

''Sorry.'' Tucker's grin cast a shadow of doubt on the sincerity of his apology. ''I just can't quite shake the image of Shelly knocking you on your ass.''

''She didn't knock me on my ass.'' Ryan hesitated a moment. ''I caught myself on the back of a chair before I fell,'' he admitted, then bit back a smile at Tucker's shout of laughter. ''Hey, she's stronger than she looks, and she caught me by surprise.''

''Caught you right in the eye, too. Face it, Ry, you got beaten up by a girl.''

''Yeah, and it was damned depressing,'' Ryan said, grinning. ''Could have done permanent damage to my fragile male ego. The only thing that keeps me from running like a rabbit is the fact that Shelly's bound to hate this whole idea at least as much as I do.''

''Could be.'' Tucker dropped his cigarette and ground it out with the toe of his boot. He shot Ryan a teasing look from under the brim of his hat. ''On the other hand, you're quite a catch. She might like your grandfather's plan to build an empire.''

Ryan arched one brow. ''With a guy she punched out in high school?'' He shook his head. ''I don't think so.''

However Shelly felt, the evening loomed unpleasantly on his horizon. He couldn't get out of it, but maybe he could make things a little easier on himself. He eyed Tucker thoughtfully. "What are you doing tomorrow night?"

"You figure you're going to need somebody to protect you in case Shelly comes at you again?"

"I *am* in a weakened condition." Ryan lifted the cast for emphasis. "Actually, I was thinking that another body at the table might slow down Grandad's matchmaking efforts a bit."

"I've never seen anything slow down Nathan Lassiter when he's got his mind set on something." Tucker reached for his cigarettes, tapping the pack against the side of his thumb to slide one out. He grinned crookedly as he put it in his mouth. "It might be fun to watch you squirm, though."

"Nice to know I can count on you," Ryan said dryly.

"Hey, what are friends for?" Tucker said, grinning. He turned and nodded to the mare, who was still watching them warily. "So, tell me about this horse of yours."

undry
store walk
Indian the Os
to enother the
seen in to ma
had been plan
in its usual c
junction with
floor.
"Hey, Kyra
and saw a woman
paperback wh
friendly smile.

Chapter Five

The bell over the door jangled cheerfully as Ryan walked into the General Store. According to the fading white sign with red lettering out front, it was actually Goodman's Sundries and General Store. No one seemed to remember who Goodman had been, and most folks would have been hard put to describe a sundry, so, over the years, the name had been whittled down to General Store. The stock ran the gamut from stationery to cowboy boots. You could buy a fifty-pound sack of flour or a yo-yo, a TV dinner or a rifle. There was even a small, glass-enclosed jewelry case with a selection of pieces made out of locally mined jade.

When he was a boy, Ryan's mother had once taken him to F.A.O. Schwartz, but he hadn't been nearly as impressed by the famous New York toy store as he was the first time his grandfather took him to the General Store to buy real Western boots to replace the citified riding boots his mother had seen fit to pack. The sheer variety of merchandise had made his eyes widen. It still did, he thought, as he found himself nose to nose with an old-fashioned cigar store Indian that stood just inside the door.

"Hey, Ryan. How're you doing?" The plump, red-haired woman behind the counter set down the paperback she'd been reading and gave him a friendly smile.

"Not bad, Bonnie. How 'bout yourself?" Bonnie Rayczek had been a year behind him in school. Her brother, Bobby, had been a couple of years ahead of him and had once bloodied Ryan's nose for bringing Bonnie home from a date at five in the morning. He'd apologized when he found out that Ryan's truck really had broken down, and neither Bonnie nor Ryan had ever felt the need to clarify how they'd passed the hours they'd spent waiting for someone to drive by and offer them a lift into town.

That had all been a long time ago—a lifetime, he thought. Bonnie had married Jack Dillard right out of high school, and they now had four children, ranging from twelve down to five. Bonnie worked part-time for her parents, who owned the store. She liked to joke that her husband was Willow Flat's token celebrity. He wrote mystery novels about a computer hacker who was nearly as handy with a gun as he was with a keyboard and had a habit of stumbling over dead bodies. Ryan had read a couple of them, skipping the computer jargon and raising his brows a bit over the idea that a guy who spent his days peering at a monitor had muscles like Stallone and handled a gun like Bill Hickok.

"In a few hours I'll be doing great," Bonnie said in answer to his question. Her smile was quick and infectious. "My mom is taking the kids for the next two days, and Jack's promised to take me to Cheyenne for our anniversary. Two nights in a fancy hotel, a dozen roses, good food and not a dirty dish or a runny nose in sight. I may never come home."

"How'd you pry Jack away from the computer?" Ryan asked. Jack was notorious for getting absorbed in a book and forgetting little things like meals and children waiting to be picked up from school.

"I told him I'd divorce him and make sure he got custody of the kids."

Ryan winced. "You're a hard woman."

"Yeah, but I get results," she said, grinning.

"What's with the new addition?" he asked, jerking his head at the wooden Indian.

Bonnie snorted. "Dad bought it. I don't know what he thinks he's going to do with it. Damned thing weighs five hundred pounds if it weighs an ounce. I think he's got some idea of setting it outside the door to give the place a little atmosphere."

"Well, at least you don't have to worry about anyone slipping it in their purse and stealing it."

"I'd help them load it in the truck if they'd just take the stupid thing away."

"I'll steal it for you." He lifted the cast on his arm. "But you'll have to wait until I get this thing off next week."

"I may hold you to it," she said, grinning. Bonnie settled her weight a little more comfortably on the stool. It was the middle of the day in the middle of the week, and business was even slower than the book she'd been reading. She welcomed a chance to chat. "You headin' back to the circuit once the doc gives you the go ahead?"

"I haven't decided what I'm going to do," he said, keeping his response deliberately vague. Considering the friction between him and his grandfather, he was no longer sure what his plans were. He made it a point to shift the conversation in another direction. "I hear your oldest did you proud in the Little Britches Rodeo last summer."

"Sure did." Bonnie's round face glowed with maternal pride. "Marisue brought home first place. She says she wants to get serious about it, so we've been keeping an eye out for a likely looking barrel racer for her."

"I hear of anything, I'll let you know," Ryan promised.

"Thanks."

The bell jangled again, and they both turned toward the door. Ryan felt a little shock of pleasure when he saw Maggie Drummond walk in. For the past week, he'd alternated between regret that he hadn't told her he wanted to see her again and relief that he'd kept his distance. The quick warmth of her smile when she saw him gave regret the upper hand.

"Hey, Maggie. How're you doing?" Bonnie's smile was warm and friendly.

"Good. How 'bout yourself?"

"I bribed Mom into taking the kids for a couple of days, and Jack and I are going to Cheyenne. We're going to paint the town red."

"Don't forget to hide his laptop computer," Maggie said, obviously aware of Jack's tendency to get lost in his work.

"I'm holding it hostage. If he so much as mentions murder, even if he just reads about one in the paper, I'm going to let our youngest loose in Jack's office. Timmy's a mechanical genius of sorts. He can take anything apart. Can't put a thing back together, of course, but he's hell on wheels when it comes to takin' 'em apart. I figure he could have the computer reduced to scrap in under ten minutes. Give him twice that and the fax machine and printer are goners, too.''

"You're tough," Maggie said admiringly.

Ryan grinned. "That's what I told her."

"Have you two met?" Bonnie asked, glancing questioningly between them.

"Ryan gave me a ride into town when my transmission died a couple of weeks back," Maggie said. She smiled at him, and Ryan found himself noticing that slightly crooked front tooth again, just as he had the first time they'd met. He didn't know why he should find the tiny flaw so oddly appealing, but he did.

"How's the car?" he asked.

"It runs much better with a working transmission," she said, widening her eyes in amazement.

"No kidding? I've heard that rumor but I never really believed it," he said, mock solemn, and was ridiculously pleased when she smiled again. Damn, she was cute, he thought, his own smile widening as he looked at her. Doug had said that she made a man think of home-cooked dinners and picket fences, and there was some truth in that, but she also made him think of laughter under the covers on a cold morning, of seeing that smile first thing in the morning.

"What can I do you for?" Bonnie asked Ryan when the silence lengthened, and he was suddenly aware that he'd been standing there smiling at Maggie like a schoolboy in the throes of his first crush. Pulling his gaze away from Maggie, he met the speculative look in Bonnie's eyes and abruptly remembered that she was credited by some with being the biggest gossip in the state. There wasn't an ounce of malice in her, but she felt a compulsion to know everyone's business, and what she didn't know, she was willing to speculate about.

"Sara said she called in an order for groceries," he said, trying to look as if he hadn't just been thinking about how much he would like to take Maggie Drummond to bed.

"I've got a delivery due in any minute now that has some of the stuff she wanted on it. Can you wait a bit? Soon as the truck gets here, we'll start unloading."

"No problem." Ryan smiled ruefully. "At the moment, my most useful talent is picking up supplies. I can kill some time around town and come back."

"Not a whole lot of time-killing things to do around here," she commented. Her eyes shifted to

Maggie, who had moved away and was looking in a refrigerated case. "You could maybe head down to Bill's and play some pool. Or something. You goin' in to work today, Maggie?"

"It's my day off." Maggie came forward and put a plastic-wrapped sandwich and a soft drink on the counter. "I'm going to have a picnic in the park."

Park? It took Ryan a moment to remember the two-block-square patch of grass and trees that sat between the tiny newspaper office and the Blue Bell Motel, which catered to tourists passing through on their way to hike and camp in the nearby Wind River Mountains. In a place where open land was the rule rather than the exception, the small park had never made much of an impression on him.

"There's a family of chipmunks there," Maggie continued. "I like to photograph them."

For the first time Ryan noticed the tote bag slung over her shoulder.

"The kids loved those shots you took of them with their horses the day you came out to our place. Maggie's as good as a professional with that camera," Bonnie told Ryan.

"I don't know about that, but I've certainly got a world-class collection of rejection slips." Maggie's grin was appealingly self-deprecating.

"At least you're the best at something," Ryan said.

Bonnie's eyes were bright with speculation as she looked back and forth between them. "Hey, why don't you two have lunch together?" she said.

Startled, they both turned to look at her. She smiled brightly as she pulled Maggie's purchases toward her and started to enter prices in the register. "You said you were just going to kill some time, Ryan. You might as well have some company while you're doing it."

Ryan nearly groaned out loud when he saw the gleam in her eyes. What was it about him that made people feel compelled to try to pair him up with a woman? First his grandfather and his scheme for marrying him off to Shelly, and now Bonnie pushing him in Maggie's direction. Other men managed to stay single without everyone in the county feeling compelled to dabble in their love lives. He was starting to feel like a balky calf with a couple of cow dogs nipping at him, trying to nudge him back in line with the rest of the herd. He didn't need help arranging his life, he thought resentfully. He was perfectly capable of asking Maggie out, if and when he decided that was what he wanted to do.

"You're welcome to join me if you'd like," Maggie said, her smile just a little shy, as if she expected him to refuse. Ryan hesitated for less than an instant. He wanted to have lunch with her, damn it. It would be stupid to refuse just to prove he could.

"If you're sure the chipmunks won't mind," he said, and was pleased when Maggie's smile widened.

Ryan left his pickup parked in front of the General Store, and Bonnie promised to have Sara's grocery order loaded in it as soon as the delivery arrived.

"I'll hold out the frozen stuff until you're ready to leave. No need to hurry. I'll be here until five," she said, her hazel eyes bright with speculation as she looked between the two of them.

"Thanks, Bonnie." Ryan followed Maggie out the door. As they walked past the big front window, he glanced inside and saw Bonnie reaching for the phone.

"She's very nice, but she does have a tendency to gossip," Maggie said. Glancing down at her, he saw that her gaze had followed his. Obviously she'd followed his line of thinking, too.

"You do her an injustice," he said ruefully. "Bonnie is a world-class gossip. If Yale gave degrees in gossip, she could have graduated summa cum laude."

She laughed and shook her head. "She doesn't mean any harm by it."

"No. She just can't resist sticking her nose into everyone else's business. She was the same way when we were in school. If you wanted to know anything about anyone, you could just ask Bonnie. You'd think four kids would be more than enough to keep her occupied, but it doesn't even seem to have slowed her down."

"I've heard it said that people always manage to find time for the things they truly love," she said, tongue in cheek.

"That's certainly true in Bonnie's case," Ryan agreed, grinning. He nodded to Lee Hardeman, who edited the weekly *Willow Flat Herald*. The old man was sitting outside the newspaper office, enjoying the sunshine and watching the cars go by.

"Howdy, Ry."

"How's Abby?" Ryan asked, slowing his stride a little.

"Doin' fine." Lee's smile was pleased. "I'll tell her you asked after her."

"You do that."

"His wife?" Maggie asked as they passed the newspaper office and reached the north end of the park.

"His mule."

"Excuse me?" She stumbled over a crack in the

ancient sidewalk, and Ryan's hand shot out, catching her arm to steady her. "Abby is a *mule?*"

"That's right," he said, enjoying her reaction. He enjoyed the feel of her bare skin beneath his fingers, too, and left his hand where it was. "Lee's very fond of her."

"I hope Abby appreciates you asking after her."

"I'm sure she will. For a mule, Abby has a rather refined sense of etiquette."

"For a mule," Maggie repeated. She giggled, a soft, girlish sound of mixed amusement and mischief. "I'm not sure just what might constitute good etiquette to a mule."

"That's one of those questions that's probably better left unanswered," Ryan said.

"Probably." She stepped off the sidewalk onto the grass and caught back a sigh of regret when Ryan let his hand drop from her arm as he followed her. There had been a pleasant sense of casual intimacy in the light touch. If she'd been inclined to dangerous fantasies, she might have let herself imagine what it might be like if the intimacy were not so casual.

But this was nice enough in itself, even without fantasies, she thought as she pulled an old blanket out of her tote bag and shook it out before spreading it over the scrubby grass.

She sank down cross-legged on one corner of

the blanket and swept out a hand in invitation. "Choose your own seat. This is an informal luncheon."

Ryan grinned as he dropped to the blanket, folding his long legs under him with surprising grace. "That's a relief. I think my tux is at the cleaners."

Maggie reached in the bag that held their sandwiches and tried not to notice that his eyes were even bluer than the wide sweep of Wyoming sky above them.

A low rock wall edged the end of the park next to the motel. Actually, the word *wall* was a little grandiose, since it contained no mortar and only the most minimal effort had gone into its construction. It was nothing more than a fairly tidy running heap of stones, a convenient place to stack the rocks that had been pulled out of the ground when the motel's parking lot was built.

The height varied from a little under two feet to something over three, giving it an undulating look. In her more fanciful moments, Maggie thought it looked like the back of a sea serpent thrusting up from the scrubby grass. Over the years, the ever present wind had blown soil in among the stones, and small plants had rooted there. In the summer, lizards sunned themselves on top of the wall, and chipmunks had found homes among the rocks.

The tiny ecosystem delighted Maggie. She'd spent endless hours photographing the wall and its inhabitants—the delicate wildflowers that showed themselves for a few brief moments in summer, the beady-eyed lizards doing push-ups on the rocks in the sharp gray light just before a thunderstorm or the crisp shadows and angles of a sunny day. But her favorite subjects were the chipmunks. Their tiny, masked faces and self-important bustle as they went about their business never failed to enchant her.

Today they were making themselves scarce, but Maggie couldn't muster up any real disappointment. Today she was content to watch the bees hum through the scraggly remains of a perennial bed that some civic-minded citizen had planted a couple of years before. The harsh Wyoming winters had taken their toll on the plants, but a few had survived and were making a brave stand. They wouldn't win any prizes, but she liked the cheerful color, liked even more the toughness underlying the delicate beauty of the flowers. They were survivors. You had to admire that.

She stole a quick look at her companion. Ryan lay propped on one elbow, across the blanket from her. A plain white T-shirt clung to the solid muscles of his chest and the flat plane of his stomach. His jeans were faded almost white with age, and the hems were worn almost ragged. They fit as if made for him, molding his narrow hips and clinging to his long legs. The black boots showed signs of wear, too.

Maggie had no trouble recognizing the tingle of unabashed lust that settled in the pit of her stomach. There was something intensely male about him, a heat—a scent, almost—that tugged at her in a way she'd never experienced before. But along with the female hunger came another familiar urge—she itched to see him framed through a camera lens. Black and white, she thought, picturing it in her mind. Black-and-white film would do wonderful things for the strong angle of his jaw, the high curve of his cheekbones. On the other hand, black and white wouldn't show the clear blue of his eyes or the odd burnished highlights where the sun caught in his hair. Either way, she knew he would make a wonderful subject.

She wondered if he would mind being photographed. Then wondered if it would be a wise thing to do. She usually felt a strong connection with whatever she photographed, as if the lens served to sharpen and focus her emotions. She was already drawn to Ryan Lassiter, had already spent far too much time thinking about him. She didn't really need anything to encourage her thoughts to wander in his direction.

Ryan watched the play of expressions across her face and wondered what she was thinking. He hadn't known her long, but it was long enough to recognize the slightly out-of-focus look that meant her thoughts had gone off on a tangent. She was prettier than he'd realized the first time he saw her, he thought, cocking his head a little as he looked at her. Or maybe she'd grown on him—the soft, kissable mouth, the chin that held just a hint of stubbornness, those big gray eyes that tended to reflect her thoughts.

Not only was she pretty, but she was that rarest of all things—a good listener. You never had the sense that she was waiting for you to finish talking so she could say something, and she didn't just listen politely, her mind drifting to other things. She actually heard what you were saying.

There was a hazard in that, he decided, taking a drink of Coke from the can. Having someone who really listened encouraged a man to talk too much, to say more than he'd intended. He'd found himself telling her about the mare, about his hopes of breeding her and maybe developing a good line of cutting horses. Unselfconscious about her ignorance, she'd asked him questions, wanting to know what a cutting horse did, how they were trained.

Some of the women who followed the circuit thought the quickest way into a cowboy's bed was a display of pretty confusion and a breathy request for explanations of some piece of equipment or the rules of an event. It apparently worked with a lot of the riders, but he'd never really understood the appeal until now. Maggie's interest was genuine, and so were her questions, and he couldn't deny that it was nice to have a woman hanging on his every word.

His mouth twisted in a self-deprecating smile. Hormones and egos, he thought—men were slaves to them both. And Maggie Drummond had a definite effect on both.

"A penny for your thoughts," he said, abruptly tired of his own.

Maggie started, her eyes darting to him and then away, her brain scrambling for a response. She could hardly tell him she'd been thinking that she was far too attracted to him for her own good. Her eyes fell on the wall, and she said the first thing that popped into her head.

"What do you call a bunch of chipmunks?"

"What?" Ryan's brows shot up.

"You know, there are names for groups of things. A gaggle of geese. A rook of crows."

"A herd of cows," he offered, but she gave him a scornful look.

"That doesn't count. *Everyone* knows that one."

"Sorry." He tried to look abashed, but the truth

was, sitting here, pleasantly full after having eaten a fairly decent ham sandwich, with the sunlight picking out the gold highlights in Maggie's hair, it was hard to look anything but content.

"A covey of quails," she said, speaking half to herself.

Ryan wondered what she would do if he smoothed his finger over the frown lines between her brows.

"A pod of whales and a pride of lions," he contributed, digging a little deeper.

"Commonplace," she sniffed, though her eyes were starting to laugh.

"A souse of sows," he said, challenging.

"No fair making them up," she protested, biting her lower lip to hold back a grin.

"I'm not." He tried for an offended look. "It's a term ranchers use."

"Ranchers don't raise pigs. Farmers raise pigs."

"Just enough to butcher for our own use," he lied without hesitation. To the best of his knowledge, no pig had ever set hoof on the Double L.

Maggie wrinkled her nose at the thought of butchering. "A souse of sows?" she repeated, unconvinced.

"It's not used much anymore," he admitted.

"I can see why."

"A den of thieves," he suggested, and grinned when she gave a choke of laughter.

"Doesn't count."

"I don't see why not," he protested.

"I brought up a serious trivia question, and you're making light of it." She made her mouth prim and disapproving.

"Isn't that a contradiction in terms? Can you have serious trivia?"

"A serious *intellectual* question," she revised, giving him a repressive look. "Perhaps the challenge is too much for you?"

"A pack of wolves," he said sullenly.

"Not even worth mentioning." She dismissed his example without hesitation.

"You're a hard woman," he complained, put upon.

"And you're lazy. Come on. There's got to be a term for a group of chipmunks."

Ryan thought for a moment and then grinned suddenly. "A chatter of chipmunks."

"A chatter of chipmunks?" Maggie dissolved in giggles, her eyes sparkling with delight. "You win. If that isn't the term for it, it ought to be."

"Thank you." He accepted her concession of defeat with a gracious bow of his head.

"But I still don't believe there is such a thing

as a souse of sows," she added, giving him a narrow-eyed look.

"It's not mentioned in many reference books," he admitted cautiously.

"No!" She widened her eyes in mock surprise, and Ryan grinned.

With the shade from a nearby tree casting shadows across his face, both softening and emphasizing the sharp angles of jaw and cheekbones, his eyes bright with laughter, he was very nearly beautiful, and Maggie found herself almost compulsively reaching for her camera. Color film would have to do. "Would you mind if I took a couple of pictures of you?"

"You must be getting desperate," he said, but he offered no objection when she turned the lens in his direction.

This was a new side of her, he thought, watching her slim fingers move over the camera, checking the light and adjusting the lens. There was smooth confidence in her movements, no hesitation or uncertainty. She moved quickly but without hurry. Concentrating, she caught the tip of her tongue between her teeth. His eyes dropped to her mouth, and he was startled by the quick jolt of hunger that went through him. At just that moment the camera clicked, and he wondered what she would see when the picture was developed. Would it be obvious that he'd been wondering what her mouth would feel like under his? Leery of letting his thoughts travel too far down that particular path, he sought a distraction.

"Detroit to Willow Flat is a considerable change. How did you end up here?"

"My mother inherited a house." She shifted the angle of the camera and snapped another shot. "Her aunt died, and she decided to come out here and look things over. I... We hadn't ever really had a chance to get close, so I decided to come with her. I had a nothing sort of office job, so it wasn't like I was leaving much behind."

The shutter clicked again, and then she lowered the camera, her eyes meeting his for a moment. She smiled a little and shrugged. "Actually, she thought Aunt Margaret had left her a ranch. It was...a disappointment when it turned out to be just a house. It's been...hard for her to adjust her thinking."

The hesitant way she spoke made him wonder what she wasn't saying. "You live with her?" he asked.

"Umm." She nodded and brought the camera back up, concealing her face. Hiding behind it? "Her and my older sister. I like it here."

"But they don't?" he asked, reading between the lines.

Maggie adjusted the lens and snapped another picture before lowering the camera. She kept her head down, her fingers shifting restlessly over the plastic case. "Neither of them is crazy about it," she said finally, and something in her tone suggested that it was an understatement.

"So why don't they leave?"

"Money." She snapped the lens cap in place and lifted one shoulder in a half shrug. "Mom worked in a warehouse—doing paperwork mostly. One of the lifts had an oil leak, and she slipped and fell. She gets disability, but it's not exactly a fortune. She can live more cheaply here than she could in a city, especially since the house is paid for."

"What about your sister?" Ryan wasn't sure why he was probing into her family background. It didn't exactly fit in with his decision to keep his distance from her, but, then again, that decision was getting a little ragged around the edges. Maybe, if she'd been some bleached blonde with an inflatable chest, he would have been able to stick to that resolution. But the feelings she brought out in him were more than simple lust. She... interested him. Damn it.

"I guess it's money with Noreen, too," Maggie said, answering his question. "She's a waitress at the Dew Drop, and the pay's not great. I guess it's hard to save up any money." Maggie looked down and fussed over putting the camera back in the inexpensive nylon case. The truth was, she didn't really know why Noreen stayed in Willow Flat. If she couldn't save the money herself, she could easily have talked one of her many lovers into loaning it to her. Some of them would probably have been willing to take her wherever she wanted to go. Yet she stayed. Maggie figured Noreen had her reasons. She always did.

"Families are never quite as simple as 'The Brady Bunch' made it look," Ryan said, reading more into her expression than she'd intended.

"No." Her head bent, she fingered a worn place on the camera case. She doubted if there was a family anywhere that was less like "The Brady Bunch" than hers.

"What about your father?"

"He left a few months after I was born." She looked up with a smile that didn't quite reach her eyes. "Apparently I was a very fussy baby and he couldn't take the noise."

Who had laid that guilt at her door? he wondered. Her mother?

"I doubt if he left just because of that."

"No. Probably not."

"But you feel guilty anyway," he said shrewdly.

"Not intellectually." She glanced at him again

and caught the lift of his brow, and her smile took on a self-deprecating edge. "It would be pretty dumb to feel guilty for something that happened when you were an infant."

"Incredibly dumb," he corrected, and laughter chased the shadows from her eyes.

"If you ever consider a career change, don't go into therapy. I don't think you're allowed to tell your patients they're incredibly dumb."

"I didn't say *you* were dumb. I said it would be dumb to feel guilty over something that happened when you were a baby. Men don't dump their families because a baby cries too much. They dump them because they're assholes."

Maggie laughed again. "Is that an official diagnosis?"

"It should be." Ryan thought of his own father, something he rarely did anymore. Duncan hadn't walked out on him—not officially, anyway—but the end result hadn't been much different. A few guilt-induced visits over the years, awkward phone calls from around the world to wish him a happy birthday or a Merry Christmas. The difference between his parents and what Maggie's father had done was only a matter of degree. He'd just been lucky enough to have his grandfather to take him in. Something told him Maggie hadn't been as lucky, despite the fact that she still had one parent.

Thinking of his grandfather reminded him of the
fact that he was supposed to be picking up groceries for Sara, some of which she wanted for dinner
tonight—the dinner Nathan had planned in order to
offer him up to Shelly Taylor on a silver platter.
Or maybe it was Shelly who was being offered to
him. Either way, the thought of it was enough to
give him heartburn in advance.

"I ought to go see if Bonnie's delivery came
in," he said reluctantly.

Maggie tamped down a quick surge of disappointment. She couldn't expect the afternoon to last
forever. But she couldn't hold back a wistful little
wish that it could have lasted just a bit longer.
Pushing the feeling aside, she stood up.

"I probably ought to head home, anyway," she
said, though there was nothing waiting for her there
but a few unimportant chores and the endless chatter of her mother's television shows.

"Sorry if I scared the chipmunks away," Ryan
said, rising with smooth, masculine grace.

Maggie wasn't sorry. She'd enjoyed this small
slice of time with him, enjoyed it more than she
should have, no doubt. "Maybe they just weren't
in the mood to have their pictures taken today,"
she said lightly.

"Camera shy?" he suggested with a lopsided
smile that made her wish she had her camera in

her hands again. "There's nothing worse than a coy rodent."

He arched his back to stretch the kinks out of his spine, and she allowed her eyes to skim over him, admiring the solid width of his shoulders. He wore a wide gold-and-silver belt buckle that pressed against the flat planes of his stomach, and she wondered if he'd won it in a rodeo competition, but the thought drifted out of her head as she let her gaze wander down the long, long length of his legs before moving back up. She could see dark whorls of chest hair shadowed against the thin, white fabric of his T-shirt, and her fingers curled inward, as if she could feel the crispness of that hair against her palms, along with the heat of the skin beneath.

He really was a beautiful example of the male of the species, Maggie thought. Looking at him, she felt a heavy, liquid heat low inside, a sexual awareness—female to male.

She realized abruptly that he'd stopped stretching and was standing there, feet braced slightly apart, arms at his sides, watching her. Maggie's eyes jerked upward, meeting his for an instant before she looked away, color flooding her face. Good going, she told herself as she bent to snatch up the blanket. Nothing like being caught ogling the man. Maybe, for her next trick, she could drool over him.

Ryan watched her shake out the blanket with unnecessary vigor, but he could still see the look in her eyes in the moments just before she'd realized he was watching her. The sexual awareness had been unmistakable. It wasn't the first time a woman had looked at him with hunger in her eyes. The rodeo groupies who haunted the arenas weren't shy about making their desires known. He'd been propositioned more times than he could remember. On a few memorable occasions, words had been bypassed in favor of a more direct approach. In a bar in Abilene, he'd had a woman buy him a drink and send her bra along with it. In Sante Fe, a redhead with seriously big hair had walked up to him and put her hand on his crotch while she made an explicit and rather inventive suggestion about how they might spend the next few hours.

None of those invitations had inspired anything more than a mild distaste—and, in the case of the redhead, acute embarrassment. But one glimpse of the shy hunger in Maggie's big gray eyes and arousal stirred, quick and hard. It was one thing to keep his distance when he was the only one who wanted—and he could almost convince himself that he didn't really—but it was something else to do it when she looked at him like that.

"I think it's already dead," he said, when she continued to shake the blanket as if her life depended on freeing it of every single crumb.

Without giving himself time to think, he reached out and caught the end of the blanket in his good hand, tugging lightly to pull her toward him. Surprised, she looked at him, her eyes uncertain. She could have released the blanket. Could have turned away and ended the moment before it began. But he knew she wouldn't.

This was crazy, he thought, pulling her closer. He'd made up his mind that he didn't want to get involved with her—with anyone—and he knew her just well enough to know that kissing her was involvement. He could stop this now, he told himself. Before it went any further, before he did something they both might regret. He could say something light, make a joke. She would smile, and the tension would be gone as quickly as it had sprung up. But it was a mistake to think about her smile, because that made him look at her mouth, and once he'd done that, there was no way he could go another minute without tasting it.

Maggie gasped in surprise when Ryan yanked suddenly and had her stumbling against him. The blanket dropped to the ground, forgotten, and she stared up at him, her hands flattened against his chest. He threaded his fingers through the streaky blond mass of her hair, feeling it curl around his hand as he tilted her head back. Crazy, he thought again as her eyes went smoky gray. Madness, he thought as he took her mouth.

Maggie had been thinking about this since the first time they met—thinking about it, wanting it and pretending not to. But no amount of daydreaming could have prepared her for the quick rush of heat that shot through her, weakening her knees and melting her already shaky defenses. She'd been kissed before, but not like this. Never like this.

The sunshine, the low hum of the bees working the flowers, the rattle of a truck driving past the park—all of it faded away. There were only the two of them in all the world. Ryan's hand shifted, tilting her head as he deepened the kiss, and Maggie opened her mouth to him, needing to taste him as much as he needed to taste her.

She'd had an orange soda with her lunch. He slid his tongue across her lower lip, tasting the lingering sweetness and finding it ridiculously erotic. Then again, at that moment, there wasn't much about Maggie Drummond that he didn't find erotic. The soft curves of her body, her scent—a mixture of soap and shampoo—the way her fingers curled against his chest, gathering little handfuls of his T-shirt, holding on as if he were the only solid thing in the universe.

Maggie felt the weight of his cast settle carefully against the curve of her lower back, urging her closer, and she went willingly, her body bending to his, pliant as a willow. She'd never before been so aware of the fundamental differences between male and female. He was all hard planes and angles, corded muscles and five o'clock shadow. She wanted to burrow closer, to let the feel of his arms around her block out the rest of the world.

The quick rush of hunger had Ryan's head spinning. What had begun in curiosity had turned into something much more than he'd expected. She was so much smaller than he was, he should have felt awkward holding her. But he liked the feel of her in his arms, liked the way her body felt tucked against his. Liked it too damned much, he thought, aware of his growing arousal. This wasn't the time or the place. They were in a public park, for God's sake. But instead of drawing back, he spread his fingers wide, cradling the back of her head, deepening the kiss.

It had been a long time since he'd wanted a woman like this, a long time since he'd forgotten everything but the need to lose himself in a woman's kiss. Years since he'd felt this kind of hunger, this kind of need. Years, he thought dazedly.

Years.

The realization of just how long it had been made him abruptly aware of where he was and what he was doing, of who the woman in his arms was.

And of who she wasn't.

Maggie swallowed a whimper of protest when she felt Ryan's arms loosen around her. She'd been kissed before—or thought she had—but it had never been like this, never made her feel boneless and very nearly dizzy with the force of her own needs. Just a kiss, she reminded herself as his hand slid from her hair and his mouth left hers. Just a kiss, she repeated more firmly as she forced her fingers to release their grip on his shirt.

And the *Titanic* was just a little shipwreck.

Her lashes seemed unbelievably heavy as she opened her eyes and stared up into his face. Maggie felt a quick rush of pure, feminine satisfaction at the slightly glazed look in his eyes. It was nice to know that she wasn't the only one affected.

As soon as he released her, Ryan wanted to take hold of her again. The strength of the urge made him take a step back. He wasn't ready for this. Whatever *this* was—and he sure as hell wasn't ready to put a name to it—it was too much, too soon. He was trying to put his life in order, not add complications to it. Especially not a complication with beautiful gray eyes and an incredibly kissable mouth.

He bent to scoop the blanket up off the ground, shaking it a little before handing it back to her. He should say something, something casual. So he'd kissed her. So what? He wasn't a monk, and she wasn't the first woman he'd kissed in the past four years. Only the first to scramble his brain when he did. The thought made him uneasy. He cleared his throat and looked away from the temptation of her mouth.

"I guess I ought to head back, see if Sara's order is ready."

Though he didn't move physically, Maggie could sense him stepping back mentally. Not that she blamed him, she thought as she folded the blanket. She went down on one knee to push it into her tote bag, grateful for the excuse to look away from him. She could use a little distance herself.

Not for anything would she let him see that her stomach was still jumping with awareness or that her knees were not quite steady. When she stood up and looked at him, her smile was easy, her eyes clear.

"My car's parked in front of the store. I'll walk back with you."

Chapter Six

They didn't talk much on the walk back. Maggie commented that they were having a nice stretch of weather, unusually warm for this early in the year. Ryan agreed that it had been very nice. There didn't seem to be much to say after that.

Lee Hardeman was still sitting outside the newspaper office, and he and Ryan exchanged greetings again, this time without mentioning Abby, the mule. Maggie thought it was strange that the old man should still be sitting there until she glanced at her watch and realized that it had been less than an hour since they'd walked past the first time. It seemed as if so much had happened that more time should have passed. She had to remind herself that a kiss hardly constituted a cataclysmic event, but she wasn't sure she believed herself, not when she could still feel the aftershocks from it.

Ryan slowed his pace as they neared the store. Maggie's compact was parked next to his truck. He remembered it from the first time they'd met, when he and Doug had given her a ride into town. Just a couple of weeks ago, he realized, mildly astonished. For some reason, it seemed as if he'd known Maggie longer than that.

He waited on the sidewalk while she opened the passenger door and put her tote bag on the front seat. She was smiling as she shut the door and turned back toward him. Ryan found himself half wishing she wouldn't smile. It made him look at her mouth, and, when he looked at her mouth, he remembered the taste and feel of her. That made him want to kiss her all over again. And that was just what he couldn't let himself do, though he was having a hard time remembering why.

"This was nice," Maggie said, then blushed, afraid he might misinterpret her comment. She rushed to clarify her meaning. "The picnic, I mean. The picnic was nice. And everything." Her voice trailed off.

"It was a nice picnic," Ryan agreed solemnly. He waited a beat. "But 'everything' was even nicer."

He said it for the sheer pleasure of watching her

blush deepen, and she didn't disappoint. Her eyes met his for an instant, then flickered away. She focused her gaze on his collarbone.

"Me, too," she said, her voice strangled. "I mean, I thought so, too."

He wanted to see her again, Ryan decided abruptly. It might not be the smartest thing to do, but, then again, if you were smart all the time, life got pretty damned dull. He'd spent the past four years risking life and limb on the chance that he would win enough money to get him down the road to the next arena. This was just a risk of a different sort.

"I hope the delivery got here," Maggie said a little too brightly, and he realized that he'd let the silence stretch uncomfortably.

"Maggie—" He started to reach for her hand and then caught himself. If Bonnie Dillard looked out the window and saw him holding Maggie's hand in broad daylight, right there in front of God and everybody, by nightfall half the state would hear that they were engaged, and the other half would hear that they were having a torrid affair.

Good, Lassiter. Kiss her in broad daylight in a public park where anyone could see you, but draw the line at holding her hand. That's real smart.

So he hooked his thumbs in his pockets, aware of the awkward weight of the cast on his arm. And the cast wasn't the only thing about him that was awkward, he thought as his eyes met Maggie's. She was looking at him questioningly, waiting for him to say something beyond her name. His mind a complete blank, Ryan stared at her. It had been a long time since he'd asked a woman for a date. He wasn't sure how to go about it anymore.

"Maggie, I—"

"Maggie! Isn't this handy?"

The voice was a husky contralto, low and smooth and very female. Maggie looked past him, and Ryan caught a flash of something in her eyes that was there and gone too quick for him to read.

"Noreen." Her voice was flat, without emotion and not particularly welcoming.

"In the flesh."

Ryan turned toward the voice, his eyes widening a little when he saw the woman walking toward them. She was tall—maybe five-nine or so—and she was wearing a pair of strappy red sandals with spikey little heels that brought her closer to six feet. She was slim, but with curves in all the right places, and she'd poured those curves into a pair of lipstick red jeans and a skinny white knit top that left very little to the imagination. Practically nothing to the imagination, Ryan amended when she got close enough for him to see the shadowy outline of her nipples through the thin white fabric.

Her hair—a pale silvery blond—was worn loose and full, tumbling onto her shoulders in the kind of disarray that was guaranteed to set a man to thinking about steamy sex. As if reading his thoughts, she lifted one slim hand and pushed her fingers through the heavy mass in a gesture that thrust her next-to-naked breasts forward. With an effort, Ryan lifted his gaze from that undeniably impressive display. The look in her eyes told him that the move had been deliberate, and that she was pleased with herself for getting his attention.

"I thought you were working today," Maggie said. She hated the way Noreen was looking at Ryan. Hated it even more that he was looking back. "You said Colleen called in sick."

"She did, but she got to feeling better and came in to work. I was going to walk home, but if you're heading that way, I'll catch a ride with you."

"What happened to your car?" It was a struggle, but Maggie managed to keep her tone even. The last thing she wanted to do was allow Noreen to see that she was disturbed by her sudden appearance. It was never a good idea to put any kind of a weapon, no matter how outwardly innocuous, into her older sister's hands.

"I ran out of gas." Noreen slanted a laughing glance at Ryan. She ran her fingers through her hair again. "I know it's a classic, ditzy blonde thing to do, but I just wasn't paying any attention to the gauge.''

"Could happen to anyone," he said neutrally. This time he kept his eyes on her face. Somehow, he didn't think there was a ditzy bone in that well-kept body.

"I still feel silly." She pursed her lips in a little moue of embarrassment that drew attention to her full mouth, which was painted the same color as her jeans. Then she gave him a sudden, dazzling smile. "Since Maggie doesn't seem much inclined to introduce us, I'll do the honors. I'm Noreen, Maggie's older sister—but only by a couple of years," she added with a husky chuckle.

Maggie resisted the urge to clarify that it was actually seven and a half years. Experience had taught her that she couldn't begin to compete with Noreen when it came to bitchiness, even if she'd wanted to.

"This is Ryan Lassiter," she said, completing the introductions Noreen had begun.

Noreen smiled and held out her hand. "I'd been hoping to meet you. I know you rescued Maggie when her car broke down a couple of weeks ago. I thought it would be nice if someone in the family thanked you."

"Maggie thanked me," Ryan said, feeling her

fingers cling as he pulled his hand from hers. *This* was Maggie's sister?

"I was hoping I'd bump into you in town sometime," Noreen said. She narrowed her eyes, as if the sun was bothering her, and then shifted her position slightly so that the sun was more to the side. It could have been a coincidence that the move also put Maggie half behind her, effectively blocking her from the conversation.

"I'd like to buy you a drink. A way to say thank you," she added when Ryan's brows rose.

"It's not necessary," he said. He couldn't help but think that Lucrezia Borgia must have had a similar look in her eyes when she invited her victims to have a glass of wine.

"Maybe not, but it would make me feel good." Noreen trailed her fingers over the scooped neckline of her top, drawing his eyes to the cleavage so generously displayed. "I work at the Dew Drop, usually the evening shift. You can come in anytime." She let her gaze linger on his mouth for a minute before lifting her eyes to his. She wet her lower lip, and her voice dropped to a husky purr. "Anytime at all."

"I just might take you up on that," he lied, giving her a friendly, noncommittal smile.

There was no denying that she was beautiful. And he could hardly hold it against her that she so obviously knew it. You couldn't look like that and not know it. High cheekbones, delicately arched brows, that full lower lip that made a man wonder what it would be like to kiss her. Eyes that were a pale, crystalline blue, fringed by thick dark lashes. He'd seen pictures of icebergs that were nearly the same color. And that held just about as much warmth.

She put him in mind of a camping trip that he and Tucker had gone on when they were in their teens. Hiking through a small ravine, he'd found himself practically nose to nose with a rattlesnake sunning itself on a ledge. The snake had been far enough away that he didn't have to worry about it striking but close enough to give him a start. They'd stared at each other for a while before he moved on up the ravine, walking a little more carefully this time. There was something about Noreen Drummond that brought that long-ago encounter to mind.

Ryan glanced at Maggie, but she was studying a crack in the sidewalk as if fascinated by the meandering path it wove across the aging concrete. He sure as hell couldn't ask her for a date now, not with Noreen standing there looking all sultry and available. He would talk to Maggie some other time, he decided, and felt both relief and regret at the delay, which meant he was either a coward or a damned fool—he could take his pick.

"If I don't get those supplies home, Sara's going to skin me alive," he said, wanting to put an end to the awkward little scene.

"Are you sure I can't buy you that drink now?" Noreen eased subtly closer, her tongue coming out to moisten her lower lip again. The gesture reminded him irresistibly of that snake, sitting there watching him, forked tongue flicking out now and again as if trying to decide whether or not he might be edible.

"Some other time." To be polite, he made an effort to sound regretful.

"I'll hold you to that," Noreen purred, and Ryan fought the urge to check himself for fang marks.

He glanced at Maggie, but she was still absorbed in her study of the crack. When she didn't look up, he mumbled a general farewell and then beat a hasty and, he knew, cowardly retreat into the General Store.

"Well, that was nice timing," Noreen said as the door closed behind him, cutting off the cheerful jangle of the bell. "I had been hoping to bump into him."

Maggie lifted her head but was careful not to look in the direction of the store. If Ryan was looking out the window, ogling Noreen, she didn't want to know about it.

She realized she was holding her car keys so tightly that the metal was biting into her palm, and she forced herself to loosen her fingers. It had to be something in men's genes that made them so susceptible to women with skinny butts, big boobs and screw-me-now perfume. More likely it was what was in their *jeans,* she thought viciously, remembering the way Ryan's eyes had widened at the sight of Noreen's cleavage. Not that she could entirely blame him, when Noreen was practically waving her breasts under his nose.

"Do you really need a ride home?" she asked. Years of practice at concealing her emotions enabled her to keep her tone even.

"Yes." Noreen's grimace was much less attractive than her practiced pout. "The engine's making a funny noise. I didn't want to drive it in case it's something serious. Dave Lufton said he'd take a look at it for me this weekend."

Dave Lufton was one of Noreen's more regular dates. He was a couple of years younger than Noreen and worked at the feed store. At six foot five, with shoulders a mile wide and a pleasant but vaguely bovine expression, he looked like he ought to be eating grain rather than moving bags of it. Maggie had met him a couple of times and thought he seemed nice but not terribly bright. Since he was neither wealthy nor related to anyone who was, she'd wondered why Noreen went out with him until, in a burst of girlish confidence, Noreen had commented that Dave was extremely well endowed and boasted amazing endurance in bed. Maggie hadn't been able to look at him since without fighting an overwhelming urge to stare at his fly.

"I think I made quite an impression on Ryan," Noreen said as she slid into the passenger seat.

"I'm sure you did." Maggie started the car and backed it out of the parking space. To the best of her knowledge, Noreen had never failed to make an impression on anything male. She jerked the gearshift down abruptly so that the little car practically leaped forward in shock.

"Why didn't you tell me he was so good-looking?" Noreen asked.

"I said he was attractive."

"A gross understatement." Noreen licked her lips, her expression unabashedly hungry. "He's a major hunk, and his family is absolutely loaded. You don't come across a combination like that every day."

Maggie braked to allow an incredibly bowlegged old man to walk across the street, his rolling gate making him look like he'd just stepped off a ship.

She glanced at her sister. "A lot of ranchers are land rich but cash poor, you know."

"Land can be sold," Noreen said casually. "A place the size of the Lassiter spread must be worth a fortune. Isn't there some saying about turning dross into gold? Well, just imagine turning all those cows into diamonds and first-class travel." Noreen's husky laugh made Maggie want to smack her right in her Revlon-red mouth.

She tightened her fingers on the steering wheel and tried not to wish it were her sister's neck. It was a good thing that none of the ten commandments said anything about honoring your siblings. Not even divine law could make her feel anything but intense dislike for Noreen.

"The ranch has been in his family for generations. I doubt if Ryan would sell," she said, keeping her tone academic.

"A man will do anything if you just know what buttons to push." Noreen's tone was cynical. She slanted Maggie a sly look. "Or which ones to open. I know this may shock you, little sister, but the way to a man's heart isn't really through his stomach. It's definitely through his zipper. Most men haven't figured out yet that they've got two heads and only one of them is above their waist. Control the one below the belt and you can get anything you want."

"Sex isn't the solution to every problem. And don't smoke in my car," she added sharply when she saw Noreen pull her cigarettes from her purse.

"Sex is either the cause of or the solution for just about anything that comes up between a man and a woman." Noreen dropped the cigarettes back into her purse and turned her head to look at Maggie, her eyes bright with curiosity. "You sound like you're taking this rather personally."

"Not really." Maggie shrugged as she turned onto their road.

"You don't have your eye on Ryan Lassiter, do you?" Noreen's smile turned sharp with malice. "It would be a big mistake. Even if I don't net him—and I will if I set my mind to it—you're hardly the sort a man like that is going to notice."

Maggie's jaw ached with the effort of holding back the urge to tell Noreen that Ryan had noticed her enough to kiss her quite thoroughly. She would have liked nothing better than to see that smug little smile wiped off her sister's face. But the fleeting satisfaction wouldn't be worth the price, and Noreen always extracted a price.

"I don't have any particular interest in him," she lied calmly as she parked in the gravel driveway next to the house. "I just think your view of the world is a little narrow. There's more to life than sex."

"Sure there is." Noreen's smile was cold. "There's money."

She pushed open her door and got out. Maggie did the same, and they looked at each other across the roof of the car.

"Let me give you some advice." Noreen slid a cigarette between her scarlet lips and lit it with a slender silver lighter, a gift from some long-forgotten lover. When she lifted her eyes and looked at Maggie again, they were cold. "Don't set your sights on Ryan Lassiter."

"Warning me off?"

"For your own good, little sister." Noreen exhaled a cloud of smoke. Her mouth curved, but her eyes were chips of ice. "Even if I decide against reeling him in, you'll just make a fool of yourself if you try for him. A man like that wants a great deal more from a woman than you'd ever be able to deliver."

She turned away without waiting for a response. Maggie's hand clenched on the handle of the car door as she watched her sister walk across the yard to the house. Noreen's bright red jeans were a jarring splash of color against the faded white paint and the pale greens of new spring growth.

"Ryan's not a damned fish," she muttered as the front door shut behind her sister. "Nobody's going to reel him in."

It took a conscious effort to pry her fingers loose from the door handle so she could open the back door and get out the tote bag that held her camera and the blanket she and Ryan had used for their picnic. Her chin set in an expression that might have surprised her older sister. Ryan hadn't kissed Noreen. He'd kissed her. And if she had anything to say about it, it was going to happen again. And Noreen could take her skinny butt, her see-through tops and her pouty mouth and go straight to hell.

She slammed the car door for emphasis.

Ryan had met Shelly Taylor shortly after coming to the Double L. She was the same age as he and Tucker, but that was the only thing the three of them had in common. Shelly was a Girl with a capital *G*. She'd been born and raised on a ranch but, other than her skill with horses, you would never know it. Most ranch children—boy or girl— spent ninety percent of their time in jeans. They wore jeans to school, jeans at home and, as often as not, jeans to church. Shelly wore dresses—frilly pink dresses with ruffles, simple white dresses with the merest touch of pink lace, powder blue dresses with full skirts and big bows on the back. Her silky, light brown hair was always curled, her peaches- and-cream skin was always clean, and her shoes were always shiny. Even her tennis shoes had little flowers on them.

Ryan had disliked her on sight, and the feeling was mutual.

Because they lived on neighboring ranches, they generally went to school together, with either Sara or the woman hired to look after Shelly driving them. Several hours of forced proximity each week did nothing to change their opinions of one another. He thought she was a prissy little Goody Two-Shoes. She thought he was a pig.

A few weeks into the school year, Ryan brought the conflict out in the open. He hadn't planned it, but there was Shelly, and there was the mud puddle. What normal ten-year-old boy could resist? As he walked past her, he "tripped" and managed to shove Shelly and her sunshine yellow dress into the sea of mud.

If he'd been sly enough to keep up the pretense that it was an accident, it might have ended there. But she'd looked so funny, sitting there covered in mud, that he couldn't hold back his laughter.

Pushing her had been an impulse. He'd given no thought to her reaction, but, if he *had* thought about it, he would have expected tears, maybe a tantrum. Her face did turn red, but she didn't shed a tear as she picked herself up out of the mud and sloshed out onto dry ground, her pretty white anklets now dirty brown and drooping down over the tops of her formerly shiny little black shoes.

She didn't look so prim and proper now, he thought gleefully. There were streaks of mud on her pink cheeks and even blobs of it in her silky brown hair. She was covered in it literally from head to toe. Grinning, he stood and watched her approach.

Shelly stopped on the edge of the mud puddle and shook the water from her once crisp skirts. She brushed her hair back with one muddy hand, lifted her head and looked at him with fire in her eyes.

"You did that on purpose."

"I tripped," he said, uneasily aware that the excuse wasn't likely to go over very big with any of the teachers. Or with his grandfather. Shelly's dad was a good friend of his grandfather's, he remembered. But it was too late to back down now. All he could do was stick to his story. "I tripped," he said again. "It was an accident."

"You did it on purpose." Shelly's mouth tightened, and her eyes seemed to glitter.

Now she was going to go bawling to some teacher, Ryan thought. She was a crybaby. Girls were all crybabies. He got ready to sneer when the tears started to fall. But Shelly didn't cry. Instead, she balled her delicate little hand into a serviceable fist and plowed it straight into his stomach with all the force she could muster. It was more than enough.

Ryan's budding sneer vanished in a rounded O of surprise and pain as he doubled over, his breath whooshing out. He saw stars, and, for just a moment, the world seemed to revolve around him.

"You're not nice," Shelly said fiercely.

Ryan felt her hands on his back, but there was no time to react. One surprisingly fierce shove and he was face first in the mud. Sputtering and cursing, he rolled over and sat up, but Shelly hadn't waited to gloat. By the time he wiped the mud out of his eyes, she was marching off, muddied but unbowed.

For the next few years they gave each other a wide berth. Then, in their senior year in high school, he suddenly noticed that Shelly was still wearing dresses and that the legs under the short hemlines were the best in school. About the same time, Shelly noticed that Ryan's shoulders filled out a shirt very nicely. And all the girls agreed that he had the sexiest eyes. At seventeen, that was reason enough to put aside past hostilities.

They'd dated most of that year. And fought most of that year. It was peer pressure that kept them together, more than anything else. All Shelly's friends thought Ryan was a hunk, and all Ryan's friends envied him going out with the prettiest girl in school. They would have been a match made in heaven—if only they'd liked each other.

After their prom date ended in a near brawl, they'd gone their separate ways with no regrets on either side. Ryan had gone off to college, and Shelly had gone off to conquer Hollywood. They'd seen each other a few times since then. The ranching community was large in terms of space but relatively small when it came to people, and the friendship between Ryan's grandfather and her father had made it inevitable that they would bump into each other. The last time Ryan had seen her had been at Sally's funeral. She'd known Sally all her life, had been best friends with her oldest sister. Ryan had done his best to forget that day, but he had a vague memory of Shelly, with tears in her eyes, telling him how sorry she was and how much they would all miss Sally.

It was the memory of her honest grief, more than his grandfather's demand that he be there, that made him shower and change into a clean shirt and then present himself at the dinner table. Shelly was an old friend, if you stretched the term a little. Ryan frowned at his reflection in the mirror, remembering the black eye and the sucker punch in the stomach. You might have to stretch it quite a bit. He shrugged. Well, he'd liked her father, at least.

He finished snapping the front of his black Western-style shirt and then shoved the tails into the waist of his jeans. He just hoped his grandfather wasn't going to try any heavy-handed matchmaking while he was passing the mashed potatoes. Although maybe it would be better if he did, Ryan thought with a sudden grin as he combed his hair. If Shelly's temper was what it used to be, the evening might end with more of a bang than Nathan expected.

Cheered by the image of Shelly giving his grandfather a well-deserved black eye, Ryan tossed the comb on top of the dresser and left the room grinning. Hell, if Shelly actually popped Nathan one, he might have to reconsider marrying her. He was whistling under his breath as he went downstairs.

When the doorbell rang, Ryan happened to be closest to the door. He caught the anticipatory gleam in his grandfather's eye when he got up to answer it and knew Nathan was hoping he would take one look at Shelly and fall immediately into love—or lust. He doubted if Nathan cared which it was, as long as the end result was the joining of the two ranches.

When he opened the door, he had to admit that Nathan's plan was not without merit. The pretty girl he remembered had grown into a beautiful woman, one definitely worthy of inspiring lust at first sight. Time had erased the softness of youth from her features, highlighting her cheekbones and clarifying the line of her jaw. Contacts had taken her eyes from soft hazel to clear green, and her light brown hair had been skillfully highlighted so that it held ashy blond tones that created a flattering frame for her face.

She was still wearing skirts, he noticed with amusement, but the one she wore tonight—a snug band of thigh-length black knit—bore no resemblance to the frilly dresses she'd worn to school all those years ago. And the tall black heels were not even kissing cousins to those neat little black shoes.

"Ryan. It's been a long time." She held out a perfectly manicured hand. "You're looking good."

"You, too," he said sincerely. He pushed the door shut and took the hand she offered. Her fingers were long and slim, her skin silky soft. Maggie's hand was smaller but less fragile feeling. There was strength in her small hand, that oddly appealing sturdiness that she would probably hate him for seeing. With an effort, he dragged his mind back to the woman in front of him.

"I was real sorry to hear about your dad. He was a good man."

"Thank you." Shelly's smile wobbled for a moment. "He always did like you."

"Even the best of men show occasional lapses in taste," Tucker said as he stepped into the entryway behind Shelly, coming to his rescue in the time-honored tradition of best friends, Ryan thought, both amused and grateful.

"Tucker." Shelly's mouth tightened, her eyes flashing with some emotion that was there and gone too quickly for Ryan to read.

"Good to see you again, Shelly." Tucker's smile was wide and suspiciously friendly. "It's been a while."

"Two days," she said, but her cool tone was at odds with the color that had come up in her cheeks.

"Just long enough for me to miss your smiling face." Since she wasn't even close to smiling, Ryan thought it reasonable to assume that Tucker's comment wasn't intended to be taken at face value. He glanced from one to the other, but there was nothing to be read in either Tucker's bland smile or Shelly's stiffly polite mask.

"Is there some reason you're all standing in the hallway?" Nathan asked irritably from the living room doorway.

"No reason at all." Shelly moved toward him with a speed that suggested gratitude for the interruption.

Behind her, Ryan looked at Tucker, one brow raised in question. Tucker gave him a half smile but shook his head, and Ryan knew him well enough to know that he wasn't going to offer any explanation for the obvious tension between the two of them. He always had been a closemouthed SOB, Ryan thought. If you had a secret, you could count on Tucker McIntyre to keep it—a trait he usually admired. But he had to admit that he wouldn't have minded if tonight Tucker broke his usual habit long enough to explain.

Good God, he was starting to sound like Bonnie Dillard. Ryan shuddered and ran his good hand over his face. He had to get this damned cast off and get himself back to work full-time. Otherwise, pretty soon, he would be leaning across the counter at the General Store, swapping gossip with Bonnie, speculating on the state of other people's marriages and exchanging recipes for pound cake.

"Are you taking root out here?" Nathan stuck his head into the hall and frowned at his grandson. The boy was standing there, staring at nothing, looking like a wax dummy, while Tucker was getting Shelly a glass of that damned imported water Sara had bought for her. Stuff tasted like Alka-Seltzer. Still, it ought to be Ryan in there pouring her fizzy water and making conversation, getting to know her. The boy would have to be blind as a bat not to see what a looker Shelly was. Wasn't like he was suggesting he marry Gravel Gerty, for God's sake. Behind him, Shelly laughed at something Tucker said, and Nathan's irritation rose a notch.

"Have you gone deaf?" he snapped.

"What?" Ryan blinked and shook his head a little. "Sorry. I was thinking about something."

"Well, think about the fact that we've got a guest," Nathan said, lowering his voice as Ryan approached. "A damned beautiful woman and an old friend of the family."

"Not to mention owner of a ranch you want," Ryan murmured as he walked past his grandfather and into the living room.

Nathan turned to look after him, frustration a solid knot in his chest. It wasn't the ranch he wanted, damn it. It was his grandson's happiness and peace of mind. He was never going to find either as long as he kept running from what he'd lost. He'd known Shelly all his life. There was no reason why he couldn't fall in love with her if he just set his mind to it.

Sara had prepared dinner and left it simmering in the oven for them to serve themselves. Since Shelly was an old family friend, Sara hadn't felt it necessary to dust off any of her cookbooks and cook up something fancy. Ranching was hard work. Men who spent their days wrestling balky steers and mending fences burned a lot of calories, which meant meals tended to be on the hearty side. Dinner was slow-simmered short ribs, served with roasted potatoes and two sides of vegetables, and a heaping basket of Sara's special whole wheat rolls. The wooden bowl of salad was the one concession to Shelly's presence.

Ryan glanced at Shelly as he set the basket of rolls in the middle of the table and saw her eyes widen a little at the amount of food on the table.

"Not exactly California cuisine," Tucker said, catching her expression.

"Not exactly," Shelly agreed. "It smells wonderful."

"Not a stalk of arugula in sight," Ryan said as he pulled out his chair and sat down.

"I don't think arugula comes in stalks," Tucker corrected him. "Isn't it a nut of some kind?"

"It comes in stalks." Ryan let his drawl thicken. "I seen me some in a fancy grocery store one time."

"It's a nut," Tucker insisted stubbornly. "In California, they sprinkle them on everything from scrambled eggs to ice cream." He looked to Shelly for confirmation.

"Actually, it's a leafy sort of thing," she said

cautiously. "I think. To tell the truth, I'm not sure I've ever seen it in its natural state."

"I don't care what it is as long as Sara didn't put any of it on the table," Nathan said, ending the discussion on a pragmatic note.

"I think you're safe, Grandad. There wasn't an arugula nut, stalk or leaf to be had in town."

"Good. Pass the rolls, please."

Ryan's eyes met Shelly's as he handed the basket to his grandfather, and he was surprised by the gleam of laughter he saw there. He didn't remember Shelly having much of a sense of humor. Of course, that had been fifteen years ago—a lifetime. A person could change a lot in that amount of time. God knew, he had. It had been foolish to think that Shelly would have stayed the same.

"It was supposed to be a sort of Robin Hood meets the Black Stallion kind of movie, only it was set in Peru in the 19th century. I had the Maid Marian role, but I was definitely playing second fiddle to the horse." Shelly's smile was rueful.

"Why Peru?" Tucker asked, as he splashed Scotch over ice cubes and handed the drink to Nathan.

Dinner over, the four of them had moved into the living room for after-dinner drinks. So far, the evening had been surprisingly painless, Ryan thought, settling into the deep leather seat of an armchair. He could even say it had been pleasant. Shelly had a good supply of stories about life as an actress, and she didn't hesitate to poke fun at herself—yet another change. The Shelly he'd known would never have laughed at herself.

Ryan cradled his coffee cup in his good hand and stifled a yawn. There was a small fire crackling on the hearth, contributing more atmosphere than heat. Lamplight cast a golden glow across the room, gleaming off old wood and throwing gentle shadows over the worn spots in the old leather furniture. He probably shouldn't have had that second piece of pie, he thought, aware of a not unpleasant feeling of lethargy creeping over him.

"The director had this vision of the whole cast sweeping across the pampas," Shelly said, accepting a cup of coffee from Tucker. "He thought it would make a great opening shot."

Nathan frowned in confusion. "I thought the pampas was in Argentina."

"It is." Shelly's grin was quick and infectious. "Freddy was furious when he found out it was in the wrong country. It took a while to convince him that it hadn't been moved from Peru just to spite him."

"Did they change the script?" Tucker asked,

pouring a shallow layer of brandy into a snifter for himself.

"Are you kidding?" Shelly raised her brows in amazement that he should ask such a question. "This is Hollywood. If they want the pampas in Peru, it will be in Peru. Besides, the budget didn't run to much by way of location shoots, anyway. The closest we got to South America was about an hour or so north of L.A., in Lancaster."

"I've heard Lancaster is a dead ringer for the Peruvian pampas," Tucker said solemnly.

"Close enough, I guess." Shelly's mouth twisted ruefully. "Freddy was convinced he was making the next *Dances With Wolves*. If he'd put as much energy into making the film as he did into writing his Oscar acceptance speech, he might at least have managed to turn out a coherent movie. As it was, nobody—including Freddy—could figure out what the story was. Straight to video was more than it deserved."

"It must have been frustrating." Tucker leaned one shoulder against the mantel, and the firelight sifted warm golden shadows through the brandy in his glass.

"The first thing an actor develops is a high tolerance for frustration," Shelly said, shrugging lightly. "Most of your time is spent sitting around waiting—for makeup, for wardrobe, for a shot to be set up, for a set to be changed. It's not quite the glamorous life most people think it is.''

Or that she'd thought it would be? It didn't sound as if life had turned out quite the way she'd thought it would. But then, whose had? Ryan wondered, rubbing his thumb absently against the empty place where a wedding ring had once been. Wasn't there some quote about the fact that life was what happened while you were making other plans?

"So, what are you planning to do now?" It was the first time Nathan had spoken in a few minutes, and the sound of his grandfather's voice snapped Ryan out of the pleasant lethargy that had been creeping over him. The evening had been so low-key, he'd almost managed to forget the old man's dynastic aspirations.

"I'm not sure, exactly." Shelly shrugged again. "In acting parlance, I'm between roles, which sounds better than saying I'm out of work." She took a quick sip of her coffee. When she spoke again, the words were a little rushed, as if she had to hurry them out or not say them at all. "Actually, I've pretty well decided to come home." Her laugh was self-conscious. "I guess I'm getting a little too old for the Hollywood game playing. Besides, High Reaches won't run itself."

Ryan nearly shuddered when he saw his grandfather's pleased expression. If Shelly only knew what she was opening herself—both of them—up for.

"Ray's always done a good job with the place," he said.

"He has." Shelly sighed and set her cup down. She crossed one magnificent leg over the other, a move that edged her skirt up a dangerous half inch. Ryan didn't even notice. "When Daddy died, I figured Ray would just keep on taking care of things for me, but he's making noises about retiring, maybe moving up to Idaho. Andy's got a place up there now, you know. Ray wants to be closer to his grandchildren, I guess."

Ryan refused to acknowledge the triumphant look his grandfather sent him. "I'm sure he'll stay around until you find another foreman," he said, as much for Nathan's benefit as Shelly's.

"I hope so." Shelly sighed. "The truth is, Ray's not really crazy about the idea of working for a woman. And I don't think it helps that he remembers setting me on my first pony. I guess that makes it a little hard for him to think of me as his boss."

"You ought to get married," Nathan said firmly, abandoning subtlety in favor of a head-on approach. "It's tough for a woman to run a ranch alone. Tough for anyone," he added, with a token nod in the direction of political correctness. "I'm not saying it can't be done, but it's tough. You ought to look around, find yourself a good man, one who knows ranching.'' Ice cubes rattled in his glass when he waved it in his grandson's direction. ''Here's Ryan running around loose, for example.''

Ryan closed his eyes for a moment, caught between anger, embarrassment and a quick, unexpected urge to laugh. God, you had to hand it to the old man, he sure knew how to get down to brass tacks.

When he opened his eyes, he looked at Shelly, half expecting her to respond with a flash of that temper he'd once known so well. But she looked more startled than angry. When she glanced at Ryan, he smiled ruefully and lifted one shoulder in a slight shrug. She laughed a little.

''If I'm ever in the market for a husband, I'll keep that in mind.''

Tucker spoke quickly, asking her a question about an actor she'd mentioned working with, changing the subject before Nathan could say anything else and reminding Ryan of why they'd been friends for so many years.

When Shelly set aside her empty cup a short time later and said that she had to be going, he was unabashedly glad to see her go. If she was smart, she would keep her distance and give Nathan time to recover from this temporary insanity.

"I'd nearly forgotten how early the day starts out here," she said, smiling. "Ray wants me to ride out with him in the morning and take a look at some cattle he'd like to isolate for some kind of breeding program. I'm just hoping he doesn't expect me to offer any brilliant opinions, especially not first thing in the morning."

"He just wants someone to listen while he talks," Tucker said comfortably. "Ray always has liked the sound of his own voice. I'm heading back to the bunkhouse. I'll walk you out to your car."

Nathan sent Ryan a quick, sharp look that Ryan took as a suggestion that *he* should be escorting Shelly out to her car. He ignored the look, barely restraining a sigh of relief when he saw Shelly walk out the door with Tucker.

"You could have said something," Nathan snapped the minute they were alone.

"About what?"

"About anything. You hardly said a word to her."

"I guess I didn't have anything to say." Ryan stacked his cup and Shelly's together.

"She's a damned fine-looking woman."

"Yes, she is."

"Well?" Nathan put a wealth of impatience into the single word.

Ryan picked up the cups with his good hand and

turned to look at his grandfather. He was tired, there was a headache building in his temples, and his arm itched underneath the cast, a refined form of torture that set his teeth on edge. For a moment, temper warred with self-control. Self-control won, but only because he knew Nathan's interference came, at least partially, out of worry.

"This isn't the dark ages. You can't arrange marriages," he said, speaking slowly and distinctly.

"I'm not suggesting you marry her," Nathan said, ignoring the fact that he'd already suggested exactly that. "You could ask her out, at least. It's not like you're seeing another woman."

"Maybe that's because I don't *want* to see one." Ryan knew he was lying even as he said it. He'd been thinking about Maggie ever since this afternoon, cursing himself for not telling her he wanted to see her again. He'd never had trouble asking a woman out before. Then again, other than Sally, he'd never cared all that much about what their response might be. With Maggie, he cared. It was not a comfortable thought.

"I'm going to put this stuff in the kitchen and then go up to bed. I'll see you in the morning." He didn't give his grandfather a chance to continue the discussion but turned and left the room.

The evening could have been worse, he thought

as he climbed the stairs. He could have come down with food poisoning.

"I don't really need an escort to my car," Shelly said, as the front door shut behind her.

"Bunkhouse is on the way." Tucker pulled out his cigarettes and shook one loose from the pack. Despite her comment, he noticed that she waited while he lit the cigarette. He also noticed that the moonlight turned her hair to silver and made deep, mysterious pools of her eyes. And he noticed that, in heels, she was only a little shorter than he was, which put her mouth at a nice level for kissing. If a man was so inclined.

Narrowing his eyes against the smoke, he shook the match out and dropped it into one of the empty planters along the front of the porch. In his lifetime, the planters had never held anything but dirt and an occasional cigarette butt. According to his mother, old Mrs. Lassiter had had a real green thumb and her gardens had turned the big ranch house into a showplace every spring and summer.

"Are you going to walk me to my car or stand there smoking?" Shelly asked impatiently.

"I figured I could do a bit of both," he said thoughtfully, then grinned when she huffed out an irritated breath and stalked off the porch. He followed, lengthening his stride a little until he caught up with her.

She was wearing perfume, something warm and earthy that carried a hint of musk. It made him think of sex, which was, no doubt, exactly what it was intended to do. It irritated him that it had drawn the expected reaction. Just like that swatch of a skirt. There was just enough to it to make a man think about sliding his hands up under it and—

"Oh!" Shelly stumbled on the uneven ground and started to fall. Tucker's arm shot out and caught her around the waist, jerking her back against the hard length of his body.

They were plastered together from chest to thigh. She was reed slim in his arms, all soft skin and thudding heartbeat. He caught the glitter of her eyes in the moonlight and wondered what was in them. His fingers splayed open across her lower back, feeling the heat of her through the thin fabric of blouse and skirt. Her breath seemed to catch, and there was a moment when her body felt fluid in his arms. And then her palms flattened against his chest and she was pushing against him. She took a quick step back as soon as he released her.

"Thank you," she said breathlessly.

"My pleasure," he drawled, and had the pleasure of knowing the comment annoyed her.

They covered the remaining few yards to her car in silence. Shelly got her keys out of the tiny purse she carried. "Thank you for walking me to my car," she said politely.

"Sounds like Nathan has plans for you and Ryan," he said, surprising himself.

"I don't know what you mean," Shelly said stiffly.

"Sure you do." Tucker dropped his half-smoked cigarette. The tip glowed red in the darkness for an instant before he ground it out with the toe of his boot. "He wasn't real subtle about suggesting the two of you should get together."

"What does that have to do with you?" She opened the car door and stood on the other side of it, using it as a shield between them.

"Not much, I guess," he admitted. Tucker told himself that this discussion was purely for Ryan's benefit. "I guess, considering the history between you and Ryan, I half expected you to tell the old man just what he could do with his suggestion."

"Ryan and I had something very special once," she said.

"Was that before or after you blacked his eye?" Tucker asked with polite curiosity.

He heard the breath hiss between her teeth and prepared to duck if she took a swing at him. Instead, he could almost feel her gathering the threads of her control. When she spoke, her tone was painfully even.

"I wouldn't expect you to understand," she said stiffly.

"Would Ryan?" he asked dryly.

"I don't know why I even bother trying to talk to you," she snarled, abandoning dignity for honesty. "You're the most obnoxious man I've ever met in my life."

"Nice to know I'm the best at something," he said, grinning.

With a frustrated snarl, she slid into the car and slammed the door. When the engine roared to life, he stepped back cautiously. Considering her temper, he wouldn't be surprised if she tried to run him over. But either age had mellowed her or she didn't want to risk damaging her car, because she didn't attempt vehicular homicide but simply swung the car in a wide circle and drove out of the yard without so much as a glance in his direction.

Tucker pulled out his cigarettes as he watched the taillights recede. Tapping one loose, he struck a match and cupped his hands around the flame as he lifted it. Inhaling, he lifted his head to watch the last faint trace of red disappear as Shelly turned onto the highway.

If Ryan was looking for Shelly to help him discourage his grandfather, he could be in trouble.

Chapter Seven

Some days it just didn't make sense to get out of bed. When she woke to find a dead mouse on the pillow next to hers, courtesy of a proud and purring Max, Maggie should have known better than to get up. Of course, since the sight of the mouse had sent her springing from the bed as if jabbed with a cattle prod, it had probably been too late, even then, to stop the day from taking its course.

Perhaps when she dropped the blow-dryer in the sink she could have decided to at least stay home. But no, she'd unplugged it, fished it out of its watery grave and deposited it in the trash, telling herself it was old anyway and wasn't it a good thing it hadn't been turned on.

Or she could have taken the hint when she'd

realized that the milk was sour only *after* she poured it on her cereal. It didn't take a seer to read the signs that the stars were not in her favor. But, instead of creeping back to her bed—now sans mouse—and pulling the covers over her head, Maggie dumped out the cereal, had an apple for breakfast and headed out to work.

It was a mistake.

It wasn't that anything went terribly wrong. It was more a case of nothing going particularly right. Saturdays were usually busy, and this one was no exception. Bill's opened for breakfast at seven o'clock. At a quarter after, the woman who was supposed to work the morning shift with Maggie called to say that her youngest had been up most of the night with a stomach flu and she couldn't leave him. By eight Maggie felt as if she'd worn a path to the kitchen, delivering orders and picking them up.

Local ranchers were joined by truckers driving north into Montana and Idaho or south into Colorado, and campers heading into the nearby mountains. Everyone was going somewhere, and they all wanted to eat their breakfast as quickly as possible so they could get back on the road.

Maggie poured coffee, brought cream and sugar, and took orders: *eggs over easy, bacon crisp, extra butter on the toast; eggs scrambled, sausage and some of them fried potatoes; eggs over hard, a slab of ham, a mess of potatoes and throw in a handful of them hot peppers Bill keeps hidden.* She smiled, exchanged greetings, scribbled orders, tried to remember who was getting what and poured more coffee.

They ran out of sugar halfway through the morning. After a brief acrimonious exchange between Bill and the cook, who also happened to be his brother, about the importance of keeping track of supplies, one of the customers volunteered to make a trip to the General Store to get a sack of sugar. No sooner was that small crisis resolved than Maggie dropped a coffeepot. Considering how the day had gone, the only surprise was that it hadn't been brim full of scalding coffee. As it was, getting her feet and ankles splattered with lukewarm coffee seemed par for the course, as did cutting her finger while picking up the broken glass.

The morning continued pretty much as it had begun. There were no major disasters but plenty of minor annoyances. Spilled coffee, a salt shaker lid loosened by some clever child that came off and turned a plate of bacon and eggs into a salt lick, the cash register drawer stuck shut—it was just one of those days when nothing seemed to go quite the way it should.

It was past one o'clock before Maggie had a chance to sit down. She couldn't quite hold back a sigh of relief as she settled onto a bar stool. Bill was behind the bar, talking on the phone. Walter and Ernie were playing pool. No one was signaling for coffee, dessert or their check. There were a couple of tables that needed to be cleared, but they could wait.

Flexing her toes inside her coffee-stained sneakers, Maggie listened to Mary Chapin Carpenter telling the world that she felt lucky and wished she could say the same. At the moment, all *she* felt was exhausted.

"Delivery truck broke an axle somewhere outside of Casper," Bill said, wheeling his chair over to her end of the bar. "They said they can't get a new truck out here until Monday. You figure we'll have a riot if we run out of beer?"

"Considering the way things have gone today, I'd expect a riot even if you *didn't* run out of beer." Maggie gratefully accepted the glass of Coke he set on the bar in front of her. She took a deep swallow, letting the carbonation burn through the dryness in her throat. When she set the glass down, she fixed him with a serious look. "Do you believe in omens?"

Bill's eyebrows rose in surprise. "I don't guess I've ever given it much thought. Why?"

"Max left a dead mouse on my pillow this morning," she said gloomily. "I think it was a sign. What can you really expect from a day that starts out like that?"

"It wasn't a great start to the mouse's day, either," Bill returned, grinning.

Maggie laughed and shook her head. "I suppose it wasn't." She took another swallow of the soft drink and felt some of the tension ease out of her shoulders. The threat of a headache lurked behind her eyes but it wasn't insistent enough for her to expend the effort to get an aspirin.

Bill lit a cigarette from the pack he kept behind the bar, one of five he allowed himself each day. Mary Chapin Carpenter gave way to Hank Williams crooning that he was so lonesome he could cry. Had to be Walter's quarter, Bill thought. Walter had once met Hank Williams, and there wasn't anyone he'd met in the forty-odd years since who hadn't heard the tale of their encounter, usually more than once.

Bill glanced across the bar at Maggie and debated with himself before speaking. He generally kept a strict policy of noninterference in other people's lives. In his experience, interference, no matter how well-intentioned, was more likely to create a problem than to solve one. Then again, he'd grown fond of Maggie. He didn't want to see her get hurt.

He exhaled smoke and spoke casually. "Burt Miller came in yesterday."

"How's his arthritis?" Maggie asked. "It was bothering him a bit last time I saw him."

"Seemed to be doing better." Bill flicked ash off the cigarette. "Said you told him walking might help it some."

"I read an article in a health magazine." Maggie flexed her toes back and forth and fantasized about taking off her shoes.

"Well, Burt went out walking the other day. Said he saw you and Ryan Lassiter in the park."

Maggie's toes froze midflex. From Bill's tone, it was obvious that Burt hadn't seen the two of them just sitting on a blanket eating sandwiches.

"Did he?" She could feel the color creeping up in her cheeks, giving the lie to her casual tone.

"You can tell me it's none of my business." Bill was already wishing he hadn't brought the subject up. It *wasn't* any of his business. It was just that there was something so damned...vulnerable about Maggie. She was so busy looking out for everyone else that he wasn't sure it occurred to her that she could use some looking after herself.

"I'd never tell you that," she said, reaching out to touch his hand where it rested on the bar.

"Well, you probably should," he said gruffly. "I just don't want to see you get hurt. Like I said before, Ryan's a good man, but he comes with a load of baggage. Any woman who gets involved with him ought to know that."

"We're not involved." She caught his arched brow and flushed. "Well, we're not," she insisted. "We just happened to bump into each other at the store. That's all."

"From what Burt said, you bumped into each other at the park, too," Bill said dryly. He lifted his hand when she started to speak. "It really isn't any of my business. You don't owe me—or anyone else—an explanation. Like I said, I just don't want to see you get hurt."

"I appreciate that." Maggie might have said more, but one of the customers called her name and, when she glanced over her shoulder, held up his cup for more coffee. Swallowing the urge to groan, she slid off the bar stool. "Back to the salt mines," she murmured.

The interruption was probably a good thing, she thought, as she got the coffeepot and made the rounds of the few occupied tables, refilling cups. There wasn't really much point in discussing her relationship with Ryan, especially since she wasn't sure they had one. It had been over a week since their picnic, and she hadn't heard from him. She refused to allow herself to be hurt by his silence. At least she could be sure he hadn't called Noreen. Her sister would have taken great pleasure in letting her know if he had.

Maggie glanced up as the door opened and felt a twinge of disappointment when Virgil Mortenson walked in. She hadn't seen him in several days, and she'd allowed herself to hope that he was spending the time contemplating the foolishness of drinking his life away. Stupid, she told herself. It was stupid to think that a problem as serious as Virgil's was just going to go away. With a sigh, she walked over to his booth.

"Virgil. Haven't seen you in a while."

"Hi, Maggie." He shot a quick look up at her and then looked away. "I've been gone a few days. Went to see my sister over to Casper."

"I didn't know you had family in Casper."

"Just a sister." He picked restlessly at a loose piece of veneer near the edge of the table. "She's older than me by a good bit. Half raised me, I guess."

"The two of you are close?"

Virgil shrugged. His eyes slid to her face and then away. "Used to be. Hadn't seen her in a while."

"It must have been nice to visit with her." This was the most conversation Maggie had ever heard out of the man, and she had a feeling it was going somewhere, but she couldn't figure out where.

"She says I'm a damn fool," Virgil said abruptly. "Says I ain't worth spit."

Maggie blinked. Now what was she supposed to say to that? "I doubt if she means it quite like that," she said cautiously. "I imagine she's worried about you."

"Ain't nothin' to worry about." Catching her disbelieving look, he flushed and jerked one shoulder in a half shrug. "I got a job and a place to live, don't I?"

"Maybe your sister thinks there's a bit more to life than that."

"Maybe." An inch square chunk of veneer suddenly broke off in his fingers and he stared at it in surprise for a moment before giving her a sheepish look. Her lips curving in a reluctant smile, she held out her hand.

"Sorry about that," he said, giving her the broken piece.

"Can I get you something to eat, or did you just feel like ruining the decor?"

"I'll have a hamburger," he said.

Maggie's smile widened. "Rare with a side of fries? You want something to drink with that?"

"Water will do."

"No milk?" she asked teasingly. He flushed and

grinned a little, giving her a glimpse of the man he had once been.

"Water's good enough."

Maggie's smile lingered as she walked away from the table. She wasn't foolish enough to think Virgil was miraculously cured, but at least he seemed to be getting closer to admitting that there was a problem. That had to be an improvement.

Gravel crunched under the tires as Maggie pulled her car into the driveway. It was midafternoon, and she had the next two days off. She shut the engine off and leaned her head back against the seat, savoring the silence. If she never again heard anyone ask her for a cup of coffee, never had to clean up another spilled drink or carry another stack of dishes, she could die a happy woman.

She released her breath on a long sigh and opened her eyes. Clear, shadowless sunlight filtered through the clouds that had built up over the mountains. It was supposed to rain, but she was hoping it would hold off until evening. She'd promised herself an afternoon with her camera, and Bill had told her about a road that led into the foothills, where she was likely to see some wildlife. Something a little bigger than a chipmunk, hopefully. She frowned. Thinking about chipmunks reminded her of Ryan and churned up more emotion than she wanted to deal with at the moment.

Maggie shook her head as she reached for the door handle. She wasn't going to think about Ryan or Virgil or her aching feet another minute. All she wanted right now was to relax and take some pictures. The light was wonderful. If the rain would just hold off long enough for her to get her camera and drive out to the area Bill had told her about, the day could at least end on a decent note.

She was almost past the living room archway when the silence penetrated. The chatter of the television was such a constant that its absence was actually startling. Lydia even left it running on the rare occasions when she left the house, because she didn't like to come home to silence. The only time she turned it off was when she went to bed and even then, she turned on the small set in her bedroom.

Curious, Maggie shifted course toward the living room. She heard her mother's giggle as she stepped into the room. Lydia was sitting on the edge of the sofa, leaning forward to look at something on the coffee table. Noreen was sprawled bonelessly in an easy chair, her long jeans-clad legs stretched out in front of her, her eyes narrowed against the smoke that spiraled lazily upward from the cigarette in her hand.

"Look, it says there's dancing every night under the stars." Lydia's voice bubbled with excitement. "I love to dance."

"You should get yourself a dress with a floaty skirt, something that clings to a guy's legs when you dance. That kind of thing turns them on."

Lydia giggled. "Something pink. I love pink."

"Pink it is." Noreen saw Maggie just then, and her pale blue eyes glittered with sudden amusement. "Look who's here."

"Maggie!" Lydia's eyes flared wide in sudden alarm, and she leaped to her feet, putting herself between Maggie and the coffee table as if trying to hide its contents. "When did you get home?"

"Just now." Maggie looked past her to the colorful brochures scattered across the scarred blond wood of the table. She smiled questioningly. "What's going on?"

"Mom's got good news," Noreen said. Her mouth curved as she exhaled a cloud of smoke.

"Mom?"

Lydia's eyes darted back and forth, as if looking for an escape route. "I... Well, I thought... I mean, we both—"

"Mom's putting the house up for sale." Noreen cut through Lydia's stammering. She sat up and leaned forward to stub her cigarette out in the dented metal ashtray that sat on the edge of the coffee table. "She's going to take the money and go to L.A., get herself an apartment, some new clothes, take a cruise and hook up with a good-looking man with enough money to support her in style."

"That's right." Now that the news was out, Lydia's spine straightened and her chin came up. She shot Maggie a defiant look. "That's what I'm going to do."

"And what if she doesn't find this good-looking, wealthy man?" Maggie looked past her mother and directed the question to Noreen. "What's she going to do then?"

Noreen lifted her slim shoulders in a shrug. "Nothing ventured, nothing gained. Besides, I'm betting Mom can rope herself an old coot without much effort."

"Not too old," Lydia protested with a giggle.

"Not too old." Noreen's smile widened. "With a new haircut and some nice clothes, she'll have them panting after her."

"And while you're helping her buy this wardrobe, I suppose you'll help yourself to some new things, maybe tuck a few dollars away in your own bank account?" Maggie didn't try to hide her dislike.

Noreen's eyebrows rose in surprise at the bite in

her sister's voice. "If Mom wants to give me a little something, I won't say no."

"Of course I'll want to give her something," Lydia said, flashing Maggie an indignant look. "Why wouldn't I? She's my daughter."

So am I, Maggie thought. But she didn't say it out loud. What was the point? She waited for the hurt she always felt when her mother made it clear—yet again—that she came in a very poor second to Noreen. But there was no hurt there. Instead, there was...nothing.

Startled, she looked at Lydia and Noreen and realized that something had shifted inside her. She felt as if she were looking at them from the other side of a fence. It had always been that way. For as long as she could remember, her mother and Noreen had been on one side of that fence and she'd been on the other, always apart. Standing there, in the shabby little living room, it hit her suddenly that she was the only one who'd ever been interested in finding a way through that fence.

"It's my house," Lydia said defiantly. She snatched up a cruise brochure and held it clutched in one hand like a weapon, ready to fend off any arguments Maggie might offer. "I can do anything I want with it."

Maggie looked at her and saw a once pretty woman who looked older than her fifty years. Dark roots showed along the part in her hair, and her makeup had been carelessly applied—streaks of blusher angled across her cheekbones, mascara clumped her thinning lashes together, and a heavy line of black eyeliner made her eyes look smaller than they were. A girlish pout emphasized the lines of discontent that bracketed her mouth. Noreen sat behind her, her full lips curved in a smug little smile, her eyes bright with malice, smoke curling up from her cigarette.

She was tired of both of them, Maggie realized suddenly. Tired of her sister's shallow, grasping nature, tired of her mother's refusal to grow up, tired of pretending that she had anything to say to either of them. Blood alone couldn't make a family. The realization left her almost light-headed with relief. She didn't have to try anymore, didn't have to wonder what was wrong with her. She didn't have to care.

"You're right," Maggie said. She looked at Lydia and felt nothing at all. No anger. No regret. Just nothing. "It *is* your house, and you can do anything you want with it. I'll start looking for another place to live."

She had the satisfaction of seeing shock wipe the smug smile from Noreen's mouth. But she found she didn't much care about that anymore, either. It just didn't matter. She turned and walked away without waiting for a response.

Maggie kept her mind a careful blank as she went to her room and got her camera. She knew there were things she needed to think about, decisions she would have to make, but, for now, she just wanted to get out of this house.

She heard Lydia's voice and caught the sound of her own name as she walked down the hall. She sounded upset, and Maggie felt a vague sense of amusement that her acceptance of her mother's plans had probably caused more distress than if she'd argued. Lydia fell abruptly silent when Maggie walked past the doorway, but Maggie didn't slow her pace or glance into the room. She picked up her purse from the table where she'd dropped it when she came in—*God, was that less than ten minutes ago?*—and walked out the door.

She started the car but didn't immediately put it in gear. Resting her hands on top of the steering wheel, she looked out the windshield at the blue line of the mountains, her eyes blank, her thoughts tangled. She felt hollowed out inside, empty. A chapter of her life had just closed, she realized.

Where was she going from here?

Ryan paused just inside the door of Bill's Place to let his eyes adjust to the low light. Outside, the

late afternoon sun was slanting under a heavy layer
of thunderheads, casting a sharp, oddly clear light
across the foothills.

"Hey, Ryan." Bill wheeled his chair out of the
kitchen, a plastic tray of clean glasses balanced on
his lap.

"Hey, Bill. How are things going?" Ryan settled onto a bar stool and watched Bill wheel his
chair up onto the ramp and set the tray on the
counter behind the bar.

"Better than they were. It was one of those
mornings." Bill rolled his head from side to side,
stretching the kinks out of his neck. "Hey, when
did you get the cast off?" he asked, nodding toward Ryan's arm.

"This morning." Ryan flexed the muscles in his
arm, felt the weakness there and was impatient with
it. Time would take care of that, he reminded himself.

"You want to arm wrestle?" Bill asked, grinning.

Ryan laughed. "Not quite yet. I figure a five-
year-old girl could probably whip me right about
now. Thanks," he said as Bill set a glass of Coke
in front of him.

"You going back on the circuit, now that you're
back in fighting shape?" Bill asked. He began unloading the tray, the clink of glass against glass a

muted counterpoint to George Strait singing about Adelida on the jukebox.

"I don't know." Ryan slid his fingers down the sides of the glass, feeling the dampness of condensation there. "Wasn't going to, but I'm not so sure anymore." Because it was Bill, he could ask the question. "Do you still miss it?"

"Me?" Bill arched his brows in surprise, his hands going still. "No. Not for a long time now. Missed it like hell when this first happened." He thumped the heel of his hand lightly against one arm of the wheelchair. "I know it sounds crazy, but I missed the damn bulls almost as much as I missed walking." His smile was lopsided. "I never felt more alive in all my life than when I was on top of all that angry beef."

"Bull riders are all crazy," Ryan said, smiling a little. He knew what Bill meant. Those eight seconds under the lights were like nothing else on earth. There was nothing but you and the animal beneath you. But there was more to life than rodeo. He'd had his time in the arena, and he wanted something else now.

"No regrets?"

"About this?" Bill thumped the wheelchair again. "None I can't live with. It's the mind that makes a man a cripple. Never the body. I had a good life before I landed in this. I've had a good life since. Can't stay on the circuit forever, any-way."

"No, I guess not." Ryan stared broodingly at the rows of bottles that lined the back of the bar. Everything had seemed much simpler when he was lying in the emergency room waiting for them to set his arm. He would go home and settle into place at the Double L. But it wasn't working out that way. He and his grandfather had been at odds from the start, and now the old man had this crazy notion that he was going to marry Shelly Taylor, an idea he pushed at every opportunity. Even his damned horse was still eyeing him as if he were the devil incarnate.

He could buy a place of his own, he thought. He had a healthy bank account—conscience money from his parents over the last twenty years. He'd never touched any of it, didn't even know exactly how much was there, but it would certainly be enough for a down payment on a place of his own. Maybe someplace in Montana. There was some pretty country up there.

Except he didn't want to live in Montana. And he didn't want a place of his own. The Double L was home—*his* home, damn it. That was where he wanted to stay, where he wanted to start breeding and training a line of fine cutting horses, where, someday, God willing, he wanted to raise his children. His grandfather was certainly right about one thing—it was time to let go of the past, but that didn't mean he was going to let the old man direct his future.

"Maggie isn't here," Bill said, making Ryan aware that he'd been looking at the kitchen doorway, half expecting her to walk through it, though he already knew her car wasn't in the parking lot.

"What makes you think I'm looking for Maggie?" he asked, irritated at having his thoughts so easily read.

Bill arched a bushy gray brow. "Seemed a likely possibility, what with the way you two were going at it in the park the other day."

"We weren't 'going at it.' I kissed her." Ryan scowled. "Doesn't anybody in this town have anything better to do than go around minding each other's business?"

"You stand around in a public park, in the middle of the day, kissing a girl, and somebody's bound to notice," Bill observed mildly.

Ryan couldn't argue with the truth of that, but he didn't have to like it. He drank some of his Coke and scowled some more. Bill set the empty tray aside and reached for his cigarettes. He tapped one out and lit it, savoring the taste as he eyed Ryan through a thin curtain of smoke.

"You got any plans as far as Maggie's concerned?"

"Christ, are you asking me what my intentions are?" Shock had Ryan gaping at him.

"More or less," Bill said calmly. "I'm fond of her. She's too busy looking out for everyone else to do it for herself, and her family ain't worth spit."

"I met the sister," Ryan said, remembering Noreen's pale eyes and painted-on clothes.

"That one." Bill snorted with contempt. "She worked here for a while, but her take on serial monogamy was a little too loose for my taste. New man just about every night. Didn't want that kind of trouble in my place, so I fired her skinny ass. I'll tell you what, though." He gestured with the cigarette. "She's cold as ice under all that surface heat. I know more than one cowboy who ended up handing his paycheck over to her. If she was honest, she'd hang out a red light and advertise in the yellow pages." The cigarette jabbed again in Ryan's direction, ash quivering on its tip. "The mother now, she hardly ever sets foot out of the house, as far as I can tell. I've seen her a time or two—reminds me of Bette Davis in some of her later movies—frizzy blond hair, bad makeup and rump sprung pants." He shook his head. "And then there's Maggie, sweet as honey and honest as the day is long. I haven't figured that one out yet."

"Hard to figure families, sometimes," Ryan said. He frowned at his half-empty glass. "And to answer your question, I don't have any particular plans where Maggie is concerned. Not that it's any of your damned business."

"Probably not," Bill agreed comfortably. "But I don't want to see her hurt. Maggie's not the sort for casual affairs. Probably get me hung by some women's lib group, but the fact is, she's the marrying kind. The kind of woman who needs picket fences and—"

"Flowery curtains and a fire in the fireplace," Ryan finished irritably, remembering Doug's words the day they'd met Maggie.

"That's about right." Bill was undisturbed by the other man's sharp tone.

Ryan finished the last of his drink and set the glass back on the bar with a sharp snap. "I'll consider myself warned," he said.

"Not warned," Bill said calmly. "More of a reminder. It's on the house." He waved away the bill Ryan pulled out of his pocket. "A fair trade. You didn't pop me in the nose when I poked it in where it didn't belong."

Ryan grinned reluctantly and shoved the bill

back into his pocket. "Are you kidding? I figure you could still take me."

"Could be." Bill watched Ryan slide off the bar stool. "I told Maggie about that meadow up on Bartleson Creek," he said casually. "I think she was taking her camera up there this afternoon." He drew in smoke and exhaled slowly. "Just in case anyone's interested."

"Just in case," Ryan repeated dryly. Lifting one hand in farewell, he left the bar.

While he was inside, the clouds had finished sliding across the mountains, swallowing up the sunlight. The wind had picked up, and rain was starting to spit. Thunder rumbled in the distance. This time of year, thunderstorms rolled up fairly often, sometimes bringing rain, sometimes just putting on a show before drifting off. This one looked like it was carrying a fair amount of moisture.

Ryan put the key in the ignition of the truck and started it. Maggie might not be prepared for a storm, he thought, gravel crunching under the tires as he backed out of the parking space. Three years wasn't really long enough to get a feel for the vagaries of Wyoming weather. Flash floods could be a danger. Roads sometimes washed out. And a plague of locusts might descend and devour her car, he thought, both amused and irritated at his own capacity for self-deceit. Why couldn't he just admit that he wanted to see her?

By the time he turned off the highway and onto the narrow dirt road that cut across the south end of the Rayczeks' place, rain was falling steadily and Ryan was feeling foolish. Lightning flashed, thunder rumbling hard on its heels. No doubt Maggie had seen the storm coming and headed home a long time ago. Even a weather-challenged Californian could have seen it coming. He was driving out here for nothing, he thought, as the truck rattled across a cattle guard. He was going to feel damned stupid if he was the one who ended up caught in a flash flood, or if he got the truck stuck in the mud, leaving him with a long, soggy walk back to town. As soon as he came to a wide spot in the road, he was going to turn around and head back to town. There was no way Maggie was still out here.

He topped out on a long, shallow hill, and there was the familiar blue compact sitting halfway down the other side. Not sure if he should be relieved or sorry, Ryan steered the truck to a halt next to the car, unconcerned that he was blocking the road. Two vehicles were more traffic than this road normally saw in a month.

Ryan felt a twinge of concern when he didn't see Maggie sitting behind the wheel. Unless she had an underwater camera, it didn't seem likely that she would be out trying to take pictures in this weather. His eyes skimmed over the car, found the flat rear tire and moved on, widening in disbelief at the bedraggled figure sitting on a rock beside the edge of the road.

He set the emergency brake automatically and slid out of the truck. Rain pelted his head, sliding under the collar of his black work shirt and dripping off the brim of his hat. Maggie watched him approach, but she made no move to rise.

"What's wrong?" He crouched down, reaching out to slide his hands over her arms, left bare by the short sleeves of her shirt, seeking signs of injury. "Are you hurt?"

"I have a flat tire." She blinked at him through lashes clumped together by rain. *And tears?* he wondered, seeing something lost and alone in her eyes.

"I saw it. Why are you sitting out here?"

"I couldn't break the lug nuts loose." Her breath hitched, confirming his guess that she'd been crying. "I know how to change a tire, but I couldn't get the damned nuts loose."

"Let's get you inside," he said, wrapping one arm around her shoulders and drawing her to her feet.

"And I locked myself out of the car," she said,

letting him lead her across the road. "I couldn't change the tire, and I locked myself out of the car, and then it started to rain." Her voice wobbled pathetically.

Not that he could blame her, he thought, torn between laughter and sympathy. A flat tire, a stubborn lug nut, locking her keys in the car and then the rain—it was enough to drive anyone to tears.

"Let's get you dry, then we'll worry about the car." He put his hand under her elbow, giving her a boost up into the seat.

Maggie scooted under the steering wheel and across the truck's bench seat. "I'm getting your upholstery wet," she said as Ryan slid in behind her and pulled the door shut. He pulled off his hat and balanced it on the dash behind the steering wheel.

"It'll dry." He reached into the storage area behind the seat and pulled out a towel that looked fairly clean. "Here. You can dry off with this." A little more scrounging turned up an incredibly wrinkled blue flannel shirt. He sniffed it cautiously. It smelled a little dusty but seemed in reasonably good shape otherwise, unless you counted the fact that the collar was worn through and one cuff was half torn off. Under the circumstances, he didn't think Maggie would care about the garment's worn condition.

Maggie used the towel to wipe water off her arms and then blotted the worst of the moisture from her hair, grateful for the excuse to keep her head lowered while she grabbed for the tattered threads of her self-control.

She didn't have a very clear memory of how she'd ended up sitting on a rock beside the road, rain and tears pouring down her face. She remembered peering through the window to see her keys dangling in the ignition just as the first drops of rain began to fall. She hadn't even been surprised, had in fact, thought that it was the obvious thing to happen considering the way the day had been going. What else could you expect from a day that started out with a dead mouse on your pillow and ended up with the realization that your only blood relatives were shallow, grasping people whom you would really rather not know?

Her eyes stung with fresh tears, and Maggie tried to sniff them back discreetly. Ryan must already think she was a loon. She didn't have to add to her already stellar performance by sniveling all over him. She rubbed the towel over her hair with more vigor and squeezed her eyes shut, willing back the tears.

"You're going to end up bald if you keep that up." Ryan's hand closed over hers, stilling her movements. He tugged at the towel, and Maggie's fingers tightened convulsively over the thin terry cloth for a moment before releasing it. He dropped the towel on the seat between them and brought his hand back up, ignoring her small resistance as he set his fingers under her chin and tilted her face up.

Maggie thought about keeping her eyes squeezed shut in the childish hope that, if she couldn't see him, he couldn't see her, but she couldn't quite convince herself that it would work that way. With a sigh that caught in the middle, she opened her eyes and looked at him.

The storm filled the cab of the truck with clear, gray light that seemed to catch in the blue of his eyes. Late afternoon stubble shadowed the hard line of his jaw. Maggie wanted to stroke her fingers over that very masculine roughness and then maybe brush back the thick wave of dark hair that fell onto his forehead. He was, she thought, almost beautiful. And she must look like something the cat had dragged in, with her mascara running and her eyes red from crying and her hair sticking out from her head like Don King caught in a high wind.

"One of those days?" Ryan asked, and the sympathy in that midnight dark voice had tears filling her eyes again.

"It started out with a dead mouse on my pillow

and went downhill from there,'' she said, trying to smile.

"A dead mouse?'' His eyes widened in surprise.

"And then I dropped my hair dryer in the sink and the milk was sour and Michelle called in sick, and I dropped a coffeepot and everyone wanted coffee or their eggs cooked more or the bacon cooked less.'' Her voice was starting to hitch, but she was on a roll and couldn't stop now. "And Virgil came in and...said he went to see his sister...and he actually...talked to me, and I thought...he was doing better, but then he ordered a Jack...Daniel's. I know he's not my responsibility, but I just...hate the way he's wasting himself.'' She took the handkerchief he held out and swiped at her eyes. "When I got home, I found out my mother is...selling the house and going on some...cruise. She thinks she's going to...trap a studly dude and live happily...ever after. And Noreen's encouraging her...but she just wants...the money. And she's going to be left with...nothing. And...she doesn't love me.'' She was starting to sob now, but the words still tumbled out. "I've spent all these damned years trying to make her love me, but she doesn't even want to and I...I don't care anymore. I said was moving out.'' Maggie could hear her voice rising and knew she was going to hate herself later, but nothing short of clamping her hands over her mouth could stop the flow of words now. "And I'm twenty-three and...I don't have any ambition and I don't...want to be a waitress for the rest of my life." She ended on a squeak as her voice became completely suspended by tears. Sniffling, she buried her face in the handkerchief.

Mildly dazed by the flow of words, Ryan stared at her for a moment, his mind blank. "Do they carry studly dude traps at the feed store?" he asked finally, saying the first thing that popped into his head.

Caught midsob, Maggie choked out a laugh. "Even more important, do they carry bait?" She drew a shuddering breath and forced a smile. "I'm sorry to be such an idiot. It's just been one of those days."

"It sounds like finding a dead mouse on your pillow was the high point."

Maggie's smile was less shaky this time, and the tears receded another notch. "Just about."

"If you don't mind my asking, how did you end up with a mouse on your pillow? Did the little guy just walk up there and expire?"

"It was a present from Max. My cat," she explained, when his eyebrows rose.

"Breakfast in bed, anyone?" Ryan felt unreasonably pleased with himself when she gave a watery chuckle.

He was pathetically grateful that she'd stopped crying. It was a cliché, but he would rather face a raging Brahma bull than deal with a woman's tears. His mother had used them as a tool to get her what she wanted, and by the time his parents left him with his grandfather, he'd grown indifferent to her tears. Sally hadn't cried often, but when she did, her tears were as stormy as her temper and usually gone just as quickly. She'd given in to them easily and forgotten them as soon as they ended. Maggie struggled against her tears as if they were an enemy to be vanquished, as if giving in to them was a weakness to be fought.

She dabbed his handkerchief under her eyes in a futile attempt to repair the damage wrought by rain and tears. "I must look like a raccoon," she muttered self-consciously.

He tilted his head and eyed her thoughtfully. "There's a passing resemblance," he said, and the unexpected honesty startled another laugh from her.

"Put this on." Ryan helped her slide into the shirt, laughing when the dust made her sneeze. He rolled the cuffs back to expose her hands, but there was nothing he could do about the fact that the body of the garment was nearly big enough for two of her. One corner of his mouth kicked up in a smile. With her hair tumbling around her face in damp curls, dark smudges of mascara under her eyes, and his shirt swallowing her small frame, she looked like an orphan in an old silent movie. All it needed was a villain to twirl his mustache and laugh evilly.

He took the crumpled handkerchief out of her hand and held a corner of it up to her mouth. "Lick."

Maggie obediently licked, then sat still while he rubbed the damp cotton gently under her eyes. "You got your cast off," she said, realizing suddenly what was different about him. "When did you get it off?"

"This morning." He sat back and looked at her critically. "Better."

"Thanks." She reached out to touch his arm. "How does it feel?"

"Puny." He smiled at her concerned look. "It takes a little while to get the strength back. I've been through this before."

"It must be nice to have it off, though."

"Can't say I miss it."

"No." Exhausted by the emotional storms, Maggie sat back against the seat and listened to the rain drum against the roof. The lightning came more frequently now, and the rumble of thunder followed almost immediately on the heels of each flash.

"The storm's getting closer," she murmured, half to herself.

At some point she was going to feel horribly embarrassed by all this, Maggie thought. She had made a complete fool of herself. If there had been any chance that Ryan wanted to see more of her, she'd put an end to it. Tomorrow she would regret that. But right now she was just grateful for his kindness, and she felt too drained to worry about anything else.

"What are you doing out here?"

"Bill thought you were coming out this way to take pictures."

So he'd come looking for her. She allowed herself to savor that, though she knew it would only add to her regrets tomorrow. "There was a doe with her fawn," she said sleepily. "I think I got some nice shots of her."

"Good." Ryan reached out to take her hand, toying with her fingers absently. "You like it here, don't you? In Wyoming, I mean."

"Very much." She liked the feel of him holding her hand, too. "I can't imagine living in a city again."

He slid his fingers between hers, loosened his hold, then tightened it again. She rolled her head against the seat to look at him. He was looking down at their clasped hands, his dark brows drawn together in a frown. She wondered what he was thinking and then decided she might not like the answer to that question.

He looked up suddenly, his blue eyes pinning her to the seat. "Do you like to gamble, Maggie?"

"I haven't done much of it," Maggie said, confused. Did he want to play cards? "I played poker once, but I could never remember whether a straight beat a flush or vice versa."

"I'm not talking about poker." His fingers tightened over hers, and his smile had a reckless edge to it that made Maggie's pulse speed. "What do you think of Vegas?"

"I've never been there," she admitted, feeling as if she'd stumbled into the middle of a movie without a script.

"How would you like to go? Now. Tonight."

"Now?" She gaped at him. "What for?"

"What do people usually go to Vegas for?"

"To see Siegfried and Roy?"

Ryan laughed and caught her other hand in his, tugging her around until she sat sideways on the seat, facing him. "To get married. They go to Vegas to get married."

"I've heard that rumor," she agreed cautiously.

Had they given him some kind of drug when they took the cast off?

"Let's do it," he said, still with that reckless light in his eyes.

"Do what?" she asked blankly.

"Get married." When she just stared at him, those soft gray eyes wide with shock, he grinned crookedly. "I'm asking you to marry me, Maggie."

Chapter Eight

*S*tress, Maggie thought. *That's what it is. I'm having a stress-induced hallucination. Or maybe I've been struck by lightning and this is some kind of life after death experience.*

She frowned down at the dusty flannel shirt that draped across her lap like a skirt. Shouldn't she be wearing a long white robe? How could she possibly have a meaningful after-death experience while dressed like a lumberjack?

"Maggie?" Ryan squeezed her hands, and she struggled to force her rambling thoughts to focus. At least it was a pleasant hallucination. She could have imagined she was being interviewed by Jerry Springer or was trapped in an old television sitcom. Having Ryan ask her to marry him was certainly better than listening to Darrin whine at Samantha, or finding herself on that stupid floral bus with the Partridge Family.

"I know it sounds a little crazy," Ryan was saying.

"A *little* crazy?" Maggie's laugh held traces of hysteria. She tugged her hands free and ran them through her damp hair, tousling it into an even wilder tumble of curls. "Try insane, nuts, utterly mad, ridiculous—" She broke off and looked at him, her heartbeat accelerating as it sank in that he'd actually just asked her to marry him.

"You're serious, aren't you?" she whispered.

"I'm serious." Ryan's grin was rueful, but his gaze was steady. He didn't look like a man who'd just lost his mind.

"I don't—we can't—it's—" Aware that she was starting to babble, Maggie stopped and took a slow breath, pressing one hand to her chest, trying to slow her pounding heart. "Why?"

Good question, Ryan thought. It would be nice if he could give her a logical, rational response. He didn't even know where the idea had come from. Suddenly it had been there, and it had—inexplicably—made sense. He was going on nothing but gut instinct—and maybe just a touch of insanity, he admitted. Buying time, he reached for the hand that lay on her knee. Toying with her fingers, he

wrong with wanting a home and a family.'' Ryan was suddenly aware of how much he wanted just those things himself.

His grandfather was right, he thought. He had been running for the last four years. Hell, the old bastard was even right about it being time for him to get married again.

But he wasn't going to tie himself up with Shelly Taylor. Even if she proved willing, he wasn't interested. Shelly, with her long legs and near perfect features, left him cold. Looking at Maggie, with her hair tousled into layers of damp gold curls around her face and her nose pink from crying and that ridiculously fascinating crooked front tooth, he felt something stir in the pit of his stomach—a hunger, a need. Something he couldn't—wouldn't—put a name to. Not just yet, anyway. Whatever it was, he was willing to take a chance on it. And determined to persuade Maggie to take the same chance.

He slid his fingers up her wrist, felt her pulse scramble under his touch. ''There's a small house on the Double L. It's already got a picket fence, and after we're married, you can hang flowered curtains in every window. You can turn the spare bathroom into a darkroom.''

''Ryan—'' Maggie stopped and grabbed hold of her wavering store of common sense. She couldn't possibly be tempted to say yes. Could she? "I can't believe you're serious," she said finally. "You haven't given me a single reason why you'd want to...why you're suggesting that we should—"

"Get married," Ryan supplied, when she had trouble with the words.

"It isn't as if we're in love with each other," she said, careful to keep any hint of question from her tone.

"There's...something between us. That's a start."

So much for any fantasy she might have harbored that he was madly in love with her, Maggie thought ruefully. It was hard to think with him stroking his thumb over the inside of her wrist. She tugged halfheartedly on her hand but didn't insist when his fingers tightened.

"That's not a reason to get married," she said crossly.

"Isn't it?" His free hand came up, sliding under the thick tangle of her hair, his fingers cupping the back of her neck, holding her still as he leaned closer. Not that she was going anywhere, Maggie thought, closing her eyes as his mouth brushed lightly against hers. Ever since that day in the park, she'd been wanting this to happen again.

Ryan kissed her once, and then again. And again. Brief, fleeting touches that promised and teased them both. God, he'd been wanting to do this again. She smelled just the way he remembered, of shampoo and soap—gentle scents that suited her more than any perfume could have. He'd avoided seeing her again, he admitted to himself. He'd avoided it because he didn't want to want her like this. Didn't want to feel this hunger, this need that he could not—would not—put a name to.

But the hunger was there, and need was a fire in his gut. He wasn't going to question or analyze or debate the whys of it. There was no logic to it, no reasoning. He wanted her—not just for this moment but as a part of his life. Marrying her was insane. Mad. A recipe for disaster.

And he would do whatever it took to get her to say yes.

There was nothing teasing about the next kiss. He took her mouth like a conqueror claiming tribute, demanding a response, a surrender. Maggie gave him both.

Her hands came up, fisting in the black fabric of his shirt as her head fell back, her mouth opening to his. Ryan took what she offered and demanded still more. His teeth scraped against her lower lip, and then his tongue was exploring her mouth, tasting her. Taking her.

Maggie felt more than saw the searing white flash of lightning against her closed eyelids, heard the roll of thunder that came immediately after, but nature's tantrum couldn't begin to compete with the heat lancing through her veins and the roar of her own pulse in her ears.

She'd been kissed before. She was nearly sure of it. But it had never been like this. No one had ever kissed her as if the taste of her was everything in the world, as if he had to have her. Her arms crept upward, sliding around his neck as she gave herself over to the swirling magic.

Ryan felt her surrender shoot straight to his loins. He forgot that he was trying to persuade her. Forgot everything but the taste of her and the need for more. More. He could never get enough. His hand swept up her side, his palm cupping the soft weight of her breast. Maggie shuddered and made a soft little sound in her throat, and he cursed the layers of fabric between them—his old shirt, her shirt and bra. He wanted to touch, wanted to taste. He twisted, angling his body into hers, pressing her against the back of the seat.

His elbow smacked against the steering wheel. He tried another angle and banged his knee against the gearshift. Frustration shot through him and then was edged out by humor. It had been a long time since he'd seduced a girl in the front seat of a pickup truck. Seventeen years ago, the logistics of it hadn't seemed nearly so difficult.

With an effort, he grabbed hold of his rapidly fading self-control and dragged his mouth from Maggie's. Leaning his forehead against hers, he managed a raspy laugh.

"We keep this up and I'm going to end up in a cast again."

She made a soft little humming sound in her throat, and her fingers flexed against his shoulders, almost but not quite pulling him toward her. Ryan came within a heartbeat of saying to hell with logistics. But he was after more than this, he reminded himself. A lot more. It took an amazing amount of effort, but he drew back and looked into her dazed eyes.

"Take a gamble, Maggie. Don't analyze it. Don't think about it. Just come to Vegas with me."

Staggered by the strength of the need still humming through her body, Maggie struggled to think clearly. She forced her eyes away from him, but it didn't help. Rain fell in sheets outside, making the interior of the truck dangerously intimate, as if the two of them were trapped in a small world all their own.

"We hardly know each other," she whispered, trying to tell herself that it mattered.

"We can get to know each other after we're married." Ryan brushed her hair back from her face, his fingers lingering on the sensitive skin behind her ear. "Come on, Maggie, take a chance."

Maggie shivered and fought the urge to turn into that light touch. She had to think. He hadn't said he loved her, hadn't promised her eternal happiness. A picket fence and a darkroom. What kind of incentives were those to inspire a woman to throw over a lifetime of common sense?

Who was she kidding? The real incentive—the only one—was sitting in front of her. She was more than halfway to being in love with him already. In the short time since they'd met, he'd worked his way into more than a few of her daydreams. Now, here he was, suggesting a way to make a few of those dreams a reality. Except, in the dreams, he'd been offering love and eternal devotion, not a picket fence and a darkroom.

"Take a chance, Maggie." Ryan slid his hand up her arm, inside the loose sleeve of his old shirt. "Gamble with me," he whispered.

When Maggie was very small, her mother had flirted briefly with becoming religious. At the time, she'd also been flirting with a deeply religious paint salesman from Georgia though Maggie hadn't quite grasped the connection. She just knew that she was suddenly expected to spend her Sunday mornings sitting in a church basement that smelled faintly of mildew, listening to a tall, earnest young man talk about the wages of sin. She'd come away from those sessions with the vague idea that sin paid some sort of salary, like the wages her mother earned working at the diner, and a confirmed dislike of basements.

After a few months the paint salesman had gone back to his wife and four children in Georgia, Lydia had decided that religion wasn't all it was cracked up to be—though she did like the fact that it gave her a chance to dress up once a week—and Maggie's Sunday mornings had been freed.

Nearly twenty years later and over a thousand miles away from that small Detroit church, Maggie suddenly remembered that earnest young man warning a room full of bored, restless children that you had to be on guard, because the devil rarely showed his true colors. Instead, he would sneak up and start whispering temptation in your ear.

She closed her eyes against the image of Ryan wearing horns and a tail.

"We can't just run off to Vegas."

"Why not?"

There were a million reasons, but something about the way he was smiling at her drove all but the weakest of them from her head. "Clothes. We'd need a change of clothes."

"We'll buy whatever we need when we get

there." He brought her hand to his mouth and nibbled on her knuckles.

"My car," she gasped, feeling sanity slipping further away. "I can't just go off and leave my car sitting here."

"I'll call the ranch and have someone come get it."

"The keys are locked in it." The scrape of his teeth against her inner wrist was sending shivers all the way to her toes. "They won't be able to get inside."

"One of the Double L hands did time for car theft. I'm sure he can get into your car."

"Oh." Maggie closed her eyes again as he pried open her fingers and kissed her palm. She wondered dizzily if a resident car thief was a sign that she was meant to throw caution to the wind.

"It's crazy," she said, trying—and failing—to sound firm.

"So? Crazy can be fun."

"You're not talking about fun. You're talking about marriage." Maggie opened her eyes and then wished she hadn't. He was too close. She felt as if she might drown in the deep blue of his eyes.

"Marriage can be fun," Ryan told her. He brought his free hand, the one no longer encumbered by a cast, up to her face, brushing his fingers lightly over her cheekbone. "Come on, Maggie. Take a chance."

She wasn't going to do it. It didn't matter if he melted every bone in her body, which he was in a fair way to doing. The whole idea was insane. She might not be beautiful or wildly talented or particularly brilliant, but she had plenty of common sense. She wasn't going to go dashing off to Las Vegas to get married to a man she barely knew, no matter how much temptation the devil whispered in her ear.

Duvall Avery ran the Chapel of Everlasting Happiness, a small establishment just off the famed Vegas strip. Marrying happy couples put food on the table, but his real love—and greatest talent—was impersonating the King. He wasn't the only choice if you wanted the ceremony performed by Elvis, but he was—according to him—the best. According to him, when he sang "Love Me Tender," Elvis's own mother would have thought it was her son. And his version of "In the Ghetto" had been known to bring an audience to its knees.

Since Duvall was five feet five inches tall and nearly the same across, Maggie found the image of him shimmying across a stage wearing a spangled jumpsuit a bit difficult to absorb.

"Every idiot with a microphone and a tape recorder thinks he can do the King,'' he was saying as he pushed open the door to the chapel and reached in to flick on the lights. "They think all they've got to do is dye their hair black and curl their lips. A few even manage to sound a little like him, but if you want to really catch the essence of the man, you've got to do more than twitch your hips and wipe your forehead with a silk scarf. You've got to really understand the soul of the King to capture a piece of his magic.''

He turned in front of the altar and eyed them hopefully. "Some folks like to have the ceremony performed by the King himself. That's the deluxe package. Course, it costs a bit extra, and it will take me a few minutes to get into the proper frame of mind, but some couples find it real romantic. I've got one fellow who's asked to have the King perform the ceremony for all three of his weddings.''

Ryan glanced at Maggie, but she appeared to be hypnotized by the purple neon profile of Elvis that hung to the left of the altar and had lost track of the conversation. On the right wall, the King stared out at them from a full-length, nearly life-size portrait. He was wearing a white spangled jumpsuit, and Ryan would have bet the pink slip to his truck that it was painted on black velvet. He was grateful to see that, behind the altar, there was only a slightly dusty display of silk flowers. He wasn't sure he could have dealt with another icon to Elvis.

Obviously it had been a mistake to let the cab-driver decide where they would get married. The man was either getting a kickback, was related to Duvall or had really bad taste.

Ryan looked at Maggie again, wondering if she would rather go somewhere else. She'd switched her attention to the velvet painting and was staring at it in a kind of horrified fascination, as if half expecting the King to throw a sweat-soaked scarf in her direction.

"I think we'll skip the deluxe package," Ryan told Duvall. "We're more into Garth Brooks than Elvis," he improvised when Duvall looked inclined to try persuasion. He didn't have the faintest idea what Maggie's musical tastes might be. One of many things he didn't know about her, he thought and wondered that his lack of knowledge didn't seen important.

"Garth Brooks." Duvall sniffed faintly, then shrugged. "Well, at least the man has some sense of style, and even the King dabbled in country music a time or two."

Ryan wasn't sure what kind of response the other man expected to his damned-with-faint-praise approval, but he settled for a faint smile that Duvall was welcome to interpret any way he pleased. He took hold of Maggie's hand. Her fingers felt cold, and he gave them a reassuring squeeze before nodding to Duvall. "If we could get on with things?"

"Of course." Duvall rubbed his pudgy hands together, his disappointment over being denied a chance to perform the ceremony as the King apparently put behind him. "What kind of music would you like? I have everything the King ever recorded, of course. 'Love Me Tender' is a particular favorite of many couples, though I did have one gentleman who asked for 'Jailhouse Rock'—a Mr. John Smith. Apparently Mr. Smith had recently been released from prison—Leavenworth, I believe it was—and the song had some nostalgic significance to him. I must admit that I wondered if his name might be false, but his identification looked authentic, and I suppose there must really be people named John Smith, mustn't there?"

Ryan felt Maggie's hand tremble in his and shot her a quick look, afraid the stress had become too much for her. But when her eyes met his, the only tears he saw were caused by suppressed laughter. He grinned and tightened his fingers over hers.

"'Love Me Tender' will be just fine," he told Duvall, who was poised next to a rack of CDs.

"It's a lovely song," Duvall approved. "I like the earlier versions, myself. If you don't mind." Since he was already sliding a CD into the player, it was just as well that neither of his companions had a preference. He moved to the altar and gave them both a bright look of inquiry. "Are we ready?"

Ready? Half an hour later, Maggie stood on the sidewalk next to Ryan and wondered if it was too late to say she wasn't ready. Not for the marriage certificate that was tucked in the pocket of Ryan's hastily purchased jacket, not for the wedding ring on her finger, and most definitely not to find herself actually married.

"The statue should have been a warning," Ryan said, looking at the pink, pseudo-adobe building.

Maggie followed his gaze to the three-foot-high electric statue of Elvis that sat in the window. He gazed out at them, plastic sneer permanently in place.

"I don't think I'll ever feel the same about that song," Ryan said.

Maggie didn't have to ask what song. "Love Me Tender" had played over and over again during the ceremony. Whenever the song ended, Duvall would pick up a remote control and point it at the CD player and start it over again, all without losing a beat in the words he was reciting. At another time, the absurdity of it would have had her weak with laughter. As it was, any weakness she felt was caused by sheer terror.

"I'm afraid Duvall thinks I'm a tightwad because I didn't cough up the extra bucks for the deluxe ceremony," Ryan said mournfully, and was relieved to see a smile flicker across Maggie's mouth. She'd looked so solemn all through the ceremony that he'd half expected her to say "I don't." "I wonder if I'd have redeemed myself if I'd asked him to play 'In the Ghetto' during the ceremony."

This time Maggie's smile was more definite. "It might have fooled him into thinking that you knew your Elvis."

"God forbid." Ryan shuddered. "Next thing I knew, he would've been digging out a spangled jumpsuit and curling his lip at us."

She giggled. "You don't think he really wears a jumpsuit, do you?"

"Can't do the King justice without one," Ryan assured her. "You hungry? I could eat a bear." He took her hand so casually that Maggie forgot to be nervous about it.

"I could eat," she said, and was surprised to realize it was true. The butterflies in her stomach had subsided enough for her to become aware that it had been a long time since the stale sandwich eaten somewhere in the air over Utah.

"Let's walk up to the strip and find a place to eat."

He kept hold of her hand, and she was content to leave it there. Now that the ceremony was over and they were married, she felt a gentle kind of numbness settle over her senses. None of it felt real. The warm night air, the dazzle of lights as they approached the strip, the feel of Ryan's shoulder brushing hers as they walked—it all seemed like something out of a dream. The only thing that felt real was the fact that her new shoes were pinching her toes. Which reminded her...

"Thank you for the dress," she said, running her hand down her skirt.

The shop in the hotel lobby had been well stocked with what the saleswoman referred to as "gowns with a bridal air." When Maggie nixed the idea of pearl-encrusted bodices and demitrains, she'd come up with the knee-length dress of ivory silk with a full skirt, fitted bodice and sweetheart neckline. On Maggie, the skirt was a little longer than it should have been, and she hoped it didn't make her look like a child playing dress-up. Courtesy of the hotel's salon, her hair had been washed, trimmed and tamed into a fall of soft gold curls that tumbled onto her shoulders, and makeup had been skillfully applied.

"It's beautiful," Ryan said, looking at her. "*You're* beautiful."

"Thank you."

He read the disbelief behind her polite acceptance of the compliment but decided against pressing the issue. He had time to work on convincing her that she was an attractive woman. A lifetime, he thought, and was surprised by how comfortable he was with the idea.

"I was here in December for National," he said as the lights and noise of the strip enveloped them. "There were so many people here, it looked like someone had stirred an ant hill."

"National what?"

Ryan gave her a shocked look. "National Rodeo Finals."

"Sorry." Maggie's tone was so meek that he grinned.

"I'll let it go this time." He shook his head and looked serious. "But we're going to have to work on your education. There are certain things a cowboy's wife just has to know." He ignored her jolt at the word *wife* and pulled her off the sidewalk and into one of the casinos. "We can eat here and then throw some money into the slot machines. I feel lucky tonight."

Her head spinning over the idea of being some-

was fascinated by the ordered chaos in front of her. A short, squat forest of slot machines spread out across burgundy-and-gray carpeting. There were people everywhere. Couples in evening wear, middle-aged women in Bermuda shorts, old men wearing baseball caps and baggy pants—they all stood or sat in front of the machines, looking neither right nor left as they mechanically fed in coins, all their attention for the whirling displays.

"It looks like they're offering sacrifices to some god," Maggie commented, and Ryan chuckled.

"The god of luck." He nudged her farther into the casino. "Come on. Let's sacrifice a few quarters."

"I'm no good at this kind of thing," she protested. "I never win door prizes or raffles. I'm just not very lucky."

"Luck is all a state of mind. Besides, you can't come to Vegas and not feed a slot machine," Ryan said, reaching in his pocket for change. "I think it's an actual law."

Maggie smiled at the memory. She didn't think she had it in her to become a hardened gambler, but she couldn't deny that there was a strange, hypnotic fascination about playing a slot machine. After a while you didn't really think about winning. Putting the coins in the slot and watching the little pictures spin became an end in itself.

But winning was very nice, too, she thought, remembering the bills tucked in the tiny ivory silk purse that hung from her shoulder. Five hundred dollars wasn't exactly extreme wealth, but it wasn't chump change, either. She could add it to the roof fund, she thought, and then remembered that she didn't have to worry about that anymore. As of a few hours ago, the shabby little house in Willow Flat was no longer her concern. She didn't live there anymore.

For a few hours, she'd pushed reality aside—or maybe Ryan had done the pushing. Either way, she'd drifted through the evening in a carefully cultivated fog of oblivion. But the fog was starting to get a little tattered, and it dissipated completely when Ryan pulled the key to their room out of his pocket.

Their room.

Never mind that it was actually a fairly spacious suite, or that they'd shared it briefly earlier in the day when they were getting ready for the wedding. She'd had other things on her mind then, like whether or not she had a brain and why she'd agreed to this, and why she didn't just tell Ryan that she'd changed her mind.

Now it was too late to change her mind, and the two bedrooms and a parlor suddenly seemed awfully small and cramped.

"I hate these damned key cards," Ryan muttered as he slid the card in the door and waited for the light to flash green. "Give me a good old-fashioned key any day."

Maggie's half-formed hope that the key card wouldn't work and they would have to sleep in the hall proved futile when the door opened easily under his hand. There was a lamp on in the parlor. She could see the golden glow reflecting off the gleaming surface of the coffee table and revealing the plush carpeting and softly upholstered sofa.

At that moment the Black Hole of Calcutta could not have looked more fraught with peril.

"Maggie?" Her head jerked toward him, her eyes wide and dark with some emotion he couldn't quite read. "What's wrong?"

"Nothing." She shook her head and forced herself to move. She was acutely aware of Ryan following her into the suite, and the nearly imperceptible snick as the door latch settled into place sounded as loud as cannon fire.

They were alone.

For the first time since Ryan had pulled her onto a plane for the flight to Vegas, they were alone. It was not a reassuring thought.

Ryan dropped the key card on the coffee table and looked at Maggie. She was standing next to the sofa, lamplight catching in the gold of her hair and reflecting off the rich silk of her dress. Mine, he thought, surprised by the degree of pure masculine satisfaction the thought gave him. Political correctness go hang. She was his.

She was also, from the way she was looking at him, scared to death.

"We can call room service if you're hungry," he offered.

"No, thank you. I'm not hungry." Maggie doubted she could get so much as a sip of water past the tightness in her throat.

"Always hated these things," Ryan said, reaching up to loosen his tie. "Never figured out how anyone can stand to wear one every day."

"I guess you can get used to anything." Except this. She could never get used to the idea that they were actually married.

Ryan draped his jacket over the arm of a chair and dropped the tie on top of it. He undid the top two buttons of his shirt, and Maggie forgot how to breathe. She was suddenly, painfully, aware of his size and their isolation. He could do anything he wanted to her, and she wouldn't be able to stop him.

Get a grip, Maggie. Aware that she was perilously close to full-out panic, she drew a deep breath and forced her fingers to relax their death grip on her purse. This was Ryan. You didn't always have to know someone a long time to know them well. He would never hurt her—not physically, anyway—and not intentionally. Only time would tell if he was going to break her heart.

"You look beautiful," he said quietly. Maggie's eyes jerked to his and then slid away from the warm hunger she read there.

"Thank you." Her stomach jumping with nerves, she looked for a distraction. "It's a beautiful room, isn't it?" She brushed her fingers over the muted floral upholstery on the sofa. "I love the way they've mixed the blues and grays. It's not as boring as motel rooms usually are. Of course, this isn't a motel, but I always thought hotels would be just about as dull as motels. But I guess this is a nice hotel, so it should have a little more sophisticated decor. And look at this view."

The windows just happened to be on the far side of the room from where Ryan was standing. Maggie gripped the edge of the drape in a tight little fist and stared out at the city lights as if trying to memorize the streets they mapped.

"It's hard to believe we're in the middle of a desert, isn't it?" she said chattily. "Not that everything is all that lush and green, but just that there are so many people. I didn't realize Las Vegas was so big. What's the population, do you think?"

"I could call the desk and ask them to send up an almanac, if you'd like," Ryan said dryly.

Maggie closed her eyes and leaned her forehead against the cool glass. "I must sound like an idiot."

"I was thinking you sounded a little like one of those overly cheerful tour guides," he said, and the smile in his voice was her undoing.

"I can't do this," she blurted, staring blindly out the window. "I can't sleep with you tonight."

"Okay." He didn't pretend not to understand her. "You don't have to do anything you don't want to do."

"I know I should," she continued as if he hadn't spoken. "It's our wedding night, and that's what people are supposed to do on their wedding night, but I just can't."

"You don't think you could close your eyes and think of God and country?" he asked.

The coaxing question was so startling that she turned to look at him. "What?"

"It wouldn't take all that long," he wheedled. "I could hurry."

"You could—" She gaped at him. "You could hurry?" she asked weakly.

"It's the least I could do," he said magnanimously. "What with you making such a sacrifice and all."

"I'm not—" Maggie stopped and stared. "I—you're kidding, right?"

"Don't I look serious?" he asked, crossing his eyes. Maggie started to giggle helplessly.

Ryan grinned and told himself it was nice to see her laughing. Not as nice as it would have been to see her falling at his feet, helpless with lust, but anything was better than the white-faced fear or the nervous chatter.

"You really had me going there for a minute," she said, laughter still threading through her voice.

Maggie couldn't believe he'd made her laugh, but she felt better for it. He no longer seemed so big and scary, and she no longer felt quite so far out of her depth. She sighed and ran her fingers through her hair, tousling the careful layers of curls.

"I'm sorry, Ryan. I know it probably seems stupid. It's just that...so much has happened. I feel like I just stepped off a roller coaster, and my head is still spinning."

"I understand, and it's okay," he told her, sternly suppressing the part of him that said it wasn't okay and that he didn't understand anything except that he wanted her. Now.

Instinct told him that he could make her change her mind. Remembering the way she'd clung to him when he kissed her, he doubted if it would take much persuasion. But there were still lines of strain around her mouth and less color than there should have been in her cheeks. His conscience won out, but not without a battle. Feeling downright noble, he brushed a kiss on her forehead. "Get some sleep."

"Thank you for being so understanding." Maggie wondered at the sinking little feeling of disappointment she felt. It wasn't that she wanted him to argue, but maybe he could have tried to persuade her just a little? Unless he didn't want her anymore? Was that why he was being so understanding? Because he didn't care? Maybe he was already regretting their marriage?

And maybe she was letting her imagination run away with her. She was just so awfully tired. Murmuring a soft good-night, she went to her room, pausing in the doorway to give him a strained little smile.

"See you in the morning," Ryan said, keeping a smile firmly in place.

The smile vanished as soon as the door closed behind her, and then he closed his eyes and let out a soft groan. He'd never realized how painful nobility could be. There was a beautiful woman in the next room, a woman as warm and responsive as a man could dream of. She happened to be his wife, and this happened to be their wedding night.

And all he had to look forward to was a cold shower.

Chapter Nine

Willow Flat dozed under the midafternoon sun. There were a couple of pickups parked in front of the Dew Drop on the edge of town, and a scattering of cars and pickups parked in front of various businesses along the main street, but other than that, it looked like exactly what it was—a sleepy Western town.

"Everything looks so normal," Maggie commented, speaking to herself as much as to Ryan.

"Is there some reason it shouldn't?" Ryan cocked an eyebrow in her direction.

"Not really." She shrugged self-consciously. "It's just that so much has happened, it seems strange to see everything looking just the way it did when I left."

"You haven't been gone that long," he commented.

"I know." It made her dizzy to think about just how little time it had taken to turn her life completely upside down.

Lee Hardeman sat in front of his newspaper office, smoking a pipe and enjoying the sun. He waved as they drove by, and Ryan lifted his fingers off the wheel in response. A rusty white station wagon and a big yellow dog occupied the space outside the General Store. Bonnie Dillard was sweeping the front step, and she looked up and waved, too. Maggie thought she saw the other woman's brows go up in surprise when she saw them together.

"Do you suppose they know?" Maggie asked uneasily, thinking of Bonnie's penchant for gossip.

"I'd guess the Just Married sign on the tailgate might give them a clue," Ryan said dryly, then laughed at her horrified look. "You're an easy target, Maggie. Unless Duvall is a reporter for the *Herald,* it's not likely anyone's heard the news yet. But they'll know soon enough. I never planned on keeping it a secret."

"No, of course not." Maggie hoped she sounded more definite than she felt. It wasn't that she wanted it kept a secret. Exactly. It was just that she didn't really want anyone to know about it. At

least, not until she'd adjusted to the idea herself—
say in five or ten years.

"I feel...conspicuous," she muttered, and
fought the urge to slide lower in her seat.

"Must be that big red *M* sewn to your T-shirt."

Maggie smiled reluctantly. She probably wasn't
making much sense, but then, nothing she'd done
the last couple of days made much sense, so at least
there was a certain consistency to her insanity.

Ryan turned off the main road and onto the street
where her mother's house was. Not "home" anymore, Maggie thought, twisting the wedding ring
on her finger. She'd already made the decision to
move, even before she'd leaped so wildly into this
marriage, but it still felt strange to look at the
shabby little house and know that it wasn't home
anymore.

"You really don't have to come in with me,"
she said, as Ryan pulled the truck up in front of
the house. The neighbor's dog lifted his head from
his paws long enough to bark once, then put his
head back down, satisfied that he'd frightened them
sufficiently.

"Maggie, we just got married. I think I should
meet my mother-in-law." Ryan shut off the engine
and turned sideways in the seat, resting one arm
along the top of the steering wheel as he looked at
her. "Are she and your sister likely to be upset? Is

that why you keep trying to talk me out of coming in?''

Upset? Maggie thought of Noreen's probable reaction to the news that her fat, plain, boring little sister had married Ryan Lassiter. *Upset* didn't seem quite the word to describe her feelings. She was less sure of her mother's reaction, but she couldn't quite picture Lydia shedding tears of joy over her youngest daughter's elopement.

"Not upset, exactly," she said. Astonished. Infuriated. Hysterical. Ballistic. Possibly even homicidal. But nothing as simple as upset.

"Then we don't have a problem. I'll come in. I'll meet your mother. Then you can pack your things and follow me out to the ranch. Looks like your car's ready to go," he said, nodding to the blue compact in the driveway. "Tucker said he'd do whatever it needed."

"Is Tucker the car thief?" Maggie asked.

"Former car thief," Ryan corrected her with a grin. He pushed open his door. "No, that's Reggie."

Reggie? It seemed an odd name for either a car thief or a cowboy. While she was contemplating the unlikeliness of it, Ryan came around the front of the truck and opened her door.

"Come on," he said, holding out his hand. "Time to face the music."

She would rather have faced a firing squad, but Maggie kept that thought to herself and let him help her out of the truck. This must be how prisoners felt making the long walk to the gallows, she thought, as the two of them started up the cracked walkway. She tried to think of something to say, something casual, conversational. But her mind remained depressingly blank.

At least Noreen's car was gone, she noted with relief. She'd probably already started her shift at the Dew Drop and wouldn't be home for hours yet. That was something to be thankful for. Unless…Maggie's stomach dropped. Unless Ryan *wanted* to see Noreen. Unless that was the reason he'd insisted on coming in with her.

"Noreen's not here," she blurted out. "Her car's gone. She's probably at work."

"We've already met," Ryan said easily.

Maggie nodded and tried to look as if that was what she'd thought all along. Logic suggested that marrying her was an unlikely route to Noreen's heart—or even her bed. But logic didn't seem to have anything to do with her behavior lately. If it did, she wouldn't be here at all.

She heard the television as soon as she opened the front door. Squeals of delight mingled with the overly cheerful tones of some game show host offering congratulations to yet another big winner. It occurred to Maggie that, if she hadn't already decided to move out, it might have been worth getting married just to get away from the constant chatter of her mother's shows. Maybe it wasn't the picket fence or Ryan's blue eyes that had persuaded her. Maybe it was the thought of no more Sally Jesse, Montel and Vanna.

"My mother is fond of television," she said, glancing at Ryan. That was a little like saying Imelda Marcos had been fond of shoes, but she hoped she would be forgiven the understatement.

"Lots of folks are," Ryan replied easily. He wondered at the tension in her expression. Maybe he shouldn't have insisted on meeting her mother now, but it had seemed like the right thing to do. Considering the shortcuts he'd taken the last couple of days, maybe it was a bit late to be worried about conventions, but this had seemed simple enough that he'd figured he could at least do this one thing right. But here was Maggie, looking like she was about to walk the plank, her eyes big and dark with anxiety.

Then again, maybe her reaction was understandable, Ryan thought. He wasn't exactly looking forward to breaking the news of his marriage to the old man.

Unaware that her feelings were so transparent, Maggie eyed the living room doorway unhappily.

Lydia would be sitting on the sofa, a sweater pulled around her narrow shoulders, a can of Diet Coke on the table next to her, her eyes glued to the glowing tube as she watched other people's lives flicker past. She tried to imagine how her mother might react to her news. Probably with astonishment and disbelief, not just at the suddenness of it, but at the idea that any reasonably attractive man would be interested in marrying her younger daughter.

The thought of it was enough to make Maggie want to hustle Ryan out the front door. She could sneak back in and pack her things, probably be gone again before Lydia even knew she'd been there. She allowed herself to savor the fantasy for a moment before letting it slip away. Sneaking out of the house like a thief in the night wasn't exactly a mature thing to do.

Besides, she didn't know where her car keys were.

Sighing inaudibly, she stepped into the living room, aware of Ryan following her. The drapes were drawn, as usual throwing the room into a state of perpetual gloom relieved only by the flickering glow from the television. Lydia sat hunched forward on the sofa, her eyes glued to the screen where a skinny woman with an improbable amount of bleached blond hair—and even more improbable breasts—was squealing with delight and jumping up and down. Maggie had to admire the game show host for being able to keep his eyes on the woman's face.

"Mom." She had to speak twice before there was any response. "Mom."

Lydia started a little, as if waking from a dream but she didn't look away from the screen. "Maggie?"

"I wanted to—"

"I think it was very rude of you to just leave a message on the machine saying you were going to be gone a day or two," Lydia said sharply, still without shifting her attention from the blonde, who had grabbed the host and was clutching him to her substantial bosom. "You didn't bother to tell me where you were going or leave any way to get hold of you."

"It didn't seem likely you'd need me for anything," Maggie said, a little surprised that her mother had even noticed her absence. Not much intruded on Lydia's self-absorption.

The game show was replaced by an ad for a hay fever medicine, and a series of staccato sneezes burst into the room, followed by an announcer asking if you were one of the millions who suffered from allergies. His tone was so portentous.

"Noreen talked to Bob Hesslewhite about selling the house," Lydia continued, reaching reluctantly for the remote control. Pushing the button to lower the volume, she finally turned to look at Maggie, squinting as her eyes tried to adjust to the change in light. "He says there isn't much call for houses around here, and if we want to sell it, we'd probably better fix it up some and—"

She saw Ryan standing beside and a little behind Maggie and broke off in midword, her eyes widening in surprise. "Oh my. I didn't realize you had someone with you."

"Mom, this is Ryan Lassiter. Ryan, this is Lydia Drummond. My mother." Maggie winced at the stilted formality of the introduction, but it was the best she could manage to get past the tight little knot lodged at the base of her throat.

"Lassiter?" Lydia repeated as she rose. Maggie could see the wheels turning in her brain. "Of the Double L?"

"The same." Ryan's smile was friendly. "Pleased to meet you, Mrs. Drummond."

"Oh, dear." Lydia put her hands up to smooth her frizzy hair, then tugged at the frayed edges of her old blue cardigan. "I wasn't expecting company. I must look a fright," she said, patting her hair again and trying to remember if she'd put on makeup this morning. Yes, she was nearly sure she had, but still... She shot an annoyed look at her daughter. "You could at least have given me some warning before bringing company home, Maggie."

"I'm sorry. I—"

"You look fine, Mrs. Drummond," Ryan said with a smile that could have melted ice in the dead of winter. "I'm the one who persuaded Maggie to just show up on your doorstep like this. I wanted to meet you."

Never one to resist a compliment from a handsome man, Lydia smiled. "Thank you." She preened and tilted her chin at a coquettish angle, looking at him from under lashes clumped with mascara. "You wanted to meet me?"

"Yes, I did." Though he could come to regret the impulse, Ryan thought as Lydia giggled and smoothed her hand over her hip. He couldn't help but remember Bill saying that Maggie's mother reminded him of one of Bette Davis's later roles. He could definitely see the resemblance, though the makeup put him more in mind of Tammy Faye on a really bad day.

"Mom, I have some news."

"Do you?" Lydia asked absently. She kept her eyes on Ryan, and the speculation in that pale blue gaze made him shift uneasily.

"Noreen isn't here," she said abruptly. She'd run through the possible reasons for his presence and decided that he must have come looking for

Noreen. Men were always after her oldest daughter, she thought with a mixture of pride and envy. There had been a time when they sniffed after her the same way, she remembered, with a surge of regret for the toll exacted by the passing years.

"I know she's not here," Ryan said. "I didn't—"

"She's at the Dew Drop, if you want to see her."

Ryan shifted uncomfortably and wished he'd listened when Maggie tried to talk him out of this meeting. This skinny woman with the frizzy hair and bad makeup was not at all what he'd imagined Maggie's mother would be like. Or the beautiful, if chilly, Noreen's, for that matter.

"Actually, I—"

"Mom, Ryan and I went to Las Vegas and got married yesterday," Maggie said, deciding to put an end to the scene before her mother managed to convince Ryan that he really had come to see Noreen.

It took a moment for the words to register. When their meaning sank in, Lydia's reaction was almost comical. Her pale blue eyes seemed to widen endlessly, and her mouth dropped open in shock.

"You...did what?" she asked faintly.

"We got married," Maggie said, wondering if

repetition would make the words sound more believable.

"But...but I...didn't think you'd known each other very long," Lydia protested. She looked from Maggie to Ryan and back again.

"Sometimes it doesn't take long." Ryan slid his arm around Maggie's waist and pulled her against his side. "You just know it's right."

Maggie marveled that he could sound so confident, as if they hadn't just jumped blindly into this marriage.

"Well, I...I guess so." Lydia looked around the room, as if bewildered to see everything looking so normal. "I...would you like something to drink?" She bent to pick up her can of Diet Coke, and for a moment Maggie thought she was going to offer it to Ryan. But she wrapped both hands around it and held it against her chest, as if drawing comfort from it. "There's Diet Coke and milk and orange juice. No," she frowned in concentration. "I think we're out of orange juice."

"Thanks, but I'm not really thirsty," Ryan said. He was starting to think his new mother-in-law might be a few bricks short of a full load. By the end of ten labored minutes of conversation, he was nearly sure of it. It wasn't anything obvious. She didn't climb on the furniture or hang from the curtain rods. She didn't shout gibberish or talk to an invisible friend. There was just something peculiar about the way her pale eyes never stopped moving. She would look at him, then look at Maggie, and then stare at the television screen for a long moment. The sound was still turned down, but that didn't seem to matter to her. There would be a lull in the conversation, and only then, with a visible effort, would she drag her eyes away from the screen.

He had expected her to be full of questions. Why had they gone to Vegas to get married? Where were they going to live? Maybe even something about his prospects, although she might just assume that he was eventually going to take over the Double L from his grandfather. But she didn't ask any of those things: she didn't, in fact, ask anything at all.

She said she was surprised—three times. Mentioned she'd once won two hundred dollars playing blackjack in Vegas. Said she hadn't been to Atlantic City in a long time and had heard that it was much nicer than it used to be. Asked Ryan if he ever watched "Wheel of Fortune." When he admitted he'd never seen it, she became almost animated as she explained how the game was played and expressed her admiration for what a good job Vanna did turning the letters and always looking so pretty.

"Even when she was pregnant, she always looked nice," Lydia said, pleating the hem of her sweater between her fingers. "Not every woman carries well," she said in a tone that suggested that if you couldn't look good while pregnant, you probably shouldn't have a baby. "I was lucky. I carried so small you could hardly tell I was going to have a baby at all, though I did gain a bit more weight with Maggie." She frowned at Maggie, as if in reproach, and then her eyes suddenly went wide as a thought occurred to her.

"You're pregnant!" she exclaimed.

Ryan felt Maggie jolt and looked down to see the color flood her cheeks. The comment startled him, but he was even more startled to realize that the idea of Maggie being pregnant with his child held considerable appeal.

"No, I'm not." Maggie made the denial through gritted teeth and felt her humiliation completed when Lydia's face crumpled with disappointment. She didn't have to be a mind reader to know that her mother couldn't imagine any other reason why Ryan would have married her.

"I'd better get started packing," she said abruptly and stood up. Ryan had been sitting on the arm of her chair, and he rose when she did. She couldn't bring herself to meet his eyes, sure that he, like her mother, must be wondering why he'd married her.

"You need me to hang around and help you load your car?"

Maggie shook her head. "There's nothing that's all that heavy." And even if there was, she didn't want him hanging around. A few more minutes of conversation with Lydia and he was likely to ask for a divorce before they even had a marriage.

Ryan didn't argue further. He wanted to get to the ranch well ahead of her so that he would have a chance to break the news of his marriage to his grandfather before Maggie arrived. Not that the old man's reaction could begin to compare to Lydia's for sheer peculiarity, but Ryan didn't want him to say anything that might upset Maggie.

"I'll see you in a little while, then," he said, and caught the startled look in her eyes when he bent to kiss her.

He took his time about it, lingering over the softness of her mouth, tasting the startled warmth of her response. He recognized the scent of the shampoo provided by the hotel, because he'd used it, too. It was ridiculous to find anything sexy about the knowledge that they'd used the same shampoo, and Ryan decided that had to be what happened when a man spent his wedding night alone with nothing but late-night movies and a Gideon bible for company.

He broke off the kiss reluctantly. When he lifted his head and saw the softness in her eyes, he cursed the fact that they weren't alone. But when he glanced at Lydia, half hoping she'd disappeared in a puff of smoke, she was staring at them, those pale eyes puzzled and unwavering.

"It was nice to meet you, Mrs. Drummond," he said, putting more sincerity into the words than he felt.

"Yes," Lydia said, leaving him to wonder if she was agreeing that he was lucky to have met her or meant him to interpret it to mean that she'd enjoyed meeting him, too.

Fruity, Ryan thought. The woman was downright fruity.

Nathan shoved irritably at the stack of paperwork on his desk. He hated the damned stuff. Endless lists and notes and forms. Breeding records. Tax records. Payroll records. He hated every damned bit of it. As far as he was concerned, hell consisted of a desk and an endless supply of forms and pencils. When Mary Beth was alive, she'd taken care of all the paperwork involved in running the ranch. In the thirty-some years since her death, he'd muddled through it, but he'd never learned to like it.

When Ryan was in college, he'd begun to take over the task, and for a few years Nathan had been spared the tedium. After Sally's death, when Ryan went out on the circuit, he'd dealt with the paperwork when he was home, but, as his visits home became less frequent, the job had gradually fallen back on Nathan.

And, if he was honest, as the years passed and both his irritation and worry grew, sheer pigheadedness had made him deal with the paperwork himself. If the boy didn't have enough sense to stop chasing after gold buckles and come home where he belonged, then he could just damned well stay out of the day-to-day running of the ranch.

Nathan glared at the computer that sat on one corner of the desk. Damned thing took up half the desk and, as far as he was concerned, was about as useful as a boat anchor. He'd let Ryan talk him into buying it last fall, and it was only after it was installed and Ryan was gone again that he'd admitted to himself that he'd been half hoping that, if he bought the damned computer, it might help lure Ryan home.

"Nothing like an old fool," he muttered. Ryan had offered to teach him how to use the computer, but he'd refused. Now the blasted thing just sat on the edge of the desk, squat and ugly and useless.

Nathan pushed his chair back from the desk and got up. The temperature had taken a shift toward the cool side, and there was rain in the air again. The damp weather made his bones ache. He flexed his fingers out and then curled them into a fist, testing the level of pain. He wasn't getting any younger. The pain in his joints was a warning that it was time to put his house in order, time to see to the future.

He frowned at the portrait of Quintin and Marilee Lassiter over the fireplace and thought about what they'd had to do to take and hold this land. What they'd built had lasted for generations. He wasn't going to see it die with his generation, not without a fight.

It was time Ryan settled down, time he faced up to his responsibilities. The boy hadn't liked it when he suggested that he marry Shelly Taylor, but, given a little time, he would come around to the idea. Shelly was a beautiful woman, and now that she seemed to have given up on the idea of being a big star in Hollywood, she was ready to settle down. If he was inclined to believe in fate, he might see it as a sign that Ryan had broken his arm just when she was about to come home.

Nathan's frown deepened as he considered his

grandson's latest start. Going off to God knows where on a moment's notice. He hadn't even come home first. He'd just called Tucker and said he would be back in a day or two, then asked him to go get some woman's car that was stuck over on the Rayczeks' place, and hadn't offered so much as a word of explanation. Or if he had, Tucker hadn't offered to pass it along. Tucker McIntyre could be as tight-mouthed as a damned priest when he wanted to be, a trait Nathan usually admired.

He was absorbed in thought, and the quiet knock startled him. Irritated that he hadn't heard anyone approach—another sign that he wasn't getting any younger—Nathan pivoted on one heel and scowled at the door.

"What?" he barked. His mood was not improved when Ryan pushed open the door. He hadn't heard the truck pull in.

"You got a minute?"

"So, you're back, are you?" Nathan's tone held more accusation than welcome.

"I'm back." Ryan came into the room and pushed the door shut behind him. He was irritated to realize that he was as nervous as a teenager about to confess to having wrecked the car. "I wanted to talk to you."

"Now there's a coincidence because I wanted to talk to you." If Nathan felt a sense of relief that his grandson was home, if he'd thought he might not come back at all this time, he would be damned if he'd admit it, even to himself. He was tired of this game they'd been playing. It was time to shit or get off the pot. Ryan was either a part of this ranch or he wasn't. He had to make the choice. Illogically, he focused his anger on the least important thing.

"This isn't a boarding stable. You can't just drop in and out whenever you please, leaving that damned horse of yours sitting here eating its head off and not doing a goddamned thing to earn its keep. This is a working ranch. You may have forgotten what that means, but, around here, everyone earns their keep. You can't just—"

"I got married yesterday." Ryan's bald statement cut through his grandfather's angry tirade like a hot knife going through butter.

"You got—" Nathan struggled to rearrange his thoughts to accommodate this astonishing piece of information. Questions tumbled around in his brain, tangling together so that he couldn't sort out any single one to ask.

Ryan told himself that it was childish to take pleasure at having silenced the old man so effectively, but he would have been lying to himself if he didn't acknowledge a twinge of satisfaction at the look of stunned disbelief on his grandfather's face.

"You want to run that by me again?" Nathan finally managed to say. He groped behind him with one hand, found the edge of the desk and leaned back against it.

"I got married yesterday. In Vegas."

Nathan nodded slowly. "That's what I thought you said. Anyone I know?" He'd recovered from the initial shock and was thinking clearly. "I know it's not Shelly, because I talked to her this morning, and she's coming to dinner tomorrow night. I think she might have said something if the two of you had just gotten married. Who is she?"

Ryan winced at the mention of Shelly. "Her name is Maggie Drummond. She's originally from Detroit, but she's lived in town for the past three years or so."

"So you've known her quite a while?" Nathan probed.

Letting the assumption stand would save them both a lot of grief, Ryan thought, at least in the short term. But the truth would come out sooner or later, and he wasn't a child that he had to lie to cover up what he'd done.

"Doug and I picked her up on the way into town that first day," he said without apology. He hooked his thumbs in his pockets and waited for the explosion.

"You just went to Las Vegas and married a woman you've only known a few weeks?" Angry color mantled Nathan's lean cheeks.

"That's right." Ryan offered no explanation, couldn't have given one even if he'd wanted to.

"Did you do this to spite me?"

"Of course not. How stupid do you think I am?" Ryan asked, irritated.

"That's what I'm trying to find out." Nathan's tone was dangerously pleasant. "You've just told me that you married a woman you don't know. That doesn't say much for your intelligence."

"I didn't say I didn't know her."

"Oh, that's right." His grandfather's voice was knife sharp. "You've known her a few weeks. Plenty of time to know you want to spend the rest of your life with her."

"It doesn't always take time to know someone."

"Did you do this because I urged you to marry Shelly?" Nathan demanded. His hands clenched over the edge of the desk, fingers digging into the old wood until his knuckles showed white. "Is this supposed to reassure me that you're ready to take a part in running the ranch?"

Muscles humming with tension, Ryan paced to the window and stared out. The sky was overcast, threatening new rain, and the light that filtered through the clouds was oddly clear. From where he stood, he could see most of the outbuildings that sprawled out from the main house. Barns, corrals, machine shop and toolshed—the Double L boasted more buildings than some towns he'd driven through.

Off to the left, just barely visible, was the foreman's house, where the McIntyres lived. He couldn't see it from here, but the original cabin stood in back of the ranch house, the logs silvery with age, the wooden floor worn thin by the footsteps of generations past.

This was his, damn it. His home. His history. There wasn't much he wouldn't have done to hold on to it. But that wasn't why he'd married Maggie. He still hadn't quite figured out the why of it. Or maybe he just wasn't ready to admit the why of it. Either way, his marriage to Maggie had nothing to do with the ranch, and no one was more surprised by that than he was.

He swung away from the window and looked at his grandfather. "I married Maggie because I wanted to. Not to get you off my back about Shelly or to convince you of anything. I wanted to marry her."

He hadn't said he loved her, Nathan noted. Later, he would give some thought to what that might mean. For the moment, he had other things on his mind. Dragging his hands through his gray hair, he suddenly felt every one of his seventy-three years. Married. Christ Almighty, the boy had jumped into marriage without so much as a breath of warning. And so had the girl, for that matter. What the hell kind of woman did something like that?

"Drummond," he muttered, rolling the name around in his mind. "Isn't there a gal named Drummond that works at the Dew Drop?"

"Maggie's sister," Ryan said, gritting his teeth a little as he considered what he knew of Noreen— what his grandfather was likely to know of her. "Maggie works for Bill Martin."

"Little thing with dark blond hair and big eyes?" Nathan asked, calling up a fuzzy image. His frown deepened when Ryan nodded. "Don't know anything about her, but I've heard an earful about the sister. If she's—"

"Maggie's nothing like her sister," Ryan interrupted, surprised by the quick lick of anger that went through him at the comparison. He braced his feet apart in unconscious challenge. "Anything you have to say about this, you can say it to me. But if you say anything to upset Maggie, I'll take her and be out of here so fast it will make your head swim."

Nathan's brows shot up in surprise at the sharp warning in his grandson's voice. The boy looked ready to take him on right there and then. It had been a long time since he'd seen him display that much emotion about anything. It gave a man something to think about.

"Do we understand one another on this?" Ryan asked.

Nathan nodded slowly. "We do." But he didn't really understand a goddamned thing about any of it.

"Good." Ryan let some of the tension ease from his shoulders. The worst of it was over, he reminded himself. The news was out, and the old man had taken it more calmly than he might have. He wasn't exactly breaking out the congratulatory champagne, but he hadn't ordered up a pot of boiling oil, either. You had to look on the bright side, Ryan decided ruefully.

He combed his fingers through his hair and tried to order his thoughts. There were things he needed to do. "Maggie's driving out from town," he said. "I thought we'd move into Aunt Grace's cabin."

"You planning on living there?" Another surprise, Nathan thought. When he'd married Sally, the two of them had lived in the main house.

Aunt Grace's cabin wasn't a cabin, and the woman whose name it bore had been dead for close to half a century. Nathan's father had built the small house for an older sister who had never married. She'd lived out there for more than forty years, cultivating a small rose garden, a large vegetable patch and writing letters to a seemingly endless supply of friends who lived all over the country. Nathan remembered her as an energetic, active old lady with an acid tongue and a surprisingly bawdy laugh.

After her death, the vegetable patch had been allowed to go fallow, and most of the roses had succumbed to winter cold or summer dryness, but the little house had been maintained, functioning as a guest house when the need arose.

"I figured the place hadn't seen much use in quite a while," Ryan said. He'd given it quite a bit of thought and figured that they could use the privacy. At least until they took their marriage past the in-name-only stage, which he hoped to God was going to be soon. But all he said to his grandfather was, "Maggie's a photographer, and there's a spare bathroom that could be turned into a darkroom without too much trouble."

Nathan nodded as if none of the four bathrooms in the big house could possibly have functioned as a darkroom. Whatever was behind this marriage—and he didn't for a minute believe that he'd heard the whole of it—Ryan seemed solidly committed to it. He was curious about this Maggie Drum-mond. And even more curious to see her and Ryan together.

Anyone who could force his grandson out of the mental and emotional distance he'd been keeping between himself and the rest of the world was someone he wanted to meet.

Chapter Ten

Maggie stared, glassy-eyed, at the faint outline of darker wallpaper on the kitchen wall opposite her. On the table in front of her, a misty plume of steam rose from a sturdy white porcelain mug. Rain drizzled down the night-dark window over the sink, closing the small kitchen off from the rest of the world.

There must have been a picture there once, Maggie thought, contemplating that shadowy square. What kind of picture would hang in the kitchen of a spinster lady who liked to garden and write letters? Maybe it had been a still life with a squash and an inkwell. Or a mixed bouquet of roses, carrot tops and fountain pens.

And maybe she'd lost what was left of her mind.

waited for inspiration, and, when it didn't come, he took the coward's way out and turned the question back on her. "Why not?"

"Why not?" Maggie sputtered. "Because we hardly know each other. Because it's crazy. Because normal people don't just dash off to Vegas and get married on an impulse."

"Happens all the time," Ryan argued.

"And they hit Reno six weeks later for a divorce." Maggie thought about taking her hand back. She was nearly sure that you weren't supposed to hold hands with a man while you were turning down his proposal. But his fingers felt warm and strong around hers—just the opposite of the way she felt inside, which was cold and a little weak. The cold she could attribute to the rain that was still drumming against the roof of the truck, but the weakness came straight from her heart.

Ryan Lassiter had asked her to marry him. He was sitting right there in front of her, all six-feet-two and eyes of blue of him, asking her to be his wife. And she was turning him down?

"We've never even been on a date," she said weakly.

"I just asked you to go to Vegas, didn't I? We could have dinner first, even catch a movie, if you want." He made his expression hopeful and was rewarded by a spurt of choked laughter.

"Dinner, a movie and a wedding. That's certainly a unique first date."

"Probably not as unique as you think." Ryan looked down at her hand, vaguely startled by the delicacy of it. "Not every Vegas marriage ends in divorce, Maggie."

"Not everyone who's exposed to chicken pox catches it, but the odds aren't in your favor either way," she replied.

Ryan grinned at the comparison. "Are you suggesting marriage is a disease?"

"No." Maggie shook her head and tried to order her thoughts. The absentminded stroking of his thumb across her palm made it difficult to think. "I'm not saying anything against marriage. I want to get married, have children and a home."

"Flowered curtains and a picket fence," Ryan said, smiling as if at a private joke.

"More or less." Maggie shrugged. "It's not politically correct, I guess. I should probably be planning trips to Bosnia to take Pulitzer prize-winning photographs of mass destruction, but the truth is, I like taking pictures of beautiful things, and I don't much care if my pictures never change the world." She laughed self-consciously. "I don't even care all that much if they never get published. I'm just not particularly ambitious."

"There's nothing wrong with that. Nothing

body's wife, Maggie followed him blindly into the noise and light.

"I won. I still can't believe I actually won."

"You sure did." Ryan grinned as he steered Maggie into an elevator. It was, by his best estimate, at least the fiftieth time she'd said more or less the same words in the last half an hour.

"Five hundred dollars." She looked up at him as if for confirmation.

"Five hundred and change," he said, punching the button for their floor. The doors slid shut, and the elevator started upward.

"I never win anything."

"You did this time." Her stunned amazement delighted Ryan. He reached out to tug on one of her curls. "Too bad you decided to quit. If you'd kept it up, you might have had the casino on its knees by morning."

"You can make fun of me if you like," she said with careful dignity. "But I don't recall you winning anything."

"Gloating is an unattractive personality trait."

"So is jealousy," she said, throwing him a pointed look.

The elevator stopped, and two couples in evening wear got on. Ryan stepped closer to Maggie to allow the newcomers room. One of the men pushed the button for the top floor restaurant, and someone made a comment about ordering filet mignon in sherried mushroom sauce, making it clear that they were on their way to dinner.

Maggie didn't know the exact time, but she knew it had to be approaching midnight, which seemed a little late to be going out to eat. Then again, this was Las Vegas, where the line between night and day was permanently obscured by the flash and glitter of neon lights and the clatter of slot machines. Where otherwise sane people spent hours hoping to line up three matching pieces of fruit or beat the odds at the blackjack tables.

Where rational, practical women married men they barely knew.

The elevator bumped gently as it reached their floor. The doors slid open, and Ryan set his hand against the small of her back to guide her into the thickly carpeted hallway.

She'd had fun tonight, Maggie thought, surprised. Ryan had kept the conversation light and easy during dinner, and had succeeded well enough that she'd eaten a shrimp cocktail and more than half of her blackened redfish before she remembered that she was too nervous to eat anything.

After the meal, he'd guided her into the casino and introduced her to the city's reason for being. Maggie had never been to Vegas before, and she

She closed her eyes, but opened them immediately when the room seemed to dip and sway around her. Not even nine o'clock, she thought, looking at the clock that hung over the back door. Considering everything that had happened, it didn't seem possible that barely twelve hours had passed since she woke in a Las Vegas hotel room.

The day had been crammed so full that it was difficult to sort out everything that had happened. There had been the trip back from Vegas and moving out of her mother's house, closing a major chapter of her life. Then the drive to the ranch, which had given her entirely too much time to think about the insanity of the step she was taking—of the steps she'd already taken.

By the time she drove through the wooden archway with the Double L brand burned into it, she was half convinced that the only intelligent thing to do was to not even get out of the car but to simply hand Ryan his ring through the partially open window, tell him she was very sorry but she really couldn't possibly marry him after all, and then just keep driving.

But her car had no sooner pulled into the ranch yard than Ryan was walking out to meet her, and one look at that long, rangy body and the smile in those blue eyes, and Maggie knew she wasn't going anywhere. What the hell, she thought recklessly, if you were going to gamble, you might as well gamble big.

Then there had been Ryan's grandfather. Maggie shuddered at the memory of her first meeting with the tall, lean old man with the piercing blue eyes. She'd been so nervous and tongue-tied that he was probably convinced his grandson had married either a deaf-mute or an idiot, or possibly both.

He'd been polite, she remembered. He hadn't been exactly bubbling over with warmth, but she had the feeling Nathan didn't "bubble" under any circumstances. And if his eyes had been a little watchful, she could hardly blame him for that. Like everyone else—including her—he was probably wondering why his grandson had married her.

At least he hadn't asked if she was pregnant. Maggie winced at the memory of her mother's question. She'd asked twice more after Ryan left, following Maggie into her room to watch her pack. Lydia couldn't seem to absorb the idea that Ryan had married Maggie just because he wanted to. Now, if Maggie was pregnant and he felt *obliged* to marry her, that made sense. The third time she asked the question, Maggie's temper had snapped.

"Is it so impossible to believe that an attractive man would actually *want* to marry me?" she'd demanded, leaning her hands on the edge of her suitcase and turning her head to look at her mother.

Lydia blinked owlishly at the sudden sharpness in Maggie's voice. "I didn't mean it that way." She twisted nervously at a button on her sweater. "It's just that...everything's so sudden—the two of you going off to Vegas and all. And then, well, I know he met Noreen and—"

"And after meeting Noreen, he couldn't possibly still have found me attractive?" Maggie asked, her voice dangerously soft.

"Now, I didn't say that." Lydia's voice teetered on the edge of a whine. "But she did say he was attracted and—"

"Well, she was wrong." Maggie said it flatly, as much to silence her own doubts as in response to her mother's words. The disbelief in Lydia's expression did nothing to improve her mood.

It shouldn't have hurt, she thought now. God knew, it wasn't as if her mother's low opinion of her had come as a surprise. She'd lived with it all her life, had always known that, in Lydia's eyes, she could never hold a candle to her older sister on any level. But the hurt was there. Hours later, she could still feel the ache of it in her chest, the ache of knowing she would never be smart enough, pretty enough, clever enough, to make her mother love her.

It was a measure of how tired she was that thinking about it now brought tears to her eyes. Maggie forced them back. She wasn't going to cry over it. Not now, not ever again. When she'd walked out of that house this afternoon, she'd walked away from that part of her life with no regrets. Or none she couldn't live with.

So much had happened in the last two—or was it three?—days. No wonder her head was spinning. With a sigh, Maggie wrapped her fingers around the cup in front of her and lifted it to her mouth. She nearly whimpered with delight, her mouth curving and her eyelids drooping, as she savored the hot, sugary tea.

That was how Ryan saw her when he walked into the room—her eyes almost shut, her mouth curved in a sensuous little half smile. He stopped dead as a wave of pure lust shot straight to his groin. She looked like a woman either remembering or anticipating great sex. He wanted desperately to believe that it was the latter, but he suspected that, at the moment, there wasn't anything he could offer that would excite her half as much as the cup she held so lovingly.

Eyes still closed, Maggie brought the cup to her face and pressed the warm porcelain to her temple, letting the heat sooth the nagging little ache that had been lodged there for hours.

Her lips parted in a soft sigh of pleasure, and Ryan's mouth went dry at the same time that his

eling with a Brit, who also happened to be a bull rider. He got me hooked on the stuff. I don't indulge often, but I'll never live it down if anyone finds out, so let's just keep this our little secret, okay?''

"Your secret's safe with me." Maggie solemnly crossed her heart.

Ryan grinned at her. "You hold my life in your hands now. If word of this ever leaks out, I'll be banned from the NCC—National Cowboy Club," he clarified when she arched one brow in question.

"Is that the one with the handbook and the secret handshake?'' she asked, smiling as she remembered that first day when he and Doug had picked her up.

"That's the one." The water had begun to boil. Ryan picked up a folded towel to use for a pot holder, then dumped water over the tea bag and carried the cup to the table. Maggie watched with amusement as he put three spoonfuls of sugar into the cup.

"Would you like some tea with your sugar?" she asked politely.

"Sugar brings out the best flavor in tea."

"Sugar is a junk food," she said primly.

He arched his brows. "And tea's a nutritional powerhouse?''

"You may have a point." Maggie hid her smile

behind her cup, feeling the tension slowly seep away. With everything that was going on, she kept forgetting that she actually liked the man she'd married.

Ryan was relieved to see her smile. The wary look in those big gray eyes made him feel like Bluebeard, with half a dozen wives buried in the basement. He frowned and shifted uncomfortably. No wives in the basement, maybe, but he still hadn't told her about Sally. He'd meant to—several times. On the way to Vegas. On the way to the chapel. While they were having dinner after the wedding. Today, before he left her at her mother's house. It had just never seemed like the right time.

It wasn't as if it was all that relevant to the two of them, he told himself. Or that it was a secret. If they'd come to this marriage via a more normal route, dated for a few months, gotten to know one another gradually, he would undoubtedly have told her about Sally long before they got to this point. But they hadn't, and he hadn't, and now it felt awkward. Still, it wasn't going to get any easier.

Ryan opened his mouth, then closed it again when Maggie's eyes shifted to look past his shoulder, her mouth curving in a smile.

"Max." Affection warmed her voice, and Ryan told himself that he had not yet sunk to the level of being jealous of a cat. "He looks like he's settling in," Maggie said happily.

"Should I expect to find a dead rodent on my pillow in the morning?" Ryan asked, eyeing the cat with deep suspicion. Max sat down, flicked his tail around to cover his front paws and looked at Ryan with classic feline indifference.

"I doubt if he's in the mood to go hunting tonight," Maggie said, getting up and going to the counter to get one of the cans of cat food she'd brought with her. "He didn't much care for traveling by car."

Which was a gross understatement. Max had made his opinion of the whole operation loud and clear, yowling continually throughout the entire trip to the ranch. Maggie hadn't been sure her hearing—or her sanity—would survive.

"Why is he looking at me like that?" Ryan asked when Max ignored Maggie's preparations for his dinner in favor of staring at Ryan.

"He's curious."

"Yeah? Did he ever hear what curiosity does to cats?" Ryan muttered into his tea. Ridiculous to feel uncomfortable, but there was something about that steady, unblinking stare that made him uneasy.

"Max, stop tormenting Ryan and come eat your dinner," Maggie said as she set a saucer on the floor. The cat stared at Ryan a moment longer and then rose, stretched slowly and sauntered over to the saucer.

Maggie picked up her cup and carried it to the sink to rinse it out. Outside, the rain continued to fall, a steady hiss of sound that closed them in. It had been raining when he asked her to marry him, Maggie remembered. She'd had the same feeling then—that they were cut off from the rest of the world, apart from everyone and everything.

Behind her, Ryan shifted position, and she was suddenly aware that they were alone in this house that, with luck, would become a home for the two of them, a place to build a future together. They were alone, and this was, for all intents and purposes, their wedding night. Last night he'd seemed a total stranger. Tonight she remembered the way his eyes smiled before his mouth moved, and the flutter in her stomach was as much anticipation as fear.

She put a self-conscious hand to her hair, which she'd bundled into a careless knot on top of her head. It had been convenient for moving her things in and out of the car, and for unpacking, but it wasn't exactly a romantic hairstyle. And jeans and a softly worn denim shirt weren't likely to make a man fall over with lust, either.

Maybe she should go take a shower, wash her hair, put on a dab of perfume and a sexy nightgown and... Maggie's thoughts stuttered to a halt as she ran a mental inventory of her wardrobe. Her sleeping attire tended to consist of cotton pajamas—short for summer, long for winter. She didn't own anything slinky and slithery, or feminine and ruffled. She frowned down at the cup she was holding under the running water. What kind of a bride came to her wedding night wearing blue-and-white striped pajamas? The only thing worse would be pink flannel with feet and a drop seat.

"I'd guess that's clean by now."

Absorbed in thought, Maggie hadn't realized that Ryan had moved until he spoke. Startled to find him next to her, she jumped and jerked back, her breath escaping in a little hiss of alarm.

"Sorry. I didn't mean to startle you." Ryan rinsed his cup and set it on the counter. If he'd been hoping for a sign that she was secretly hoping he'd jump her bones, he was out of luck, he thought. He hadn't even touched her, and she'd jumped as if she'd just backed into an electric fence. So much for his fantasy of pulling the pins from that ridiculously sexy knot of hair and seeing it tumble onto her shoulders.

"That's okay. I just didn't know you were there." Maggie laughed nervously and pressed her hand to her galloping heart. "I mean, I knew you were there, but I didn't know you were *here*. Right here. Not at the table, I mean.''

She barely restrained an urge to clap both hands over her mouth to stop the flow of inanities.

''Maggie?'' Ryan waited until her eyes lifted from his collarbone to his face. ''You don't have to worry,'' he said gently.

''I don't?'' Maggie frowned questioningly and wondered if she should worry that she didn't know what it was she didn't have to worry about.

''I told you last night, we don't have to rush into anything. I can move my things into the spare bedroom for now.'' *And learn to like cold showers,* he thought grimly.

Maggie stared at him, her eyes blank as she struggled to readjust her thinking. Her first urge was to tell him it wasn't necessary for him to move into the spare bedroom, but then she was swamped by a wave of doubt. What if he would *prefer* to sleep in the spare bedroom? What if he'd realized, barely twenty-four hours into their marriage, that he didn't want her? What if he was already regretting this wild leap into matrimony and thinking in terms of getting an annulment? God, did anybody but the Pope still give annulments? What if you weren't Catholic? What did you do then?

With an effort, Maggie reined in her careening imagination. What if he was simply doing exactly what he'd said—trying to be considerate of her feelings? If she were a different kind of woman, one with more experience and confidence, she could have found a way to let him know that his consideration was appreciated, but that she really wasn't averse to being seduced after all. But she wasn't a different woman. She was just plain, slightly plump, not-very-experienced Maggie Drummond. Or was it Lassiter now?

"I don't know what my name is."

Ryan had been indulging in a little self-inflicted torture by letting his imagination travel down forbidden paths, thinking of what it might be like to slide his hands underneath her shirt and find warm, female flesh. Maybe she would sigh and melt against him, and then he would pick her up and... Maggie's forlorn tone caught his attention before he registered her words.

"What?"

"My name." She shoved distractedly at a lock of hair that had escaped confinement and fallen against her cheek. "I don't know what my name is anymore."

"Maggie?" Ryan suggested cautiously, wondering if she'd snapped under the strain.

"Not that name." His careful tone and wary expression surprised her into a smile. "My last name. Is it Lassiter or Drummond? We never talked about

whether or not I was going to change my name.''
She sighed and shoved at the rebellious curl again.
Exhaustion was sweeping over her in a long, slow
wave that made her grateful—almost—that Ryan
had decided to postpone their wedding night yet
again. ''I suppose there's a lot we haven't talked
about.''

''A few things.'' He thought guiltily of his first
marriage. Tomorrow, he promised himself. This
was not the time to start what could be a long,
involved conversation.

''What do *you* want to do about the name?'' he
asked, reining in the urge to say that *his* wife used
his name. Scratch the surface and you went right
through the twentieth century veneer and got to the
basic male need to mark what was his.

''I don't know.'' Maggie pushed at the curl
again and then gave up and pulled out the two stra-
tegic pins that held her hair up.

Her hair fell onto her shoulders in a thick tumble
of dark gold curls, and Ryan's mouth went dry. To
hell with nobility, he thought savagely, his hands
lifting to bury themselves in that inviting mass.

''I don't know anything right now.'' There was
a world of weariness in her voice, and Ryan froze,
his hands still inches away from their intended des-
tination.

Looking at her, he saw again the smudgy shadows under her eyes, the delicate pallor of her skin. She looked fragile, breakable. Time, he reminded himself. They had plenty of time.

Maggie would have felt better if she'd known how close she'd come to being ravished on the kitchen table. As it was, she murmured a good-night and went to bed thinking that even if he was just trying to be considerate, it would have been nice if Ryan had pretended that he at least *wanted* to share a bed with her.

Patience, Ryan reminded himself as he watched her leave. Patience—along with nobility—was a virtue. He considered that a moment, staring absently at Max, who was carefully washing his face with one curled paw. Virtue was supposed to be its own reward, but he didn't feel particularly rewarded. He felt…itchy.

The pipes banged as the shower came on upstairs, and he closed his eyes with a groan. It was a mistake. With his eyes shut, the image of Maggie in the shower, naked, her skin gleaming with moisture, was all too vivid.

A day or two, he thought, opening his eyes to banish the image. He wasn't a randy boy anymore. He could certainly wait another day or two to consummate his marriage.

But he didn't have to like it.

* * *

"So, how's married life treating you?" Bonnie asked as Maggie wheeled her cart up to the counter and began unloading her purchases onto it.

"Fine so far." Maggie set a can of tomato juice down and wondered if it was worth making an hour's drive to the next decent-size town in order to avoid Bonnie's regular catechism. This was the third time she'd come into the General Store since she and Ryan were married, and each time she'd answered the same round of questions.

"What's it been? Couple of weeks now?" Bonnie punched in prices with one hand, scooting the entered items aside with the other.

"Right about." *Two weeks, three days and twelve hours or so*, Maggie thought. *But who's counting?*

"Could have knocked me over with a feather when I heard the news that you and Ryan had run off to Vegas." Bonnie shook her head as she keyed in a bunch of bananas and three cans of soup.

"I guess we surprised everyone." *Including ourselves.*

"Not that you don't look good together, and anyone could see Ryan was attracted. I could see it that first day when he was here and you came in. Remember?"

"Hmm." Maggie made a little humming noise in her throat and smiled, knowing it was all the response Bonnie required. She wasn't likely to forget that day. It was the first time Ryan had kissed her. And damned near the last, she thought, setting a bag of apples down with a thunk guaranteed to leave bruises.

"Still, the two of you sure did play it close to the vest. Nobody had any idea you were seeing each other. Not even me, and there isn't much gets by me," Bonnie said with simple pride.

"We just didn't want any fuss," Maggie said, and wondered how many times she'd said the same words or a variation of them in the past couple of weeks. It seemed as if everyone in a hundred-mile radius had found an opportunity to express their surprise. A number of them had dropped by Bill's Place for no reason except to tell her how amazing they found her marriage; how incredible it was that they'd managed to keep their relationship a secret. Wouldn't they all be surprised to know that there *was* no relationship—then or now. Maybe she should just have a T-shirt printed up that said *Yes, Ryan Lassiter Married Me and I Don't Know Why, Either.* She smacked a slab of bacon on the counter.

"Well, you sure managed that." Bonnie chuckled and shook her head as she rang up a box of Cheerios and a pound of cheddar cheese. "I'm surprised you're still working over at Bill's. Thought you might quit and maybe spend more time with that camera of yours. Ain't like you need two incomes. The Lassiters have always been real shrewd when it comes to managing money."

"Most women work these days," Maggie replied. Her job was the only familiar, solid thing in her life right now, and she was clinging to it like a security blanket.

"True enough. But for the life of me, I can't figure out why. Unless you've got a career you really love, like you and your photography. If you want my advice, you'll take your time off now while you can enjoy it. Once you have kids, being home will be more work than any job you ever had." She eyed Maggie curiously as she hit the total button. "You and Ryan figuring to have kids right away?"

Maggie wondered if this was Bonnie's subtle way of asking if she was pregnant, which would certainly explain why Ryan had married her. But when she looked up sharply, there was nothing but friendly interest in the other woman's expression. God, no one had warned her that marriage made you paranoid. She resisted the urge to run her hand over her face and drummed up a smile. "We haven't really decided."

"Jack and I didn't decide to have kids until we were working on number three," Bonnie said, grinning. "Sometimes nature has a way of making up your mind for you."

Only if nature was in the mood to perform a miracle, Maggie thought, counting out money. In the normal way of things, children required sex, and there was certainly none of that going on in her marriage.

"I think this is one decision Ryan and I want to make ourselves," she said, and tried not to think about what it would be like to have a child—Ryan's child. In an effort to shift the topic, she nodded to the apples Bonnie was loading into a grocery bag. "I don't suppose you have a good recipe for apple pie, do you?"

Bonnie's laugh was infectious. "Last time I made a pie, even the goats refused to eat it, and they'll eat tin cans like they were Hershey bars. When we got married, Jack made me add a promise never to bake to the wedding vows."

"It can't be that bad," Maggie protested, grinning.

"Worse." Paper crackled as Bonnie opened a second bag and began loading it. "My own children beg me not to make them cookies." She shook her head. "If you want a pie recipe, you came to the wrong place. I can sure eat them," she said, patting her ample hips. "But ovens and I just don't get along. You planning on baking up a pie to seduce Ryan?'' She grinned. ''I heard a rumor that the way to a man's heart is through his stomach. Course, you've already got his heart, but you might as well try for the stomach, too.''

''I heard that rumor, too, but it's not for him.'' If she'd thought there was a chance he could be so easily seduced, she would have turned the oven on days ago. ''We're having dinner with his grandfather tonight, and I told Sara I'd bring dessert. A friend of the family is coming—Shirley Taylor. She was supposed to come a couple of weeks ago, but our wedding postponed things.''

''Shelly,'' Bonnie corrected. ''Shelly Taylor. Her daddy and Ryan's grandad were real good friends. She headed for Hollywood right out of high school, and we all kind of figured she'd stay there. I was surprised that Shelly came home after her daddy died.''

''She's an actress?'' Ryan hadn't told her anything about his grandfather's guest, and Maggie had been picturing an older woman, had even wondered vaguely if there was a romantic attachment between her and Nathan.

''I guess so, though I've never seen her in anything. Of course, I haven't been to a movie in a month of Sundays, and I don't watch TV all that much, so I could have missed her.'' She finished bagging Maggie's purchases and leaned against the counter, her expression thoughtful. "Haven't seen her since she came back, but from what I hear, she's still quite a looker. She was the prettiest girl in school, no doubt about that."

"She was in your class?" Maggie struggled to readjust her thinking, erasing the image of a sun-weathered ranch woman and replacing it with that of a young, beautiful actress.

Bonnie shook her head. "A year or so ahead of me. She was in Ryan's class. As a matter of fact, the two of them were quite an item there..." Bonnie's voice trailed off as she remembered who she was talking to. She flushed lightly beneath her tan. "Of course, that was a long time ago."

"I imagine Ryan dated a lot of girls in high school," Maggie said, forcing casual disinterest into the words.

"That's right." Bonnie seemed relieved that Maggie hadn't taken offense. "He and Shelly dated most of their senior year, but, looking back, I think it was mostly peer pressure," she said reminiscently. "You know—he was handsome, she was pretty. And their folks kind of nudged them together."

"Their folks?"

Pleased to have an excuse to gossip—and this wasn't really gossip, because it was the God's honest truth—Bonnie settled onto the stool behind the counter and leaned her elbows on the counter. There was no one else in the store, and she had nothing she had to be doing. Maggie was a good listener, and there was no harm in catching her up on ancient history.

"Nathan Lassiter and Leland Taylor. Like I said, they were real good friends. Leland married late in life, and Shelly was his only child, so when he died, she inherited High Reaches, lock, stock and cattle. It borders right along the Double L, you know."

No, she hadn't known, Maggie thought. But there seemed to be rather a lot she didn't know these days.

"When Ryan came to live with his grandad," Bonnie continued, "I guess it seemed like a good idea—Ryan and Shelly getting married I mean. Seemed like a good idea to their folks, anyway. I was never real sure if the two of them had any real interest in tying the knot. Like I said, they dated for a while in high school, but nothing came of it. Shelly, she—"

The phone rang, interrupting her in midsentence. Bonnie jumped and scowled at the instrument. "Drat that thing. Hasn't rung all day."

"That's okay. I really should get going," Maggie said, grateful for the interruption. She wasn't at all sure she wanted to hear any more about

Ryan's past relationships. It was too depressing in light of the current non-state of their marriage.

"Good luck with that apple pie," Bonnie said as she pushed the two bags across the counter to Maggie and then reached for the receiver as the phone jangled again.

She was going to have to stop buying food, Maggie decided as she dumped the sacks of groceries onto the passenger seat of her car. She simply couldn't take another round of Bonnie's friendly probing and helpful information. Of course, if that was the problem, she was going to have to quit work and avoid people altogether, because she hadn't met anyone in the last two weeks who didn't feel compelled to comment on her marriage.

"I feel like the bearded lady in the circus," Maggie muttered as she slid behind the wheel and slammed the door shut. The only person who wasn't astonished by the whole thing was Bill, who seemed to have taken her sudden marriage in stride.

There was a headache niggling behind her eyes—an all too familiar companion lately. She wanted to close her eyes and put her head down on the wheel and just stay there until the world made sense again. But this wasn't really the best place for indulging in a nervous breakdown. With a sigh, she reached for the keys.

In two weeks, the drive to the Double L had

become familiar enough for her to allow her mind to wander. And it wandered, as it usually did these days, to her marriage. Or what was supposed to be a marriage.

Two and a half weeks and Ryan hadn't so much as kissed her. At first she'd thought he was trying to be considerate, and, even if the consideration wasn't necessary, she'd appreciated the thought. But, as the days—and nights—passed and he showed no desire to change their sleeping arrangements, she'd begun to think that he just wasn't interested anymore.

He *had* wanted her. She knew that. It wasn't something a man could hide, and that day in the truck, when he'd asked her to marry him, he'd wanted her. And he could have had her, she thought, flushing at the memory. Looking back, she knew she wouldn't have offered so much as a whisper of protest if he'd wanted to take her right there in the front seat of his truck, with the rain pouring down outside.

She didn't know why he hadn't, why he'd stopped when it must have been obvious that she was willing. She didn't know why he'd asked her to marry him—pushed her into it. And she didn't know why, now that they were married, they were living like roommates—friendly, polite roommates.

Maggie had always considered herself a morning

person, but ranch life started before the sun came up, and, that first morning, she'd awakened to the smell of coffee. By the time she was dressed and ready to face her new husband—or as ready as she would ever be—Ryan had breakfast done. If she'd worried that there might be some awkwardness in this, their first morning truly alone together, Ryan had squashed it with an easy smile and a question about how she liked her eggs. By the time the meal was over, she was starting to think that marriage might be a fairly simple proposition after all.

And if she'd been disappointed that he hadn't kissed her goodbye, it was a small disappointment. She had to give it time, she reminded herself. Every marriage had a period of adjustment, and they'd skipped so many steps along the way that theirs was likely to take more adjusting than most.

But the adjustment period wasn't going at all the way she'd expected, Maggie thought, as she turned off the highway and onto the road leading to the ranch house, tires rumbling over the cattle guard. Ryan was gone before she got up in the morning, and, though they ate dinner together, their conversation was strained and punctuated by lengthy silences. Immediately after the meal, Ryan generally shut himself into the tiny downstairs room they'd designated as an office or went down to the barn to check on "things."

It was obvious he was avoiding her. What wasn't obvious was the why of it. Did he regret marrying her? Did he think she regretted marrying him? At her most hopeful, she wondered if he was waiting for her to make the first move. The thought made her laugh, though there was little humor in the sound. If he'd wanted a wife who knew something about the art of seduction, he'd picked the wrong girl.

Maybe she should buy herself a slinky night-gown and a perfume that oozed sex. But short, plump blondes were not really built for slinking, and most perfumes made her sneeze. The image of herself poured into a sleek negligee and looking like a silk-covered sausage, nose red and eyes watery from sneezing, brought a genuine laugh.

God, she had to be losing her mind to even consider it. Maggie turned the car into the ranch yard and angled up the slope toward the house she and Ryan shared. The thing to do was to just sit down and talk to him, she told herself. Ask him what he expected from their marriage. They were adults, right? They should be able to have a calm, rational conversation about this, right?

Right. She could just see herself sitting down with Ryan and asking him why they weren't sleeping together. Sure. She would do that right after she tried the perfume and silk routine. Or maybe, for a change of pace, she would just flap her arms and take off flying.

She slammed the gearshift into park and got out, walking around the front of the car to the passenger side. But first, she had a pie to bake.

Maggie hefted both bags into her arms and used the side of her foot to nudge the door shut. After she baked she was going to shower and get dressed so she could have dinner with an actress, who was beautiful, and probably also tall and willowy, and who just happened to be her husband's ex-girlfriend. And, if that wasn't enough to blight her day, she could consider the fact that the odds were good that Shelly Taylor had slept with Ryan, which was certainly more than she could say.

Things couldn't go on this way, Maggie decided as she carried the sacks through the gate in the picket fence and up the short walkway. Balancing one bag on her hip, she pushed open the door and felt her mood lift a bit when Max trotted out of the living room to greet her, mewing inquiringly.

"Yes, I got cat food," she assured him, smiling. His purr rumbled up to her, and he wound himself around her legs as she made her way to the kitchen. One of the nice things about a cat was that there were no hidden undercurrents, no looking for layers of meaning behind their every action. She didn't have to worry about what Max was really thinking. As long as she fed him, provided him with a comfortable place to sleep and made herself available to scratch his tummy now and again, Max thought she was terrific. It was a pity human relationships couldn't be as straightforward.

"Something has to change, Max." Maggie set the bags on the kitchen table and began unloading them, while he made encouraging noises in his throat. He could have been urging her to open a can of cat food, but Maggie preferred to believe he was responding to her words. "I can't just let things go on like this forever."

She got a saucer out of the cupboard, and Max nudged his volume up a level. "It shouldn't be that difficult," Maggie said, taking out a can opener. "All I have to do is talk to Ryan calmly, ask him what he expects from this marriage. And if he doesn't want me—"

Her voice caught, and she paused with the can of cat food half open, her eyes focusing on nothing at all, as she imagined what it would feel like to have Ryan look her in the eye and tell her that he didn't want her after all. Max waited a polite thirty seconds and then meowed anxiously. The reminder started Maggie's hands moving automatically. She dumped the cat food onto the saucer and set it on the floor, much to Max's relief.

She stood watching him eat for a moment and

wondered if maybe it wouldn't be best to just leave things alone for a little while longer after all.

Ryan wanted to have dinner with his grandfather and Shelly about as much as he wanted to have a root canal without anesthetic. If he could have thought of a way to avoid it, he would have done it in a minute. But one dinner invitation had already been scrapped because of his sudden marriage, and his grandfather hadn't hesitated to remind him of it. Shelly was a neighbor and an old family friend, and she was going through a difficult spell—and Nathan hadn't hesitated to remind him of that, either. The fact that the old man was right didn't make Ryan enthused, but it did make him resigned.

Avoiding things like this was one of the best arguments he could think of for staying on the road. Social obligations were generally limited to paying your share of the tab at McDonald's and taking your turn at the wheel so your traveling partners could doze between towns. Avoiding an occasional dinner was not reason enough to hit the circuit again, he admitted, smiling a little as he ran his fingers through his slightly damp hair. Not when he'd found everything he wanted here. Or all the pieces of it, anyway.

The land, good friends, the only family he had that mattered. Maggie.

His smile faded, dark brows drawing together as he considered Maggie. There was the one element that wasn't falling into place. And it was, for reasons he hadn't quite defined, the one thing that mattered most. Hell, even his grandfather seemed to be coming around. The tension that had hummed between them for the past few years was easing. A couple of days ago, when he'd offered to boot up the computer and start catching up on the records, the old man had agreed without a single snide comment.

If his marriage to Maggie had accomplished nothing else, it seemed to have helped convince the old man that he was staying this time. The only other thing it seemed to be accomplishing was to drive him out of his mind.

Ryan sat down on the edge of the bed to tug his socks on. Marrying her had felt so right—still felt right, for that matter. Or it would if they weren't moving farther apart instead of closer together.

He didn't know what he'd expected. Hell, they'd jumped into marriage so fast, there hadn't been time for expectations. But he did know that he hadn't planned on finding himself sleeping alone two weeks after the wedding. Two weeks, and he was still sleeping in a bed that was two inches too short and a whole lot too narrow while his wife—his *wife*, damn it—slept across the hall. Alone.

Ryan yanked a shirt out of the closet. When the hanger popped loose from the rod and clattered to the floor, he scowled and left it there. It was his fault. He knew it was. He'd all but bullied Maggie into this marriage, and then his damned conscience had reared its ugly head, telling him to give her space, to give her time—that he owed her that much. And maybe he did.

But how much time and how much space? *Maybe until you find the guts to tell her about Sally?* his conscience suggested snidely, and Ryan winced. It wasn't a matter of guts. It was just that he hadn't found the right time to tell her. And if that wasn't the most pathetic excuse he'd ever heard, he didn't know what was. He shrugged the shirt on and frowned at his reflection in the mirror. It wasn't the right time that was missing, it was the right words. How did you go about telling your wife that she wasn't your first wife? In the ordinary run of things, she would have known about Sally long before this. But there was nothing ordinary about the way they'd done things.

Now, here they were, married for two and half weeks, and he still hadn't told her about Sally, and he was still sleeping alone. Two and a half weeks of seeing her fresh from a bath, her skin flushed and damp, her hair curling around her face, of knowing that she was lying just across the hall, of wondering what she wore to bed and how long it would take him to peel it off. Two and a half weeks of wanting and not having, and his self-control was stretched to the breaking point.

"We're married," he muttered to himself as he jammed buttons through buttonholes.

If only she didn't seem just as happy to leave things the way they were. If she'd shown any sign of sharing his frustration, he would have jumped her bones in a minute. But she hadn't shown any sign of wanting her bones jumped. When they were together—which was less and less often—she was friendly, pleasant, easy to talk to. If he'd been looking for a roommate, it would have been perfect.

But he wanted a wife. Ryan scowled at his reflection in the small mirror that topped the high dresser. He wanted Maggie.

They had to talk, he decided. Wasn't that the way couples were supposed to handle things? A calm, rational conversation to work out their conflicts, discuss their mutual goals?

And then he'd jump her bones.

Chapter Eleven

Shelly Taylor was everything Maggie had feared she would be and more. She was tall, slim, beautiful and depressingly pleasant. She wore a pair of gray tailored trousers and a green silk shirt that managed to look both sophisticated and casual. Her voice was low and beautifully modulated, and immediately made Maggie feel like Minnie Mouse. Even her teeth were perfect, Maggie thought, when Shelly laughed at something Nathan said.

Glancing across the table at Ryan, she saw him smiling at Shelly and wondered if he was thinking the same thing she was. Why on earth had he married Maggie, if there was a chance he could have this beautiful, witty woman? Unless Shelly had turned him down? The thought offered no consolation. For one thing, what woman in her right mind would turn down a man like Ryan Lassiter? He was not only incredibly good-looking but he was smart and kind and had a terrific sense of humor. He was even kind to animals, for God's sake.

But even if she could accept the possibility that Shelly had turned him down, where did that leave her? An also-ran, a consolation prize that offered little consolation. She'd known he didn't love her when she married him. But it was one thing to know he didn't love her, something else altogether to think he might love someone else.

Maggie looked down at her plate and reminded herself not to let her imagination run wild. She didn't know that Ryan loved Shelly. All she knew was that he didn't love her, didn't even seem to want her anymore.

Ryan divided his attention between the conversation and his wife. She was quiet tonight, he thought, looking at her downbent head. She hadn't strung more than two sentences together all night. She'd left the house before he was out of the shower, coming over to the main house to help Sara, her note had said. Avoiding him, Ryan knew.

He stabbed a piece of steak and brought it up to his mouth, chewing without tasting. They had to talk. That was all there was to it. He wasn't much for long-winded conversations about relationships.

In general, he thought it was best to let such things work themselves out one way or another. But this wasn't working itself out, and they were losing something that mattered.

It wasn't just the sex, though he was honest enough—male enough—to admit that mattered. But he also missed seeing her smile, missed the way her nose wrinkled when she laughed and the way her eyes lit when she was excited about something. He didn't just want to make love to her. He wanted to hold her afterward and wake up with her in the morning.

Everything a marriage could be, everything he knew they could have—that was what he wanted.

Nathan chewed methodically on a bite of steak. Shelly was telling some story about a Western movie a friend of hers had been in. Near as he could tell, there wasn't a soul in Hollywood with sense enough to pour piss out of a boot, which made it all the more remarkable that they were raking in so much money. Listening to Shelly, he let his eyes drift from the frown in Ryan's eyes to the misery in Maggie's. They were both putting up a good front—or trying to—but the atmosphere between them was thick enough to cut with a knife.

One thing he enjoyed about life was that, no matter how old you got, it never got dull. Take his grandson's marriage, for example. On the surface, it seemed straightforward enough. Young couple falls in love, gets married. Happened every day. But, for the past couple of weeks, Ryan had been as testy as a long-tailed cat in a room full of rockers, and Maggie looked like her best friend and her dog had both just died.

The thing was, he liked Maggie. More than that, he liked seeing Ryan all riled up about something again. Frustration was better than that damned smooth surface calm the boy had been holding like a shield for the past few years. Maggie was good for Ryan, and he had a feeling she would be even better for him once they'd worked out whatever the problem was between them.

Everyone laughed at the end of Shelly's story, and she gave them credit for being better actors than a lot of the people she'd once worked with. She doubted if any of them remembered a word she'd said. Oh well, some nights the audience just wasn't with you.

She sliced off a sliver of steak and tried to tell herself that she was appalled by the amount of red meat served at every meal, not to mention baked potatoes dripping with butter and sour cream. But the truth was, after more than ten years of nibbling lettuce leaves and trying to look excited about rice cakes, she was rather enjoying sinking her teeth into real food again. And the way Ray Wellman was running her all over the ranch, she was certainly burning off plenty of calories. The man was worse than a personal trainer, dragging her out of bed at six in the morning and then working her like a damned slave driver.

And it was no good telling herself that he worked for her. She could never quite get past the memory of him picking her up and dusting her off after her first tumble from a pony. Or the time he'd paddled her when he caught her and his son, Andy, smoking cigarettes behind the barn. He hadn't spanked them for smoking but for smoking near the hay. You couldn't ever really be an employer to a man who'd once laid the flat of his hand against your bottom.

The conversation shifted, inevitably, to ranching, and Shelly made an effort to absorb what was being said. She had so much to learn and, judging by Ray's daily threats to quit, not a whole lot of time in which to learn it. For a little while there, she'd thought maybe she and Ryan might... But he'd gotten married, and that had been the end of that.

She tried to summon up regret, but it wouldn't come. Despite what she'd told Tucker McIntyre, the best sparks she and Ryan had ever managed to strike off one another were those of pure temper. Still, it would have been so convenient if they'd managed to fall in love, or at least passionately in like.

"These days, ranchers have to diversify if they want to survive," Nathan was saying. "Either that or develop a nonfat cow." He smiled and leaned back in his chair, shooting his grandson a quick, unreadable look before shifting his attention back to Shelly. "Actually, we're looking at starting a new venture."

"Really?" She didn't have to fake interest. Ray had been browbeating her with the idea that diversification was the wave of the future, an idea her father had refused to consider.

"Horses. Ryan here's got the idea he can breed quarter horses." Nathan kept his eyes on Shelly, ignoring Ryan's startled look. "Brought home a mare to get things started. She's not much on manners, but she's got good blood."

Shelly smiled at Ryan. "You certainly know plenty about horses."

"I've fallen off my share." Whatever he knew about horses, he obviously still didn't know squat about people, Ryan thought. Last he'd heard, his grandfather had not been receptive to the idea of expanding the Double L's interests in the direction of horse breeding.

"I talked to Ben Rayczek a couple of days ago about a stud he's got that might be just what we're

looking for,'' Nathan said, pushing his plate away
and looking at Ryan with a gleam of challenge in
his eyes.

We? Ryan wondered, but all he said was, "I
know the horse. Big blood bay. Ben won't let him
go cheap.''

"If we're going into the horse-breeding business, we'll do it right,'' Nathan said firmly.

There was that "we" again. Ryan debated letting it irritate him, but the irritation couldn't quite
get past the thought of starting out his string of
horses with that blood bay as stud. He'd expected
to spend a couple of years trading and dealing before he could consider a stud of that quality. More
than that, it was a relief to know that he apparently
wasn't going to have to fight the old man every
step of the way. The dream was his, and he would
have pursued it alone, but he preferred it this way.

"Yeah, I guess *we* should start off on the right
foot," he said, putting a subtle emphasis on the
pronoun.

"Wouldn't have it any other way,'' Nathan said,
his eyes bright with humor.

Shelly made her excuses as soon after dinner as
good manners allowed. The truth was, the evening
had depressed her. Watching Ryan and his grandfather reminded her that her own father was gone

forever. And seeing Ryan with his wife reminded her that she was on the shady side of thirty and still alone, without even a career to keep her warm at night.

As she walked down the porch steps, she wondered if she'd made a mistake coming back here. Maybe she should have stayed in L.A. Even if she wasn't destined to be the next Meryl Streep, she'd been making a reasonable living—okay, a pretty damned marginal living—but she could have moved into teaching or become an agent. Lots of actors became teachers or agents.

She smelled the smoke from his cigarette before she saw him, standing at the corner of the porch, a darker shadow among the shadows.

"Hello, Tucker." She walked down the steps and stepped out of the light, becoming a shadow herself.

"Shel." He was the only one who'd ever called her that, she thought. She'd hated it when they were children, but it seemed almost…comforting now. "How was dinner?"

"Fine. Your mother knows how to set a table."

"That she does."

They stood there in silence for a few moments. That was another thing about him that she remembered. The way he could let a silence stretch without getting uncomfortable. In all her years in L.A., she'd never known anyone who could tolerate silence.

"You sticking around?" he asked after a while.

"Yes." She didn't pretend not to know what he meant. He was wondering if Ryan's marriage had done anything to change her plans. Something about the darkness or the stillness of the night made stark honesty possible. "I don't have anywhere else to go." She sighed. "The truth is, I'm a pretty mediocre actress, and good looks will only carry you so far. Mine took me about as far as they could."

"Gonna be quite a change, coming back here." He didn't offer any polite protests about either her looks or her talent, she noticed, and wondered if she should be offended.

"I feel like a change." She slid her hands into the pockets of her tailored slacks, hunching her shoulders a little against the cool air. Or maybe the chill she felt came from inside. "Even before Daddy died, I was thinking about making some changes in my life. Now here I am, with a ranch on my hands that I don't have the faintest idea how to manage, and a foreman who wants to quit, and no career, and I want—" She broke off, afraid to say the words out loud.

"You want what?" He was just a voice in the darkness, and it gave her the courage to admit something she'd barely even acknowledged to herself.

"I want children," she said in a rush, and then laughed at herself. "Sounds stupid, doesn't it? Me, with kids. Who would believe it?"

Shelly looked down toward the bunkhouse, where lamplight spilled golden through the windows. Her sigh held regret. "Ryan and I weren't likely to fall madly in love with each other, but I thought we might come to like each other well enough to put together something worthwhile. I suppose that seems awfully cold and calculating."

"Just a bit."

"So who asked you?" she snapped, stung.

"You did," he replied coolly. He dropped his cigarette and ground it out with the toe of his boot. "So essentially, what you're looking for is a ranch manager who likes kids?"

Shelly huffed out an irritated breath. "I should have known better than to expect you to understand."

"What about passion? Hunger?" She hadn't seen him move, but he was suddenly right in front of her. His shoulders blocked the starlight, closing her off from the world, making her heart flutter uneasily. He brushed his hand over the arch of her cheek, traced the line of her jaw, and she felt herself shiver with awareness.

"Passion and hunger aren't enough to build a relationship," she said, the words coming out more question than statement.

"But liking each other well enough is?" he asked, and she caught the glint of humor in his eyes as he lowered his head to hers.

"Tucker, don't—" *Stop,* she thought as his mouth crushed hers and pleasure lanced through her. *Don't stop.*

He took his time, tasting her hesitation and the growing warmth of her response. When he finally lifted his head, Shelly was clinging to him, her arms wound around his neck, her slim body plastered against his from chest to knee. With an effort, she dragged her eyes open and stared up at him.

"I'll drive you home," he said, brushing his thumb over her mouth.

She knew what he was saying, what he was asking. A cautious woman would have stepped back and told him that she could drive herself home. A cautious woman would have told him not to make assumptions. But then, a cautious woman wouldn't have chosen acting as a career. And cautious women rarely lived exciting lives.

"I left the keys in the car," she said, and let her hand stay in his as he led her away from the house.

"You made a good choice there," Nathan said, lifting his glass in a half toast toward the kitchen.

"I like Maggie."

Ryan had been standing with one arm on the mantel, his eyes on the empty fireplace. A cup of coffee sat on the mantel next to his arm. Shelly was gone. Maggie had refused his offer to help clear the table, and he'd been just as glad to retreat to the den with his grandfather. It wasn't that he minded loading a dishwasher. He figured anybody who could muck out a stall could handle a dirty kitchen, but the forced pleasantness in her voice and the unhappiness in her eyes were more than he could take.

They had to talk. Now. Tonight. He just had to figure out what he was going to say to her.

At his grandfather's comment, he lifted his head and looked at the old man. "I'm glad, but I didn't marry Maggie to please you."

"I know." The knowledge pleased him. Nathan swirled the brandy in the bottom of the snifter and eyed his grandson curiously. "For a while there, I thought you might have done it to tick me off."

"My reasons for marrying Maggie didn't have anything to do with you," Ryan said, and he was faintly surprised to realize it was the truth. Maybe the old man's nudging had put the thought of marriage in his mind, but he hadn't married Maggie or any reason except that it was what he'd wanted—what he still wanted.

"I gathered that." Nathan nodded, satisfied. He took a sip of brandy and then frowned a little. When he spoke again, his voice was gruff, as if the words scratched his throat. "I was wrong to shove you and Shelly together, but if it helped turn your head in Maggie's direction, I'm not sorry."

Ryan choked on his coffee. "Did I hear you say you were wrong?"

"Don't push it," Nathan said testily. "I've always been willing to admit when I'm wrong."

"It's the first time I've heard you say it in twenty-three years."

"Maybe it's the first time I've had to," Nathan said sharply, then smiled reluctantly when Ryan laughed. "You never did have any respect for your elders and betters."

"Show me someone who's both and I'll show some respect." As easy as that, Ryan thought wonderingly. As easy as that and the gap that had grown between them over the past few years was bridged. "Were you serious about buying that stud from Ben Rayczek?"

"If you like the look of him." Nathan swirled the brandy again, keeping his eyes on the movement. "I guess I've gotten a little set in my ways. Don't like letting go of the reins."

"I don't want you to," Ryan said honestly.

"This place will be yours one of these days. Yo
should have some say in how things are done."

Ryan didn't want to think about the time whe
the Double L would be his. "There's plenty o
time," he said, hoping it was true.

They were silent for a long moment, uneasily
aware that they were treading uncomfortably close
to actual emotions. Nathan cleared his throat.

"When are you going to straighten out whatever's going on between you and your wife?"

"When are you going to butt out of my life?"
Ryan asked, irritably.

"When you learn how to manage it better," Nathan snapped.

They glared at each other for a moment, relieved
to be back on familiar ground.

When Maggie came into the room a few minutes
later, they were arguing over what might be a reasonable price for Ben Rayczek's blood bay. She
stood in the doorway for a moment, watching them
and thinking that it must be nice to be so sure of
someone's affections that you could risk raising
your voice to him.

"Ben's no fool, and he's not going to sell that
horse for pocket change," Ryan was saying. "You
get what you pay for and—"

He broke off when he saw Maggie, his expres-

ion shifting from temper to something more
guarded. The change brought a quick, pinching
ache to her chest, but she kept her expression calm.

"I know it's not all that late, but I'm tired, so I
think I'll head back to the house. Thank you for
the wonderful dinner. Ryan, you don't have to
come with me," she said, when he set his cup
down and stood up. She laughed a little, just to
show how happy she was. "I don't think I'll get
lost between here and home."

"I'm ready to go," he said. He wasn't going to
give her a chance to go home and lock herself away
in her bedroom before he had a chance to talk to
her. Tonight he was in the right mood to break
down the door, and if he did that, they might never
get around to talking at all.

The night air held a slight chill, making Maggie
wish she'd brought a sweater. Or maybe the chill
she felt was internal, she thought.

"We need to talk," Ryan said as they moved
away from the porch light.

It was the darkness that gave her the courage to
say it. "I know. We made a mistake." She wanted
to laugh a little, just to show that it was no big
deal, but she didn't trust the laugh not to turn into
a sob, so she contented herself with a quick shrug.
"We both knew it was a risk, rushing into things

this way. Obviously, it isn't working out. So, n●
hard feelings, and we—''

Ryan caught her arm and pulled her to a stop
making her realize that she'd been walking faste
and faster, until she was only a heartbeat awa
from breaking into a run. He pulled her around t
face him, moonlight glittering in his eyes.

"I'll have a lot of hard feelings."

"What?" She'd expected him to be relieved, to
jump at the chance to end their marriage with no
recriminations.

"I don't think we made a mistake—not in getting married, anyway. I think we've made a bunch
of them since then," he said ruefully. "Or I've
made a bunch of them." He kept hold of her wrist,
both to keep her with him and because he needed
the contact. *Need,* he realized. That was the word
he hadn't wanted to use in connection with Maggie. He needed her, and it scared the hell out of
him.

"There's so much I haven't told you," he said,
speaking half to himself. He took a deep breath and
decided the best way was just to say it. "I was
married before, Maggie. I should have told you
about it, but it—''

"I know about it," she said calmly.

"You know?" Ryan stared at her. It hadn't occurred to him that she might already know about

ally, though he supposed it should have. It wasn't
s if there were any secrets in Willow Flat.

"Bill told me about her. It must have been a
errible time for you."

"It...it was." Funny how her warm sympathy
made his throat tighten, made the words hard to get
out. "I should have told you about Sally myself,"
he said. "There just... It seemed awkward."

*Awkward to tell the wife he didn't love about the
one he had?* she wondered. But there was no point
in going down that road. "It doesn't matter. I know
our marriage was a mistake and—"

"Stop saying that." He shook her arm. "It
wasn't a damned mistake."

The sharp bite of anger in his tone almost made
Maggie hope again. "We rushed into things."

"It's not the rushing that got us in trouble. It
was getting cautious all of a sudden." He shifted
his hold, taking her by both shoulders and pulling
her a half step closer, trying to read her expression
in the moonlight. "Why did you marry me, Maggie?"

She jerked, as if he'd shouted the question, and
pulled back against his hold, but he refused to release her.

"Maybe I should tell you why I married you,"
he said, when she didn't seem able or willing to
answer.

"It was an impulse," she said hastily. "You don't have to explain. I know it was a—"

"If you say it was a mistake one more time, I'm going to shake you until your teeth rattle like castanets," he told her firmly.

She sucked in a quick, startled breath and gaped up at him, her eyes wide as saucers. He wished for more light so he could see her more clearly, but maybe this was better—easier—done here in the dark.

"I married you because I couldn't imagine not marrying you. It was an impulse, and we rushed things, but it wasn't a mistake." His thumbs made small circular motions against her shoulders. "After Sally died, I figured I'd never take another chance like that, never love anyone like that again."

"I understand. I—"

"Shut up." He reinforced the order by jerking her forward and kissing her ruthlessly. When he lifted his head, Maggie could only stare up at him, her eyes dazed, her knees as weak as overcooked noodles.

"Oh, my," she breathed.

"You don't understand at all."

"Okay." She couldn't argue with him, not when her heart was pounding against her breastbone like drum and her head was spinning quite madly. "I don't understand."

Ryan grinned. "That's what I like, a nice submissive wife."

He wrapped his arm around her shoulders and turned her in the direction of the little house. He'd left the porch light on, and it cast a clear swatch of pale lemon light down the pathway.

"I'm trying to tell you that I love you," he said, and tightened his grip on her shoulders when her knees threatened to give out under her. "I'd have mentioned it sooner, but I'm only just figuring it out myself."

"You are?" Maggie wondered if it was possible to actually die of happiness. Emotion rose in her chest, thick and warm, until she thought her heart might burst with it.

They'd reached the porch, and he stopped, turning her face to him. Her eyes shone more brightly than the moon. The love in them was so plain that he wondered how he could have been so stupid as to have missed seeing it before. He wondered how he could have been so lucky as to have found something like this for the second time in his life.

He lifted his hand to cradle her face. "Getting married wasn't a mistake, even if the way we did it was the craziest thing I've ever done. With the possible exception of the time when I was sixteen and got drunk and let Tucker convince me to try bull riding at midnight,'' he added thoughtfully.

Maggie's soft choke of laughter was the best thing he'd heard in weeks. ''I'm not sure if I should be flattered or insulted.''

''It was a very big bull,'' he said, for the sheer pleasure of hearing her laugh again.

He brushed his thumb across her lower lip and saw the laughter fade as awareness came into her eyes.

''What would you say if I offered you a wedding night, Mrs. Lassiter?''

Maggie's color rose, but her eyes remained steady on his. ''I'd say yes.'' She reached up to take his hand in hers. ''Come inside.''

Epilogue

Six months later

"**I** think she's starting to like me," Ryan said. He set one booted foot on the lower rail of the corral fence and looked at the mare standing on the other side of the fence.

"What makes you think so?" Virgil Mortenson lifted one hand to stroke the mare's nose.

"She doesn't sneer quite as much when she looks at me." Ryan kept his hands in his pockets. The mare tolerated his presence, but she hadn't gotten to the point where she welcomed his touch. Besides, the early November evening was cold, with the promise of snow before morning.

"Can't say as I ever saw a horse sneer," Virgil said, giving him a sideways look.

"You just weren't looking," Ryan said. He turned to face the other man, leaning one shoulder against the top rail. At the movement, the mare rolled her eyes in his direction and snorted. Ryan gave her a mildly disgusted look. "The way she looked at me, you'd think I was coming down here with roast horse on my breath."

"That could upset her a mite," Virgil agreed, grinning.

"She's just lucky you agreed to work with her. Otherwise, I'd probably have sent her to the glue factory by now." It was an empty threat. He knew it. Virgil knew it. Hell, the mare probably knew it.

"I didn't agree to work with her," Virgil said dryly. "Your wife *told* me I was going to work with her."

Ryan grinned. "She's small, but she's tough."

"She is that."

The silence that fell between them was comfortable. From the bunkhouse came the sound of somebody singing—an off-key version of "Pretty Woman," drowned out suddenly by a muffled chorus of catcalls.

"Jim Duggan," Ryan said, smiling. "Can't carry a tune in a bucket."

"Doesn't stop him from trying. You ought to hear his version of 'Ebb Tide.'" Virgil let his hand drop away from the mare. She snorted and gave Ryan a suspicious look before wheeling and trotting off across the corral. Virgil rested his hands on the top rail, his eyes on the horse. "Not many would have hired me after the last few years." He glanced at Ryan, then looked away again. "I appreciate you taking a chance on me."

"I didn't see it as taking a chance," Ryan said easily. "You're the best there is with horses."

"There was a time..." Virgil's voice trailed off, and he shook his head a little. "It had been a long time. Wasn't sure I still knew one end of a horse from the other."

"I was."

Ryan looked at the other man. There was healthy color in his face, and his eyes were clear and steady. It had been six months since Virgil's last drink. The battle wasn't won—might never be completely over—but Ryan was willing to bet Virgil was going to beat his demons. God knew he would if Maggie had anything to say about it. When Virgil had come back to town, sober for the first time in years, it had been Maggie who suggested that Virgil was exactly what Ryan's fledgling horse operation needed. Ryan agreed, but Virgil, whether from pride or uncertainty, had turned down the job. Ryan might have left it at that—you couldn't force the man to take a job, he'd told Maggie. But Maggie disagreed, and she'd descended on Virgil's shabby little room like an avenging angel. Ryan had no idea what she'd said, but, when she came back, Virgil was with her, looking as if he wasn't quite sure how he'd come to be there. That had been four months ago, and Ryan had had no cause to regret hiring him.

Remembering, Ryan grinned suddenly. ''Hell, even if I hadn't wanted to hire you, I would have been afraid to tell Maggie so. There's no stopping her once she's got the bit between her teeth.''

''Browbeats you, does she?'' Virgil asked dryly.

''Has me running scared.'' Thinking about Maggie, Ryan felt a sudden, restless need to be with her. He controlled the urge to glance over his shoulder at the little house they shared. Maggie would be cooking dinner, unless she was in the darkroom and had lost track of time. Distracted, he lost the thread of what Virgil was saying. Something about the mare? He looked at her, a dark shadow in the gathering dusk. ''You're doing a hell of a job with her.''

Virgil wasn't fooled. It had been a long time, but he remembered what it was to have someone who completed your life, to feel whole only when you were with her.

"I reckon I'd better go if I want to eat tonight," he said, and caught back a grin when Ryan leaped at the excuse.

"Maggie will be putting supper out pretty soon."

Virgil watched him walk away, smiling a little at the eagerness in the younger man's step. There had been a time when he'd had a wife to hurry home to, a reason to look to the future. His smile faded as he turned away, absently rubbing the heel of his hand over his heart as if soothing away an ache.

Maggie's teeth worried her lower lip as she carefully guided the tip of the pastry bag along the toothpick-drawn line in the pale frosting. A somewhat wavery line of blue icing flowed forth, spelling out "Happy Birthday" on top of the cake. A final frosting dot topped the *i*. Releasing her breath in a relieved sigh, Maggie straightened her aching back and gave the cake a critical look.

Not bad, she decided. *Not a masterpiece, certainly, but not bad at all.*

She brushed back a lock of hair and huffed out another breath. Not that Ryan was likely to critique her cake-decorating skills but, still, she wanted everything to look nice. This was a special occasion, after all. Ignoring the butterflies that invaded her stomach when she considered just how special, Maggie bent back over the cake to add the last word.

Tomorrow night was the official celebration of Ryan's birthday. They were having dinner at the main house—Nathan and the McIntyres, Tucker and Shelly. Just family, Nathan had said, and Maggie had felt a warm glow at the idea. For the first time in her life, she knew what it was to feel part of a family. Never mind that she wasn't related to any of them by blood. They were family, and she wasn't standing on the wrong side of the fence anymore.

All her life, she'd thought there was something wrong with her, some flaw in her that made it impossible for her mother to love her. It had taken her marriage to Ryan to show her that the problem hadn't been with her at all. Now Lydia and Noreen were gone, off to Los Angeles with the money they'd gotten for the house. When they left, she'd accepted the fact that she might never see either of them again and had found that her only thought was that the idea caused her so little regret.

Maggie finished off the last word with a little flourish of frosting and straightened. She studied the cake carefully before giving a satisfied little nod. She wasn't likely to bump Martha Stewart off her pedestal anytime soon, but it wasn't bad for a first effort. Tomorrow night was for family, but tonight was just for the two of them, a private celebration of birthdays and…things.

Aware of a nervous flutter in the pit of her stomach, she carried the pastry bag to the sink to rinse it out. Ryan would be pleased with her news. She knew he would be. It was silly to be nervous about it.

The hiss of the running water drowned out the sound of Ryan's approach. The first she knew of his presence was when she felt an arm slide around her waist. Startled, Maggie shrieked and jerked her hands out from under the water, scattering droplets everywhere.

"That's what I like—a woman who's excited to see me."

"You scared the wits out of me," she scolded breathlessly, then squealed and tried to wiggle away when he buried his face in the side of her neck. "You're freezing!"

"It's cold outside. Looks like we'll have snow tomorrow." Ryan turned her into his arms, catching her up against his lean body. "Think about it, Maggie. We could be snowed in for days. The wind howling outside. Just the two of us. Alone." He waggled his eyebrows up and down and gave her a laughably lascivious look. "We'll have to find something to occupy our time. Any suggestions?"

"You could probably kill a lot of time shoveling snow," she said, struggling against a smile.

His face fell. "I was thinking of strip poker," he suggested.

"It doesn't seem logical to play strip poker when the wind is howling outside."

"Who died and made you Mr. Spock?" he muttered. He glanced over her shoulder. "Hey, is that a cake?"

"No." Maggie slid out of his arms and moved between him and the table. Drat. She'd planned on hiding it until after dinner, then bringing it out ablaze with candles. "I mean, yes, it's a cake, and it's for later."

"My birthday's tomorrow. Couldn't I have a piece of cake before dinner—sort of an early celebration?" Ryan sidled closer and tried to sneak a glimpse of the cake. He wasn't that anxious for a piece, though she was turning into a good baker. But he liked seeing her try to look stern—not an easy task when her hair was tousled and she had a streak of blue icing across one cheek.

"No cake before dinner." Maggie shifted to block his view. "Why don't you go clean up or something."

"I'm clean enough, and I'm starving." He gave her the look he'd perfected when he was a boy, the one that had never failed to wheedle a handful of cookies out of Sara. "Just a little bitty piece?"

Maggie stared at him, caught between laughter and exasperation. This wasn't what she'd had in mind. She'd wanted to be wearing something a little more feminine than jeans and a faded blue sweatshirt. She'd been picturing candlelight and good china, not fluorescent lights and a flour-dusted table. Then again, she'd been waiting all day to tell him, and she wasn't sure she could wait much longer. Her stomach fluttering with nerves, she stepped aside.

Ryan glanced at the cake and then looked at her, grinning. "Birthday cake two nights in a row? How lucky can I get?"

"Luckier, I hope. I mean, I hope you think it's luckier," she said breathlessly. "Because I think it is. Luckier, I mean."

Ryan raised his brows, his blue eyes bright with affectionate amusement. "You want to run that by me again? I think something got lost in the translation."

Maggie flushed and reached out to shove the cake a little closer to him. "I decorated it myself."

"Yeah, I saw that. You wrote 'Happy Birthday...'" Ryan's voice trailed off as he looked down at the cake and saw what she'd written "Happy Birthday *Daddy?*" He lifted his eyes to her face, and the happiness blazing in them soothed any uncertainty she might have felt about how he would react to the news.

"Maggie?" Ryan caught her hands in his, his fingers tense and hard. Her throat suddenly too full for words, Maggie could only smile tremulously and nod. His grip tightened. "When?"

"I took the test this morning. We're going to be parents in seven months, give or take a couple of weeks."

If someone had asked him, Ryan would have said that it wasn't possible to be any happier than he already was. In the last few months, Maggie had driven away the shadows in his soul and filled his life with sunshine and sweet smiles. It was more than he'd ever expected to have. He was sure it was more than he deserved.

"Have I told you lately how much I love you?" he asked, cupping her face in his hands.

"I think you mentioned it this morning." She curled her fingers around his wrist, her eyes bright with love. "But I've heard that actions speak louder than words," she suggested, flattening her free hand against his chest.

He grinned and bent to scoop her up in his arms.